Adult Virgins Anonymous

About the Author

Amber Crewe is the alter-ego of Nicole Burstein, who lives in North London with her family and multiple bichon frises. In the past, Nicole has worked as a gallery attendant at the Natural History Museum, a bookseller for Waterstones, and used to present the traffic and travel news on various radio stations including LBC and local BBC Radio. Her current day job is in Customer Support for a financial technology company. She completed her Creative Writing Masters with Birkbeck College in 2011 and has been trying to make the writing career happen ever since. In her spare time, Nicole is a keen embroiderer and consumer of pop culture (in other words, she does cross-stitch whilst binge watching series on Netflix). She has a total of three Blue Peter badges, has an unending appetite for sourdough bread, and has never seen any *Die Hard* films. When the world gets too much, she watches YouTube videos of rollercoasters to relax.

AMBER CREWE

Adult Virgins Anonymous

CORONET

First published in Great Britain in 2020 by Coronet
An Imprint of Hodder & Stoughton
An Hachette UK company

This paperback edition published in 2021

1

A CIP catalogue record for this title is available from the British Library

Paperback ISBN 978 1 529 33616 0
eBook ISBN 978 1 529 33617 7

Typeset in Plantin Light by Hewer Text UK Ltd, Edinburgh
Printed and bound in Great Britain by Clays Ltd, Elcograf S.p.A.

Hodder & Stoughton policy is to use papers that are natural, renewable and recyclable products and made from wood grown in sustainable forests. The logging and manufacturing processes are expected to conform to the environmental regulations of the country of origin.

Hodder & Stoughton Ltd
Carmelite House
50 Victoria Embankment
London EC4Y 0DZ

www.hodder.co.uk

To all the people who might need this book,
You're not alone

University of London Leavers' Ball
Class of 2011

Kate Mundy was drunk on promise. Drunk on a cheap bottle of white wine too (and the half a bottle of Lambrini before that), but mostly promise. Promise and expectation and the knowledge that tonight was the night it was all going to come together. Tonight was the night she was going to leave her juvenile years behind her and finally step into the adulthood she both demanded and deserved.

'You have the glow,' Lindsey told her, bumping Kate's shoulder with her own as they crowded through the lobby of the banqueting rooms.

'The glow?'

'Yeah. Like you're shining all this amazing energy.'

'If by glow you mean sweat, then definitely. We're not even in the main bit yet and it's like a sauna in here,' Kate laughed.

'No, I mean glow,' Lindsey said. 'You're putting out all these pheromones, all these signals. You know?'

'Signals?'

'Kate's gonna get laid tonight! Kate's gonna get laid tonight!' Pippa sang, the wine in her glass sloshing over the sides.

'Signals. Sex signals! You're a massive freaking green light for it right now,' Lindsey clarified as Pippa wrapped the arm not attached to a glass of wine around her.

'Sex for Kate! Sex for Kate! Sex for Kate!' Pippa yelled.

'Guys, stop it,' Kate shushed. 'That is not what tonight's about. Tonight is for cherishing what we have right now, you know, before real life gets in the way?'

Even as she said it out loud, she knew that she was lying. Knew that she was glowing in just the way Lindsey had described, and was pleased about it too. It meant that everything was still going according to her masterplan.

Pippa blew a rude raspberry in response. 'Nope,' she cried, 'tonight is the night that Katie finally gets her rocks off!'

'Sex for Kate! Sex for Kate! Sex for Kate!' Freddie Weir heard the drunk girl yelling from across the lobby and winced.

'Well there's one for you,' Baz nudged him, his voice just a little too loud.

'Leave off,' Freddie groaned.

He needed a drink. And then he needed to find Camellia. She'd said that she'd see him here, and he'd bought the ticket especially. They'd been flirting all term and tonight was the last time he'd have a chance to see her, to tell her how he really felt. At least, he thought that they'd been flirting. To be honest, he wasn't entirely sure. The one thing he knew for certain was that he liked spending time with her, and that she'd been nice to him. They always sat in the same seats in the library as they revised for finals, right next to each other. He'd even got her a Yorkie from the vending machine once, without her asking him to. That was flirting, wasn't it? And then, when she'd asked if he would be at the Leavers' Ball, and he'd instinctively nodded, she seemed so pleased. It was as if there was an unspoken promise there, a realisation that they were both on the same page and that tonight, at this ball, the rest of their lives could finally start. So where was she?

'You OK?' Baz asked. The buttons of his dress shirt were already open down to his navel, revealing a riot of dark chest hair.

'Just got to find someone.'

'Ahh, of course, the infamous Camellia?'

'Leave off, all right?'

'Whoa, easy there . . . go find your girl. And then, when you do, pound her to next Wednesday!'

Freddie winced again as he tore himself away from Baz's side. This was different. This wasn't going to be one of Baz's drunken hook-ups or next-day regrets. This was Camellia. He'd sat by her side all term, helped her understand concepts that weren't even on his syllabus, reassured her when she thought she was going to fail. She was real, she was special. Which meant tonight was going to be special too.

Kate finally stepped into the ballroom and took a moment to gaze around. Drapes covered the walls, lit by a pulsing array of blues and pinks. The music thumped, heavy with bass, and before her she saw a great sea of writhing bodies in black tie, ridding themselves of their cares and worries through flailing limbs and sweat. There were hundreds of people in here; surely one of them – just one boy – would want to sleep with her. Someone had to.

She was dragged from her thoughts by Lindsey and Pippa, who – one on each side – pulled her forward into the beating heart of the dance floor, bumping into people as they made their erratic way to the centre. Pippa did her signature move, a disjointed tilting of her head as her arms came out in front, a weird homage to 'Thriller', while Lindsey held out a bottle of wine and swigged from it liberally, glassware already completely abandoned.

'Got your eye on anyone?' Pippa asked, wrapping herself around Kate during a lull in the music.

Kate glanced around, her eyes alighting briefly on a tall, slightly gawky boy with a serious face, before honing in on another guy next to him, one she recognised as a bartender at the Union. She thought he was single; hadn't she overheard him moaning the other week about how bad his recent break-up had been? She couldn't think of a more suitable candidate. A man with nothing to lose couldn't possibly say no, and she was just about drunk enough to shoot her shot.

Come on Kate, you've got this, she told herself, as she stepped away from her friends and towards the dancing bartender.

Briefly disturbed by the sight of a fierce-looking blonde girl with a dishevelled up-do marching towards him, Freddie started to move away before realising that it was actually the guy next to him in her line of sight. He watched in baffled wonder as she stepped up close to him, and without a single word of warning, lunged in for a kiss. His sense of respect for a person who could pull a move like that battled with his discomfort at the thought of sudden, unprovoked proximity, and he moved away, craning his neck over the dance floor to see if he could spot Camellia.

He didn't even know what she would be wearing, or how she had styled her hair. Didn't have her number – not yet. But that was OK. Freddie was nothing if not a man of logic, and so he had decided that the only way to cover the entirety of the dance floor was to move in concentric circles. He'd just have to hope that if she was indeed part of the manic throng, she wouldn't be moving about too much.

Every time he looked towards a corner, or around a pillar, his heart thudded with disappointment. Perhaps there were two Leavers' Balls tonight? What if he'd got it wrong and she was at the other one?

'Freddie!' Baz called. He was on his second lap and had managed to avoid his best friend the first time, but not now. Baz's shirt was now fully undone, his round belly just protruding over his belt in a way that seemed provocative and cool rather than gross. Freddie could never get away with things like that, but he liked that Baz could. Despite the barrel-ness of his frame, he had the kind of round, open face and bright blue eyes that other people (especially women) tended to find attractively bold and charming.

'Where's this Camellia then?' Baz asked.

'Oh, I just left her at the bar. Had to go and get something.' The lie was out before Freddie even had a chance to think about it. Freddie hoped that the music was too loud for Baz to hear.

'And?'

'And what?'

'Is it going to happen then?'

'Is what going to happen?'

'Come on, mate, you know damn well what I'm talking about. Is tonight the night Freddie finally becomes a man?'

'Working on it pal, working on it.' Freddie's stomach swooped.

'See, your problem is,' Baz leaned in close, smelling of beer and late-night musk, 'that you put too much focus on it. That's what your problem is. You think that sex is the be-all and end-all. That it's the culmination of true romance and all that crap.'

'I don't think that.'

'Freddie, it's just sex! There doesn't have to be any greater meaning to it. Just two meat-sacks, slapping together and having fun.'

'That's gross Baz.'

'It's not gross. That's sex!'

Freddie gave Baz an affectionate double-tap on the shoulder before he headed past, careful to look as if he was moving with intention and not desperately searching, in case his friend was still watching him.

* * *

'I just thought, you know, if you wanted to go somewhere, I'm sure there's somewhere quieter we could go?' Kate wasn't sure her words were making sense, because the boy in front of her looked utterly startled.

'Do I know you?' he asked.

'You don't know me, but I know you. And I also know that it's loud in here, and that we could go somewhere quieter if you like?'

The rush of confidence, the thrill of the glow, was fast fading. Why did he look so scared? Isn't this what all guys wanted? To have it laid on thick, to literally have a girl fall at their feet?

'I don't know if you think I'm someone else maybe?'

'Come on, let's get out of here . . .' Kate was starting to feel as if her heels were too high, that her lipstick desperately needed touching up, and that the double-sided sticky tape she was using to make sure her dress didn't gape obscenely was coming undone. This wasn't the way it was meant to be going.

'Sweetheart, are you OK?' someone else now, a girl with a kind voice and a concerned face.

'I'm fine,' Kate said, pulling back and looking around for Lindsey and Pippa.

'I just think that maybe you should get some water or something?' the girl said.

'And I just think you should get out of my friend's face!' Suddenly Pippa was there. Too much there.

'Easy, OK? I was just trying to help.'

'I think you could help a lot more by staying out of my friend's business, OK?'

'Excuse me? It was your friend who lunged at *my* boyfriend.'

Boyfriend? Oh crap. Kate hoped that the layers of foundation she was wearing would hide her reddening face.

Kate looked around anxiously for a gap in the crowd to escape through, but her brain seemed to be slowing down just as the music felt like it was speeding up. When she turned to check that her friends were following her, she saw Pippa reaching out a palm towards the girl's face, Lindsey struggling to hold her back.

Lindsey called out, 'Help me hold her!'

'We should really get her home,' Kate said.

'No, this is meant to be your night. And you know what Pippa gets like. She just needs a glass of water and some time on the naughty steps outside.'

Kate watched as the guy she had technically assaulted and his girlfriend made their getaway. She didn't want to go home. The night was young and she had a mission to complete. But Pippa was swaying dangerously and looked as though she was about to puke.

'We should take her back to halls,' Kate said, trying not to sound too sad about it. Lindsey looked at her appreciatively with panda-like smudges of eyeliner under her already tired eyes, her usually bouncy brown curls limp and flat around her face.

'I know it sucks, but it's not as if tonight is the last chance you're going to get to have sex or anything,' she said, stroking back Pippa's damp hair.

Lindsey was right, Kate thought, but that wasn't the point. Not exactly. She knew there'd be more chances to lose her virginity – there had to be – but tonight was the last night she'd be able to truthfully say that she 'lost it at uni'. From now on, she was a bona-fide adult, a graduate who was expected to know all about the intricacies and intimacies of life. From now on, for whoever she met, being a virgin could only be decidedly and horribly weird. Damn it, Pippa.

That was it. The dream was over. The friend code trumped the sex code, always and for ever. Kate knew that.

Lindsey took one of Pippa's arms over her shoulder and Kate took the other as they left the ballroom, staggered through the lobby and back to the door. On the steps leading down to the road, she saw that tall, gawky boy again, gazing mournfully down at the ground, as if he'd just been told the worst news of his life. Kate felt a wave of sympathy. At least she wasn't the only one having a terrible night.

Freddie had seen her. She had been there the whole time. Wrapped up in the arms of someone else. Someone wearing a shirt so tight it looked as if his muscles might burst through like the Hulk on a rager.

He didn't want to be the creep who stood and watched another couple kissing, so he had moved by relatively quickly, but then he had to go back to check because there was always the possibility that his mind was playing tricks on him, that he had got the angle wrong. But nope. It was Camellia. That same short hair, tonight styled to flare out in a wild, spiky aura around her face, the nose-ring and the clompy Doc Martens (which, paired with a tulle-underskirted dress, made her look twice as cool as she usually did). There was no doubt.

She hadn't liked him, after all. Or, at least, if she had liked him, it certainly hadn't been in the way that he had hoped. A part of him wanted to march right over and demand the Yorkie back. Another part of him just wanted the earth to swallow him up.

'Taking a breather?' Baz joined him on the steps outside the hall and took out a cigarette.

'What?'

'How's Camellia? Going well?'

Freddie didn't often make bad decisions, but his heart was hurting, and he wouldn't have been able to stand any of Baz's sympathy.

'Just waiting for her, actually,' he said. He looked up towards the sky, hoping to see stars, hoping for divine reassurance. Instead he got the murky purple of night-time London clouds.

'Yeah?'

'We're going back to hers. She just needed to get her stuff from the cloakroom.'

'Come on my son! I knew you could do it!'

Freddie hoped his silence was conveying a quiet, satisfied confidence rather than how he was really feeling.

Baz was rambling on. 'See, I knew it would happen for you. So what if it was the last night? That's your style, isn't it: save the best for last. I'm proud of you, mate.'

After an affectionate pat on the back, Baz wandered off to find someone who might have a working lighter. Freddie took the opportunity to make his escape and stepped down to the road, turning right. He had no idea where he was going, he just knew that he had to get out of there as quickly as possible.

2019

I

He made a decision not to look when Wayne pointed her out and tried his hardest to stick to that decision when Baz added his approval too.

'Go on, this is a great chance! What you got to lose?' Baz said, watching him keenly.

'Everything,' Freddie mumbled back, still determined to avoid looking.

'Just be yourself,' Wayne offered. 'I mean, not yourself *right now*. But, you know, the self you are when you're just with us. Imagine you're just chatting in the pub or something.'

It was easy for them, Freddie wanted to say. Baz was all settled now, and Wayne lived in a world where nothing was above being made fun of. In the three years since Freddie had known him, he hadn't ever once seen Wayne take anything seriously, unless it was a pint, or *Call of Duty*.

'What should I say then?' he asked, hoping the tone of his voice would put them off pressing him any further. No such luck.

'She's in a comic book shop holding an issue of *Starboy* at a Brian Teller signing. What do you think you should talk to her about?' Baz replied, baffled.

Freddie finally turned his head and took her in: beautiful, in a cute way. Button features and bobbed hair.

This could be OK, he thought. *She doesn't seem all that scary*.

He took a moment for a deep breath, and in that moment came a flood of expectation. What if this was it? What if this was the moment every other moment would spin out from? One day he might be telling his grandkids about this. One year from now he might bring her here to propose, and maybe they would get married here too, surrounded by their favourite books, perhaps even officiated over by the man they had both come to this bookshop signing to see. The whole wedding party in vibrant cosplay. The photos would go viral on the internet. Ellen would end up inviting them to America to be on TV and everything.

I have to get this right. It has to be perfect.

And then, the mirror voice, just as insistent: *Why even bother?*

One deep breath turned into another, and then another, as the thoughts spiralled through his mind, battling and getting louder and louder on each turn. It was all too much.

'I think our boy might need a bit of a push.'

Before Freddie could register what Wayne had said, he found himself shoved and stumbling backwards, nearly falling over his own feet, and right into *her.*

'Oh no, oh my God, I'm so sorry,' Freddie said, scrambling upright and trying not to drop the *Starboy* single issues he was clutching.

'It's fine,' the girl said, staring at him.

'Yeah, I'm so sorry.' His palms were sweating now, his comics, packaged individually in pristine cellophane sleeves, sliding out of his hands and down to the floor as he tried to balance by placing a hand on a shelving rack that wobbled precariously.

'Let me help you with that,' the girl offered, crouching down to help collect them up.

When he bent down to join her, their faces were level, their eyes meeting briefly. Hers were brown. Wide, chocolate-drop brown.

'Do you need a tissue?' the girl asked.

'What?'

'For your face?'

God, he really was sweating. His top lip was completely slick, and one embarrassing drop threatened to actually roll off his brow and on to the floor below. It was mortifying. And now that he was mortified, that meant the sweating was only going to get worse.

'No, I'm all right thanks.' He couldn't think of anything else to say, could feel Baz and Wayne listening in behind him, the sense that he'd somehow let them down just another thing contributing to his rapidly increasing heart rate, and the adrenaline tremor in his fingertips.

An imagined lifetime of perfect romantic bliss vanished into stardust.

'I'm going to turn away now,' Freddie said when they were standing again, his comics all safely collected up.

He knew she was still watching him as he shuffled back to his friends, mopping his face with the sleeve of his jumper before Baz gave him a consolatory pat on the shoulder.

A few moments later, while Wayne was deep into explaining to a baffled stranger how underrated Brian Teller's cynical approach to Blairite Britain was in the *Starboy Ultimate Saga* during the late nineties, Freddie heard the girl behind him on the phone.

'Could you get here quickly, OK?' she was telling the person on the other end. 'I swear one of these creeps just tried to maul me. '

When he woke up, the hangover hit him like a punch. His gut moaned at him and his tongue felt dry and barbed in his mouth. Freddie tried to moisten his lips, as brittle as a mountain crag. Christ, how many pints did he end up having?

Still, at least it was Saturday. The clock on Freddie's bedside table read ten thirty, which felt about right. He may have missed most of his morning, but he didn't care. The only plans he had were to pop to the shops, then at four thirty he was due at his brother's house to celebrate his niece's first birthday.

Congratulations Lacey! He'd written on the card. *You made it one whole rotation around the sun!*

The card was tucked neatly into its envelope and was sitting right on top of his chest of drawers where he wouldn't forget it, propped up against the carefully wrapped cuddly dinosaur he had bought because he thought it looked cute, and because he imagined that if he were one year old, he'd find the soft felt teeth hilarious. Lacey had so many pink things anyway, this could be something unique that would always remind her of him.

'Well that's lovely,' he heard his sister-in-law saying. 'But why did you get her a boy present?'

Stella wouldn't actually say it, but Freddie imagined it anyway.

What if I've made a terrible mistake, he thought. *What kind of person buys a dinosaur for a little baby girl?*

It had seemed like such a good idea at the time; subversive and 'woke', as Stella liked to say. But now he wondered if he actually understood the word properly, or if he had in fact gone too far. Did he have enough time to go to the shops to exchange it? Did he even have the energy?

It'll be fine. It'll have to be fine.

He groaned and rubbed his face as he realised that he hadn't managed to brush his teeth before he got into bed, and then attempted to push past the anxiety that gave him. He hadn't remembered to take his medication either, the side effects of which he'd no doubt have to battle later.

Freddie rubbed at his eyes. Yuck. He felt disgusting. He *was* disgusting. No wonder he was alone.

He didn't remember much from the rest of the night before, not after he had seen that girl from the comic book shop come into the pub with a couple of her girlfriends and had decided that the best way to avoid Baz and Wayne trying to set him up again was to get obnoxiously drunk. Freddie vaguely recalled a couple of the people who worked at Ben Day Comics sitting with them, and at some point showing them what amounted to his most prized possession: the complete single-issue run of the first *Starboy Saga*, now all signed by the creator himself. Had he dreamt that one of the Ben Day lot had suggested that he could probably get a couple of thousand for them if he ever wanted to sell?

Oh no. The Starboys. *Where were the* Starboys*?*

Suddenly very much awake, Freddie stumbled around his bedroom, looking for any reasonable place he could have left them during his drunken stupor. Then he started looking through the unreasonable places. Oh God – where the hell had he put them?

He was still naked but for last night's boxers, when Damien found him in the kitchen, unloading the fridge of all its contents and squinting at every shelf.

Damien was a small man, but had what Freddie's mother liked to call 'presence'. He worked nights at a telecoms company, so Freddie rarely spent any time with him. When Freddie got home from work, Damien was on his way out, if not gone already. This was an arrangement that suited Freddie, as most of the time it felt like he had the entire place to himself, but it meant that when their paths did cross, he would end up feeling like an invader in his own home, with Damien's small but determined 'presence' taking up way more space than Freddie was used to.

'What do you think you're doing?' Damien asked now, the raising of his eyebrows causing deep furrows in his forehead.

'You're home?' Freddie asked in return.

'Just got in an hour ago. And I'd really prefer it if I was able to get some sleep without an absolute ruckus happening right next to my bedroom.'

Freddie frowned, sympathetic for his flatmate's need for sleep, but not able to subdue the anxiety he felt.

'Have you seen a rucksack full of *Starboy* comics?' Freddie asked. 'I took it out with me last night, and then I got drunk, and I was hoping I had left it in here somewhere before I made it to bed. '

'If they were so valuable, why would you take them outside with you?'

Damien moved to the fancy Tassimo coffee machine that Freddie wasn't allow to use, and made himself an espresso. Freddie winced at the sudden loud noise, and then marvelled at the fact that Damien wanted to drink high-concentration caffeine just before he was due to go to bed.

'Because Brian Teller was at the shop, and I got them all signed! They're in pristine condition!'

Damien looked down at him (which, considering he was a fair few inches shorter than Freddie, was quite the feat) and sighed sadly.

'I really could do without all this commotion after the shift I've just had.'

'Damien, I promise that as soon as I find them, I'll be quiet as a mouse. And I'm not even going to be here later. You'll have the flat to yourself and it'll all be nice and quiet. I just really need to find them.'

'I don't know why you care so much about those things. All lurid illustrations from seedy Soho tradesmen.'

'Comics aren't porn, Damien.'

Damien took a sip on his espresso, and let his face fall into an expression eerily reminiscent of a withering Maggie Smith.

'Look, have you seen the bag? Or the comics? Just tell me, OK?'

'For the sake of peace in this flat, I wish I had.' Then Damien took his tiny cup and retired to his bedroom, closing the door behind him with a force that wasn't angry enough to be an outright slam, but enough to make Freddie clench his jaw with worry about there being an atmosphere later.

'Damn it,' Freddie mumbled, and went back to his bedroom, digging his phone out of the pocket of his jeans. No messages. Not that he was expecting any, but there was always the hope that either Baz or Wayne had taken the bag home with them by mistake. Maybe they hadn't woken up yet, so hadn't had the chance to tell him?

EMERGENCY – anyone seen my black rucksack with the comics in them?

Freddie waited thirty seconds, and then waited thirty seconds more. No replies.

This is OK. This is all going to be OK, he told himself, willing his brain to believe it. *Just calm down, have a shower and drink some water. They'll turn up.*

He couldn't look at himself in the mirror as he brushed his teeth. He was too ashamed to meet his own eye. Was it worth it? Spending all that money and time getting wasted the night before? And for what? Broke and still one week from payday (why was January so long?) and facing the possibility of his precious comics dumped in a side alley bin somewhere. Or worse, stolen by that guy from Ben Day and sold on the dark web for Bitcoins.

Nevertheless, he brushed vigorously. And then, after about three minutes' work, feeling the anxiety tingle through his hands, he started from scratch again, working into his own gums with a torturous velocity. A whisper in the back of his brain told him that maybe, if he just kept brushing, that if he was clean enough, everything would turn out all right in the end. It took meeting his own eyes in the mirror, and taking a number of deep breaths, to resolve that this time, brushing only twice would be enough.

He distracted himself in the shower by thinking about what he was going to wear for his niece's birthday. He decided on his date jeans, so-called not because he had actually been on any dates, but because they were what he would wear should the occasion ever arise. He had been saving them, but impressing his family was as important as impressing any future romantic interest. It would potentially stop them from worrying, and who knew, maybe, if he just looked like he had his shit together, then it might magically happen? Even so, he started bracing himself for the comments. Like last time, when Stella had asked him in that tone he couldn't quite figure out where he had bought his shoes, and he could only think that he had somehow managed to buy them at the wrong place. Was there a wrong place to buy shoes?

There were still no messages on his phone once he had finished in the bathroom. Freddie wondered about calling Baz, but didn't know whether that was an OK thing to do these days. The only phone calls he'd received over the last few months were from automated robots checking to see if he'd been in a car accident that wasn't his fault. It didn't seem like something a regular, normal person would do. But this was an emergency, and emergencies changed everything.

'Hello?' It was a girl who answered the phone, a child. Freddie took the phone away from his ear for a moment to check the number. It was definitely Baz's phone. Numbers didn't spontaneously change once they were stored, but the voice on the other end was high and sweet. 'Is there anyone there?'

'Uh, yeah. Is Baz there? I mean Barry. Is Barry there?' He knew that Baz was short for Barry, he guessed that much. But was Barry also short for something? After all this time, why had his mind gone blank suddenly? Barold? Was Barold even a name?

'*Daddy!*' the girl screeched away from the phone.

Wait, was that Maisie? He remembered when Maisie had been born. Surely the amount of time necessary for a newborn baby to grow into a person who was old enough to answer the phone hadn't passed that quickly? Freddie's brain quickly did the mental arithmetic and worked out that in the time it had taken for Maisie to grow into a fully conversational human being, he had barely managed to grow at all. There wasn't one thing that had developed or evolved in his life (bar the introduction of Damien) in the time it had taken for Baz's tiny girl to gain a basic knowledge of the English language. It was frighteningly depressing.

There was fumbling, a sound like the phone being dropped and then picked up again.

'Hello?'

'That was Maisie?' was the first thing Freddie could think of to say.

'Hey Freddo,' Baz mumbled. He sounded just as hungover as Freddie felt. 'What's going on?'

'No, I mean. I'm sorry, but I was just surprised. She can answer the phone now?'

'Yeah. Maisie. Nearly five, can you believe it? Obsessed with the bloody phone. Laura has to ring sometimes just so that she can answer it. Look mate, I have a headache, you know? Is everything OK?'

'Yeah . . . I mean no. No, not really. It's about that black rucksack I have. The one I put all the *Starboys* in? I woke up this morning and I can't find it. I was hoping that you might have taken it home with you by mistake?'

'Mate, I'm sorry. I don't. Don't even remember the bag.'

'Baz, please say you're winding me up?'

'Look Freddo, mate. I have a stinking headache and I have to take Maisie horse-riding in half an hour. I don't have your comics. Have you tried Wayne?'

'You go horse-riding?'

'No. I take Maisie horse-riding. I'm going to sit in the car and have a nap. Give Wayne a bell. Or try the pub? Maybe they have a lost property box or something?'

'Yeah, no. That's a good idea. Sorry for the call. Speak soon?'

'Yup. Right. OK. Speak soon. Bye.'

Baz sounded really different over the phone. He remembered University Baz, the Asgardian lord of tits and wine. Phone Baz was tired. And a dad. A dad who took his tiny daughter horse-riding at weekends.

The pub. That was a good idea. Calling a stranger was ten times worse than calling someone he knew, and normally something that he would have avoided altogether, but just the glimmer of hope gave him motivation to push on. *Like when someone in an accident gets the strength to lift a car*, Freddie thought. This was exactly like that.

Praying that there'd be someone available to answer at the pub at this time on a Saturday morning, Freddie searched online for the details, and tapped 'call'.

2

'You haven't found a replacement yet, have you?'

Lindsey's nose looked disproportionately large on Kate's phone screen, the camera set at an angle that Kate found endearing on her ex-flatmate, but was certain would look hideous on herself. Kate had in fact spent a little too long adjusting herself on the sofa, holding her phone out at uncomfortable angles until she was certain that the screen wouldn't reveal two chins or the heaviness of the bags under her eyes. She knew Lindsey would have called her out on the latter instantly if she had been there in the room with her. Which she wasn't.

'You're a tough act to follow, you know,' Kate replied.

'What about your friend from work? Renee?'

'I asked her, but you should have seen her face when I told her the rent. I think it's out of her price range.'

It was out of Kate's price range too, and her heart made an uncomfortable lurch as she considered it.

'What about your old friends from school? Elise or India or one of that lot? Or there's always Pippa . . .'

'Are you serious? Didn't you tell me she was living in a commune in Thailand?'

'Hey, I'm not so far away from her now, maybe I should pop over and say hello.'

'I think we've both had enough of Pippa for a lifetime. But getting in touch with the others might be a good call. I've let things slip a bit with them; do you think it would be weird?'

'Only if you made it weird.'

Kate missed Lindsey so much. The flat felt horribly quiet and empty without her.

'Look,' Lindsey started. 'I know that you don't like the idea of sharing with a stranger, but I don't think you really have much choice at this point. It's get someone else in, or, you know . . .'

Or get out, Kate thought.

There was the heart lurch again.

'But anyway, I don't want you worrying about all that,' Kate said, trying to push the dangerous thoughts aside. 'Tell me about Hong Kong.'

'It's humid,' Lindsey grimaced. 'Look at my hair.'

Lindsey brought the camera out away from her face to reveal an aura of dark frizz. She made a face and started laughing.

'It looks fine.'

'It's a mess! But apart from the hair situation, it's good out here. A little hectic, they've thrown me right in at the deep end, but otherwise, it's all good.'

'If anyone can handle it, it's you.'

'The hair or the job?'

'Both, you loon.'

Kate's laugh turned into a sigh, one she hoped Lindsey didn't notice.

'There's something else,' Lindsey said, her voice softer, the whisper of an excited child.

'Go on?'

'I'm going on a date tonight.'

'What? You've only been out there a week!'

'I know. Work took me out for drinks last night, and there was this guy I met at the bar, and I don't know . . . maybe it's the new location, or the excitement and novelty? But I thought, why wait to settle in? What's stopping me?'

'Wow. Where are you going?'

'I don't know. He's picking me up in a couple of hours.'

'Lindsey, how do you do it? This is incredible.'

'It's just a date. No big deal. At worst, at least it's a way to find out a bit more about the city.'

'And at best?'

'You know I'm not going to let myself get all distracted by that kind of stuff. I'm out here to work. But that doesn't mean I can't have fun too.'

'That's the spirit,' Kate said with more enthusiasm than she felt.

The conversation collapsed for a beat. Lindsey seemed distracted by something just beyond her phone's camera, and Kate felt like she had nothing to add, like she was suddenly very far away.

'I'd better get going,' Kate said finally. 'You've got to get ready for your date, and I've got to head to work.'

'I forgot that you have to work weekends.'

'I've forgotten what weekends are.'

'Well, I hope you have a good one. I'll speak to you tomorrow, OK?'

'I want all the juicy details please.'

'Of course. Love you, hun.'

'Love you too. Byeee!'

Kate put the phone down beside her and felt the silence of the flat once more. Shelves were half full, drawers half empty. The flat echoed from having half its stuff taken away from it. At night it was especially unbearable; it didn't feel like home any more.

Staring at the ceiling, Kate thought about her options. Plan A, living there alone, was never going to be a real possibility, and Plan B, getting another good friend to move in, was proving to be more difficult than she'd anticipated. That left Plan C, the option that would involve the biggest hit to her pride . . .

But no. The emptiness was fine. Kate was fine. Everything was absolutely fine. It had to be.

* * *

Sometimes on her commute, dressed in her expensive coat and scarf from the time when she was paid a proper salary rather than by the hour, Kate could pretend that she was still someone important, with somewhere to be and people to meet. Nobody could tell that underneath was her Central Art Gallery uniform, and the only people she would be meeting that day were ones asking for directions to the nearest toilets.

The truth though, was that the coat was getting tighter and the uniform harder to hide. Kate had never been thin, at least not to a degree that she ever felt content with, but she'd never been this heavy either. It made her resist looking in mirrors sometimes, made her dread picking out clothes. Not that she felt the impetus to do anything about it. Lately it had felt a bit as though letting the world drown her was so much easier than pulling herself up and out.

Her phone vibrated with a notification just as the Tube was about to disappear underground. Expecting another marketing email from a brand she could no longer afford, Kate's heart sank at the subject line: *Your Application*. Good news never arrived first thing on a Saturday morning.

When she'd first started her job hunt, Kate had optimistically created a colour-coded spreadsheet to track the applications. But logging the rejections had become so depressing that she couldn't bring herself to open the file any more. She briefly checked this email, searching for a hint of feedback or even just a glimmer of humanity within it, but no, nowadays everything was just an automated response. She wondered, not for the first time, if her CV, and the black hole within it caused by the job at the gallery, had been rejected by an algorithm before a human being had even laid eyes on it. The gallery was only ever meant to be a stopgap, something she could do for a few months until she figured out what to do next. How had a few months become nearly two years?

Kate swiped delete on the email. She thought about tweeting her disappointment, but then she worried that a potential employer might see it and be put off. Worse than that, she worried that Lindsey might see it, and it would cause her to worry. Lindsey had an exciting new life now. She didn't need concern for her old friend holding her back.

It's fine. Everything is fine.

Renee was waiting for Kate by the staff entrance to the gallery.

'Come on, it's cold.' She was shivering in her stylish but too-thin jacket.

'Sorry, I was chatting to Lindsey. The time zone thing takes a little getting used to.'

'How's she doing?'

'Great. Fine. I think she's really enjoying herself out there.'

'Not so great and fine for you though?'

'Oh, I'm OK.'

Renee's mouth, red with bold lipstick, quirked with scepticism as she held the door open for them both.

'Really. I'm OK. I got another rejection this morning, but I didn't want that job anyway. The commute would have been painful.'

'Well, no wonder you're bummed out.'

'It's just . . . I would have been perfectly qualified to do that job a few years ago. It wasn't even manager level. I thought I stood a really good chance.'

'But you didn't want it anyway?'

'No, but that's not the point.'

'Well, until the job of a lifetime comes along, I'm pleased that we get to hold on to you for just a little bit longer.' Renee wrapped an arm around Kate's waist, and hugged her close as they zapped their passes and made their way down to the basement, where the staff changing rooms were. There were worse places to have a stopgap job, Kate knew, and worse people to work it with.

'You're looking fancy today,' Kate noticed as Renee climbed out of a slinky black dress and into her uniform. 'Hot date later?'

'Actually . . .'

The lurch. It pulled at her insides.

'No *way*. Who is he? Or she?'

'*He*,' Renee clarified with a smile, 'is someone from my course. Claude. He does these weird, giant abstract portraits. Here, let me show you.'

Renee pulled out her phone and flicked to Instagram, revealing a series of brightly coloured splatters and artful blobs arranged in vaguely face-like proportions.

'Don't show me his art,' Kate laughed. 'Show me *him*.'

Renee laughed and flicked through to some pictures of a man who looked distinctly Mediterranean, and distinctly hot, in that dark, Mediterranean kind of way, with thick-rimmed glasses that seemed to tone down the hotness to the perfect level of gorgeously approachable.

'And this man was just in your class? Just sitting there? The whole time?' Kate asked. She couldn't remember when she had last seen a man that good-looking in real life. 'He was just . . . there?'

'Well, he only switched to my particular module at the end of last year, and we kind of hooked up at the Christmas social, but I think after that he tried to play it cool, all tiny flirty moments and longing stares. Stupid stuff. I think he thought it was more romantic that way. But I got bored, so I bought him a drink and ended up asking him out last week. You should have seen his face!'

'Just like that.' Kate marvelled, thinking about how easy it seemed to be for Lindsey too.

'But I don't know yet. He's very cute, obviously, and I want to get to know him more, but quiet guys freak me out a bit, you know?'

Kate nodded like she knew.

When Renee disappeared to pop to the loo, Kate finished putting things away in her locker, fixed her lanyard around her neck, and straightened up her shirt so that the buttons didn't pull across her chest. She used to have such nice clothes, and nice make-up too. She used to get her hair done at fancy salons with juniors who massaged your head during deep-conditioning treatments. She sighed as she pulled out a small compact mirror from her handbag, smoothed her hair and quickly smudged on some tinted lip balm.

Kate met up with Renee again during the pre-shift briefing, and only half listened to the duty manager as they relayed the necessary news. She was thinking about how some people seemed to date like it was nothing. Renee did this all the time, some of the relationships so fleeting that Kate never had the chance to ask what their names were (if Renee cared enough to remember). And then there was Lindsey, barely landed on another continent and already getting interest from guys. Maybe it was because they were beautiful – far more beautiful than Kate had ever considered herself to be – but there was something else too. Something everybody else seemed to understand that Kate didn't, like a radio frequency she had no idea how to tune into.

The gallery always started quiet first thing on a Saturday, like the calm before a storm. Then, at around eleven, the public descended. But the truth was, no matter how humdrum the job could be at times, and how easy it was compared to the job she used to do, there were many parts of being at the gallery that Kate absolutely loved. Being given ample opportunity to people-watch was definitely one of them. At this time of day there were never many children, apart from the ones dragged along by family members desperate for their progeny to get away from their screens and absorb some culture. There were plenty of students, who would crouch before the famous paintings with their sketchbooks and get all the lines and tones completely wrong. There were older folk who dressed like they were going mountaineering, complete with heavy backpacks and sometimes even hiking sticks, and bored Europeans sneering that London galleries were nothing compared to the ones on the continent. There were girls in floaty dresses and tennis shoes, wandering dreamily and taking artful selfies that would appear on Instagram later, and serious boys in black turtlenecks, stepping furiously from one room to another and scowling at anything they didn't like (which was most things).

More than anything, Kate loved watching the couples. They'd wander through the rooms holding hands and pushing hair out of each other's eyes, standing before the more famous works of art and then turning to each other for a quick kiss or simply to exchange a meaningful glance. Kate tried to hate lovey-dovey stuff, told herself that she should be hardened to that kind of thing by now, but she couldn't deny there was still a tiny part of her that believed in love. She still believed, despite all the years that it hadn't happened for her, despite working so hard to stamp out any sentimentality.

'Busy today,' Renee commented when she came to relieve Kate's post. They shifted their positions every hour, and those brief moments when someone came to take over, before you moved on to take over from the next person, were welcome respite from the tedium.

'Yeah,' Kate replied.

'Did you see that girl with the eyebrows? It looked like she'd drawn two fighting caterpillars on her forehead! I'm sure she came through this room.'

Kate hadn't, but only because she had been letting herself gaze at a twenty-something couple clearly on a date. The girl was pretty in an ethereal, fairy-like way, and he was messy-handsome, meticulously scruffy and smiling. They were sitting on a bench in front of a huge, busy depiction of some mythological battle, and while she was gazing at the scene, he was gazing at her. Kate sighed.

'You need to get out there,' Renee said, following Kate's gaze. 'Online dating, or singles nights or something.'

'You know it's not for me,' Kate replied. She'd had the same conversation so many times with Lindsey, it almost bored her now. Nobody ever seemed to understand how hard it was.

'Nonsense. Besides, the more men you meet, the more likely one is to stick.'

'Sometimes I think that whole part of me has shut down, if it was ever there at all. Like, I can appreciate a good song, but that doesn't mean I can sing or play an instrument. Perhaps this is it for me. Maybe this is just something I have to accept.'

'For goodness' sake, can you hear yourself? You're not even thirty yet. And besides, you're one of the romantic ones. Things always work out for the romantic ones.'

'I'm very nearly thirty. But I love your conviction.'

'It's because it's true.'

Kate checked her watch and knew it was time to move on. She had the next person on the rota to relieve from their post.

It was lunchtime when they caught up again. In the dull quiet of the basement staff room, they stretched their legs out under a table and put their feet up on chairs on the other side, and tried not to laugh when Una reheated her tomato soup on too high a setting, causing it to furiously bubble and explode within the microwave.

'Sometimes I think that Claude's art is what would happen if Picasso and Warhol had a baby,' Renee was musing as she deep-dived through his social media.

'Do you fancy Claude, or his work?' Kate asked, peering over her friend's shoulder and twisting as she tried to take in a lava-lamp-like series of blobs that may or may not have also been a face.

'If you're daring me to engage in a debate on the separation between art and artist, you've picked a day when I'm feeling particularly confident,' Renee warned.

'Another time maybe. I've got to try and get the flatmate thing sorted.'

'Still no luck?'

'Nope. Are you sure I can't convince you?'

'Your place is amazing, so trust me, I wish I could. Knock a few hundred off a month and I'm there.'

What Kate would have given for a couple of hundred off a month. The place had been perfectly affordable until she had been made redundant. And even after that, her savings and redundancy settlement had covered a fair proportion of the costs for a few months. But for the past year, it had been Kate's parents who had done the most to take the rental burden off.

Kate felt a prickle of anxiety. She hated asking them for money. Felt terrible that they were so happy to give it to her. But the new job, and its associated salary, was just around the corner, wasn't it?

Kate looked down at her phone and started scrolling through her Facebook notifications. She knew that she hadn't been the best at keeping in touch with her old friends, but it wasn't easy when she felt so downhearted much of the time. She rationally knew that she had nothing to be ashamed of, that life happened and everybody went through rough patches on occasion, but that sense of shame didn't pay much attention to rationality. Every time she opened Instagram it felt like she was failing them somehow. But they were her oldest friends, they'd understand, surely?

However awkward it felt to start escalating Plan B and to let her friends know just how much of a pickle she was in, a big motivating factor was that it meant she didn't have to consider Plan C for a little while longer. So when she opened the Facebook app and saw the photos right there on her feed, what upset her the most, at least at first, was realising she would have to rethink everything.

3

The Rocking Horse seemed different in daylight. Or, at least, it was different from how Freddie remembered it. There was light pouring through the old-style mullioned windows, and instead of music, the only sound was the roar of the vacuum cleaner, operated by a guy still wrapped up in his parka, scarf and gloves, despite being indoors. Many of the chairs were stacked upside down on the tables, revealing a carpet busy with constellations of dark spots where chewing gum and wine stains had been trodden in over the years.

Freddie's hangover was like a metal helmet fastened around his head, so heavy that his neck and shoulders were struggling to cope with it. He had drunk a whole bottle of orange juice on the way over to the pub, hoping that the sugars and vitamin C would revive him, but instead it just felt like a gummy slime was coating the inside of his mouth and furring his tongue. He had rushed out of the house without bringing his trusty tube of travel-sized toothpaste with him, and oh boy, was he regretting that now.

'Um, are you Carmen?' Freddie asked the girl drying up pint glasses behind the bar.

She had a shockingly beautiful face, expertly made up into something simultaneously dream-like and vaguely sinister, punctuated by a gold ring septum piercing. Despite it being January, and her colleague dressing for work like he was exploring the Arctic, this girl was wearing nothing but a black vest top with her jeans, and she was quite blatantly braless.

Freddie was trying not to look, he really was. But it was hard not to look when her nipples appeared to be staring straight back at him.

'Carmen?' Freddie tried again. Her eyes narrowed as she appraised him, suspicious.

'We are closed,' she replied in accented English, nodding her head up to the clock. 'We open at midday.'

'No, we spoke on the phone? My name is Freddie?' he heard his voice doing the upward inflection thing before he had a chance to control it.

'Looking for the black bag?'

'Yes?'

Carmen disappeared out back, leaving Freddie lingering at the bar. He looked over at the wrapped-up man doing the hoovering, attempted a nod of recognition, but was ignored. Freddie turned and let his eyes drift around the pub. They were such weird places when they were empty and closed, like a theatre devoid of an audience.

His eyes fell on a nearby cork noticeboard, and seeing as Carmen didn't seem to be hurrying back to him, Freddie wandered over to see what was going on. There was a poster for the Rocking Horse's monthly karaoke night, and a couple of those posters with tabs at the bottom, some already torn off, advertising English-language tutoring and guitar lessons. Then a few boring business cards, a couple of less boring ones hinting at some *adult* services, and finally a pink note-card, the kind Freddie used to use when he was revising for exams, with a title that hit him like a punch to the gut.

ADULT VIRGINS ANONYMOUS

He looked around him. Was this a joke? Had his friends done this? Or Damien somehow? No, Baz and Wayne didn't have any idea, at least he hoped not. Damien then? They rarely talked about this kind of thing, but was it possible that in the process of living together, Damien had figured it out? No, even if there was the chance he had, Damien wouldn't have been seen dead in this pub, and he could have had no idea that Freddie would be here at this exact time and place.

ADULT VIRGINS ANONYMOUS
Are you still a virgin?
Want to talk about it in a safe space?
Meetings every other Tuesday.

You're not alone

That was the bit that got him. The bit that made his stomach try to twist inside out, made the back of his neck sweat, made him look around nervously to check for the secret cameras. Because Freddie had always been alone. Had come to presume that he was always going to be alone. Couldn't possibly entertain the thought of being otherwise. He was the last virgin left in the entire world, and it was his deepest, most shameful secret.

Freddie heard some movement behind the door and figured that Carmen must be making her way back. After checking over his shoulder one more time to see that the hoovering guy was still lost in his own private hoovering world, Freddie pulled his phone out of his pocket and snapped a quick picture of the card.

'The bag,' Carmen said, her tone profoundly bored. She plonked his rucksack up on the bar, leaving Freddie feeling somewhat bewildered. Had that really mattered so much just a short while ago?

'What's in it?' Carmen asked.

'What?'

'What's in your bag?'

'Why do you want to know that?' It was strange, being so intensely proud of a comic book collection, while at the same time being so utterly embarrassed.

'To check it's yours. Tell me what's in the bag.'

He didn't want to. He really didn't want to. It wasn't as if there would ever, in any remote universe, parallel or otherwise, be any possibility of Carmen fancying him, but still. Sure, comics were cool now, and everybody seemed to fancy themselves an amateur historian of the Marvel or DC wider universes, but he still feared the disdain that clouded people's faces when they recognised him not for a cool nerd, but the other kind. The kind who was in deep without any hope of escaping. The virgin kind. Other nerds were doing great work to break the sad stereotypes, but Freddie was not one of them. He didn't know how to be.

'Comic books?' he muttered, still not able to avoid the insecure upward inflection.

'Comic books?'

'Yes.'

'What kind?'

'*Starboy.* Lots of *Starboys.* Single issues. In their bags. Signed by Brian Teller. '

Carmen unzipped the bag and peered inside. Then she closed the zip and pushed the bag over to him.

'It's yours,' she announced, as if there had ever been any doubt about it. Then she went back to cleaning the pint glasses.

'OK,' Freddie started, taking the bag and slinging it over his shoulder. Then, a thought: 'Can I ask you something?'

Carmen looked up, bored.

'Those notices?' he asked, gesturing to the cork board. 'Are they real?'

'What?'

'I mean, it isn't like, a joke noticeboard? Are all the notices on them real? It's not something for retweets or Instagram?'

'Nothing to do with me,' Carmen said. 'Students come in. They put things up. We take them down after a while. Come back later and speak to the manager if you want to put up an ad.'

Freddie pressed his lips together and nodded. He had outstayed his welcome, but the important thing was that he had succeeded in his mission: the comics were safe. Calamity over. So why was his stomach still fluttering? Maybe it was the hangover, but he couldn't be sure.

David and Stella lived in a new-build detached house in the suburbs. It had a front lawn, which was mysteriously verdant for this time of year, when everything else was cold and grey. Had it always looked like that? As he approached, the wrapped cuddly dinosaur and birthday card safe by his side in a Sainsbury's bag-for-life, Freddie couldn't help but crouch down to inspect the mysterious grass. It was fake and plastic-feeling between his fingers. Cookie-cutter perfection without the hassle of a lawnmower. Freddie didn't know whether to admire it or find it sad.

Inside the house, past the pink balloons on the front door, the party was busy. Beyond the sideboard overloaded with presents, he could see his parents in the kitchen, deep in conversation with his brother. Freddie took in a deep breath; why did he always feel like he was steeling himself for an attack whenever he was within twenty feet of him? There were three years between them, David being the older one, and they looked alike too, except that Freddie had always been much thinner, so his features tended to be more pronounced; his nose a little larger and more pointed, the angles of his face sharper and more defined.

Freddie dodged the kitchen and went straight for the living room, where Stella was sipping Prosecco and laughing with her friends.

Baby Lacey, crawling on a play-mat on the floor, looked like a cake – whipped up, frilled and frosted with pink sugar. She had tiny pink shoes on her feet, and a bright pink bow wrapped around her tiny head, her white-blonde hair fine and wispy. Freddie supposed that the bow was to make sure that everybody knew absolutely, with no doubt whatsoever, that Lacey was a little girl. Just in case they had missed all the other pink neon signs.

There was a table laid out against the window, laden with a spread of gluten-free delicacies (some dairy-free too, as the tiny cocktail-stick labels indicated), and behind them a pretty, white-iced cake in the shape of a number one. There were drinks already poured and lined up on one side of the table: flutes of Prosecco, or a light pink punch, which Freddie presumed was the non-alcoholic choice, and went for. He was thirsty. The aches and pains of the hangover had mostly subsided, leaving him feeling generally parched, and his lips dry.

'Freddie!' cooed Stella, coming over and giving Freddie a weak hug.

'Hiya Stell,' Freddie replied.

'So pleased you could make it, darling.'

'The place looks beautiful.' The house was still new, the tang of wet paint still faintly detectable on the tip of his tongue.

'Ah well, it's a work in progress. Have you said hello to your niece yet? Lacey-doll! It's your Uncle Freddie!'

Stella steered Freddie down to the floor, where baby Lacey gazed up with wide, hazel eyes. She was a very pretty baby – there was no way that she couldn't be, considering who her parents were – but now Freddie was down here, on the play-mat with her, he really had no idea what he was meant to do or say.

'Hi Lacey,' Freddie started. 'Happy birthday?'

'She likes you,' Stella remarked, letting the baby grip one of her fingers as she guided her daughter into a clumsy stand. 'She doesn't look at everyone in that way. She knows that you're related. She knows that you're her special Uncle Freddie, don't you doll?'

Freddie offered his own finger to the baby, and was faintly pleased when she gripped back and toddled in his direction, smiling her big gummy smile.

'You stay with her, OK Freddie?' Stella instructed, getting up to mingle with her other guests, and then somehow, despite there being quite a few people already in the room, Freddie found himself alone, the only one on the floor with the baby.

'So Lacey, how's life?' Freddie started, wondering what on earth he was meant to do with her. Lacey looked up at him with big, blank eyes. 'Get any nice presents?'

It was then that Freddie remembered his own present, which he brought out of the Sainsbury's bag, and pretended to help Lacey unwrap.

'What have we got here then?' Freddie said, feeling relaxed and like he might have this baby thing down after all. Not that he would be offering to babysit anytime soon. A few minutes was fine, but he had no idea what he was meant to do with such a tiny human beyond that.

'Yeah! It's a dinosaur!' Freddie said, starting to take the cuddly toy out of its packaging.

'Freddie? What are you doing?' Stella's voice was loud behind him.

'Just giving Lacey her pres—'

'We were going to wait until *after* for the presents.'

'Oh, well, I didn't know.' But somehow Freddie felt like he was meant to.

Stella came right over, knelt down, and prised the dinosaur from Freddie's hands.

'What is this anyway?' she asked, voice soft but firm, her smile too wide and a little scary.

'Oh, well, I thought that—'

'It doesn't matter. But really, you shouldn't have opened this in front of Lacey. Now she's going to want it!'

'Well, it is for her . . .'

Sure enough, the baby's face scrunched itself up into a million little red folds, and out of her mouth came a wail.

'Now see what you've done?' Stella picked Lacey up and held her tight, rubbing circles on her back as she wailed. She must have caught Freddie's bemused expression because she then added: 'We don't do cuddlies. We're trying to restrict her exposure to cuddly, furry toys. To prevent allergies.'

'Oh, I see. I'm sorry. Nobody told me.'

'It's OK. We can fix this. It doesn't have to be a complete disaster. We're going to put the dinosaur through the wash – aren't we Lacey doll? And then we're going to get a nice big Ziploc bag, and then there's going to be no dust mites! No dusty dusties for little Lacey.'

Lacey was still heaving, her sobs painful and dramatic.

'There, there,' Stella cooed. 'Silly Uncle Freddie's very silly, isn't he? There, there, darling, we'll take you away from silly Uncle Freddie.'

Stella and David had a staggering number of attractive friends, and they were all looking at Freddie, who looked back at them while chewing his dry lips. He wondered if they talked about David's strange brother, the one who was a bit odd, not quite like the rest of them. He wondered if David had told any of them about his past, about how crazy he really was. If they all knew. Freddie could feel their judgement like hot pokers. They were looking at him, talking about him, and feeling sorry for him.

Suddenly overcome with the need to wash his hands, to feel clean, Freddie headed for the kitchen.

'Frederick!' His mother was a loud woman, both in voice and choice of clothing. Today was no different, a bright red blazer over her tight skinny jeans.

'Hi Mum,' Freddie said, wringing his hands and trying not to look over at the sink.

'So glad you could make it.'

'Of course,' he stuttered back.

'How's it going Fred?' David asked, tall and perfect, his glossy hair swooshed back off his face.

'I just need to . . .' Freddie gestured to the kitchen sink, and his brother stepped away to let him pass.

He pumped some expensive-smelling soap from the dispenser into the palm of one hand and then vigorously scrubbed as if he was a surgeon prepping for theatre, the suds reaching over his watch and far up his arms. He wondered how many dust mites were crawling all over him, how many he'd unintentionally exposed Lacey to.

'Freddie?' his mother started. 'Freddie, darling, I think your hands are clean now.'

Just one more round, he thought as he scrubbed into the gaps between his fingers, the spaces under his nails. He would feel so much better once his hands were clean, he just knew it. Lacey would be safe, and he couldn't be blamed for any more mishaps. When he stepped back from the sink, using a couple of pieces of kitchen roll to dry his hands (towels were hotbeds for germs), he found his family staring at him.

'No, it's OK, really. This is *normal* hand washing. Not *bad* hand washing. I should have done it before I went over to see Lacey. I'm sorry.'

'Why don't you sit down, son, have a cup of tea?' his father asked.

Freddie looked around, at his brother smirking for some reason, laughing at his own private joke, and his mother, orange shellac-tipped fingers clutching at a flute of Prosecco, wincing and worried.

'Seriously, I'm fine. Really.' Freddie hoped they believed him. Needed them to believe him.

'Have you eaten? Do you want me to get you a plate?' his mother asked.

'No, it's fine. I'm not hungry. What are you guys talking about?'

'Nothing important,' David replied. 'Just boring grown-up things. Like mortgage rates, what the local schools are like around here.'

'Ah, yes. Grown-up things.' Things that Freddie could never understand because he was renting in a building that used to be council flats, didn't have a good enough job to let him even dream of getting a mortgage one day, and was a million miles from ever needing to wonder about local schools.

'But how are *you*, Freddie? How are things holding up?' his father asked.

'Yes, good. Everything's fine.'

'Still renting with that Damien fellow?'

'Yup.'

'How's work? They must be close to promoting you by now, surely?' David always asked him about his job at the fin-tech company before he asked about anything else.

'No, no promotions on the horizon, but I like it. It's fairly easy-going, but you know what IT support is like, there are some challenges every now and again, and the people are really friendly.'

'Well that's great, Fred. That's just great.' David's voice was a touch too loud, which made Freddie wonder how much he'd had to drink.

'And Lacey is amazing. Has it really been a year?' he asked his brother.

'I know, right? She's going to be a stunner one day, let me tell you. And so bright, too! You wouldn't believe it. She's hit all her milestones early – it's quite possible that she's gifted.'

'That's amazing.'

'You should see the other babies she's friends with. She's miles ahead of any of them. Seriously. Lacey is going to be the most beautiful genius in the world! Runs in the family, I guess?' David looked at their parents, who smiled back at him adoringly. 'By the way, Fred, did Stella catch you? I know she wanted to have a word.'

'Yeah, the present thing. Cuddlies. I'm sorry about that.'

'What present thing?' his mother asked.

'Oh, I got Lacey a cuddly toy, but I don't think Stella liked it too much. I really didn't think about it beforehand, but I should have done. Sorry.'

'No, no,' said David. 'That's not what Stella wanted to talk to you about at all. Catch up with her later, she must be putting Lacey down now. Just make sure you talk to her before you take off, OK?'

There were family friends to greet, and old friends of David's to get reacquainted with, and then some of Stella's family to say hello to as Freddie hadn't seen them since Stella and David's wedding two years ago. He nibbled on the tasteless gluten-free bites, drank some more of the alcohol-free pink punch, and longed for someone to cut into the cake. Everyone gathered around the giant wall-mounted TV to watch a compilation video of Lacey's best bits from her first year, and then Stella went to bring the birthday girl downstairs again so that everyone could sing 'Happy Birthday' and gush about how beautiful she was.

Things were winding down when Stella finally pulled Freddie aside.

'Sorry for snapping at you earlier. You weren't upset, were you?'

'Upset?' Freddie thought about his mum's face after he finished washing his hands. 'I wasn't upset.'

'Oh, well, good then. I didn't mean to snap at you. I just want things to be perfect, and it's hard, you know?'

'Of course.'

'And I'm sorry that it might have ruined what I really wanted to talk to you about today, what I think could be your "real" present for Lacey?'

'Real present?'

'I really hope that you will catch my drift with all this, because I know your family can be closed up as clamshells sometimes, never talking about feelings or whatever, but my family is very open. We talk about everything, and I feel it's important that you have someone here who understands you, who tells it to you straight, as it were.'

Freddie really didn't like where this was going. At all.

'So, the thing is. I wanted to let you know, without you having to say anything, that *I know*.'

'You know?'

'Yes. And I know that it's hard for you. And that you'll probably never talk about it with your family. But as I said, my family are a lot more open, and probably a little bit more modern about things too. The way the world is now and everything. Does that make sense?'

'Not really . . .'

'It's so important to me that Lacey grows up with the right influences in life. I'd like to make sure that you're one of those influences. It's important that she understands all the different ways that the world works. And well, let's just say that David and I have a very *straight* world view. We want to make sure that Lacey grows up with more than that.'

For a fleeting moment, Freddie thought that Stella might be talking about geek stuff – watching *Star Trek* re-runs with Lacey, teaching her *Dungeons and Dragons* when she was old enough, lending her copies of his sci-fi *Masterworks* book series.

'I mean, David and I don't even have any gay friends, when you think about it,' Stella continued.

'What?'

'Well, I mean, there were people I knew at university, of course, and people from work. But it's not the same as family. It's not the same as making sure that your daughter is exposed to gay culture on a more regular basis. And these are things that we need to celebrate. We need to celebrate *you*, Freddie.'

'Stella, I don't think—'

'You don't have to say anything. I know that these things stress you out, and I don't want you to get all upset again. But we understand each other, right?'

'Stella—'

She brought a soft palm up to his cheek. The proximity was overwhelming.

'Think of it like the beginning of *Sleeping Beauty*, when each of the fairies bestows a gift on the baby. Except that you're the only fairy, and the gift is you.'

When Stella reached in for a hug, Freddie felt unable to do anything but receive it. He'd talk to her another time, he decided, when his entire family weren't camped out in the kitchen and there weren't a dozen or so other guests curiously watching them.

'I should get going. Weekend trains are a nightmare,' Freddie said, breaking away.

'Of course.'

'I'll just say goodbye to everyone.'

'I'm so glad we had this chat, Freddie.'

'Um, yes, great. Brilliant in fact. Thank you.'

On the train home, Freddie pulled out his phone and found a single message waiting for him from Baz.

You get your comics back?

Yup, Freddie replied. *The pub we went to last night had them. Crisis averted!*

Good good. Maisie says hello btw. She says you have a nice voice.

Freddie used a couple of emojis to smile and wave back.

Before he put the phone back in his pocket, he went to his photo album to look at the picture he took of that notice in the pub. He stared at it for a good long while, wondering what the right thing to do was.

Did his family really think he was gay? Why? Just because he didn't have a girlfriend? Because he had *never* had a girlfriend? Surely they knew that wasn't the reason. Surely they understood him, and what he had been through, better than that?

Freddie searched online for the name of the meet-up group and found the details. The next meeting was a week on Tuesday. Being alone sucked. Maybe it was finally time to do something about it.

4

The staff room was suddenly cold. And yet so hot at the same time. Kate wanted to put her phone down, or throw it far away and hear it smash, but she found she couldn't let go, and instead gripped it tight, staring down at the screen.

'Are you OK?' Renee asked. 'Has something happened?'

Kate snapped back up, managed to switch her phone into sleep mode and placed it face down on the table.

'What? No, I'm fine,' she said, trying to sound bright. She took her feet down from the chair in front and grounded them on the floor. Renee followed suit.

'Are you sure? Your face, you don't look happy.' Renee had placed a comforting hand on her arm, and Kate forced away the instinct to shake herself free from it.

'It was nothing, really,' she reassured. 'Tell me more about tonight!'

Renee looked uncertain for a short moment, her eyes narrowing with suspicion, but Kate knew that her friend wouldn't press any further, not if Kate didn't want it. And so Renee started talking about the plans she had for her date and why she had chosen the outfit Kate had glimpsed earlier: simple and black and not too smart, but not too casual either, because she had no idea what restaurant they were going to, but was safely presuming that neither of their art student budgets would stretch to anywhere fancy.

'Unless he's a secret aristocrat,' Renee wondered aloud. 'Can you imagine? A French count – do they have counts in

France? – escaping the discipline of his parents, his familial duty, by going to art school in London? He's a romantic hero!'

Maybe Kate was meant to say something, she wasn't sure. She had zoned out, gaze fixed on her hodgepodge lunch of last night's leftovers. Her appetite had deserted her.

'Kate?' Renee tried again. 'Seriously, are you OK?'

'Yeah, I think I'm just going to go and find somewhere quiet for a moment.'

'I can come with you?'

'No, I'll be fine. You finish your lunch. We only have ten minutes left anyway before we have to head back up.'

Kate found her way to the staff toilets, locked herself in a cubicle, sat down on the closed lid, and pulled out her phone. It was still the top item in her Facebook feed. A photo album, put up by Elise, the oldest of her friends, celebrating her hen party, which must have happened the weekend before. A hen party Kate should have been invited to. A hen party that implied a wedding was imminent, and one that Kate had clearly not been invited to either.

It was a spa weekend in Barcelona, and all the old school gang were there. Even India, whom Kate had never really liked and who was not a part of the original gang. India looked great, of course. Everyone did. They were all toned, and wore tight jeans and pretty tops and stylish coats – because even though it was Barcelona, it was still January – and then there were all the bikini pictures as they sat in the hot tub, or got full body massages, or drank beautiful cocktails by the indoor pool.

'The perfect way to start a perfect year!' the album had been captioned. Kate could hear Elise's voice: bright and peppy and so sweet it stung.

A photo of Elise with her arms wrapped around India, kissing her on the cheek.

A photo of Elise wearing a shiny 'bride' sash and standing outside the Sagrada Família holding aloft a bottle of champagne.

A photo just of hands, with everyone showing off their perfect, brand-new, matching pink manicures.

Shots of shots, all lined up along a bar.

Perfect, pouting group shots.

Alongside Elise and India were the whole gang: Bella and Rosie, Lucy and Georgina, and then there were loads of other people Kate didn't know. Maybe newer friends, or family Kate hadn't met or had forgotten over the years. It made her sick that she wasn't there. It made her breath catch in her chest, and her eyes fill with hot tears. They were her gang, her friends. Weren't they?

Kate cried as she imagined the conversation.

Georgina: 'But what about Kate?'

India: 'Let me guess, couldn't afford it?'

Elise: 'Well, there is that of course . . . probably. But here's the thing, I haven't invited her to the wedding.'

Rosie: 'Oh thank God, she's been so boring since she lost that job. We barely see her any more anyway.'

Bella: 'But it must be hard for her . . .' (Bella was always the nice one, and Kate chose to imagine her still being nice now.)

Elise: 'You mustn't say anything. None of you. Not a word.'

Lucy: 'I haven't actually spoken to her for ages.'

Georgina: 'Neither have I, to be honest.'

Rosie: 'Like she's fallen off the face of the earth.'

India: 'You know, I think she's still single?'

Georgina: 'Still? Has she *ever* had a boyfriend?'

India: 'I don't think so.'

Elise: 'Plus I would have had to make her a bridesmaid if she came, and I just can't imagine any of the dresses I have in mind *suiting* her, you know what I mean?'

She saw them all laughing and clinking champagne glasses, pleased to be rid of her.

Maybe it was her fault in part, but she'd always felt like she had time. Time to get everything sorted, time to get herself back on her feet and feel good about herself again. There had been issues in the past, moments of tension, but wasn't that normal? There was even that time she had thought about confronting India about her little sarcastic digs, but ultimately hadn't. They'd been going on for so long that they almost felt normal, just a quirk of India's she had to adjust to, like they had to adjust to hers.

Then came the crashing wave of insecurity: was it because she had gained weight? Was it because she was poor and working a crummy job? Was it because her parents paid half her rent every month, and sometimes more? Was it because she had never had a boyfriend?

The thought that somehow her old girlfriends had figured out her deepest, darkest secret brought on the hyperventilation, until her breathing and her tears became indistinguishable from each other. Had they finally realised that she was still a virgin? Was this why everything was going so horribly wrong?

The voice of her insecurity, always a faint hum somewhere in the background, now became angry and loud:

You're not like them.

They're all thin, you're not.

They've all had sex, you haven't.

They were never really your friends.

'Kate?' Renee was outside the cubicle, her voice soft and calm.

'I'm OK!' Kate called out, her voice full of forced cheerfulness.

'Please, open the door. Tell me what's going on.'

'You'll be late. You'll throw the whole rota off. Really, I'm fine.'

'Will you please stop telling me you're fine? You're clearly not fine.'

'It's just . . . it's just hard,' Kate confessed through the toilet stall door.

'I know.'

'I lost my job, I'm losing my flat. Nothing is going the way it's meant to. And now I've lost my old friends too.' Her voice was quiet but inside it felt like a yell. The feeling so big she imagined the mirrors in the toilet cracking, a fault opening up through the tiled floor, a dark, oppressive cloud of anxiety crashing down on them both.

'I'll talk to the duty manager,' Renee said softly, 'I'll tell them you're ill, that you're going home.'

Rubbing at her eyes to dry the tears, Kate stood up and opened the stall door.

'I can't afford to take the time off. I need all the hours I can get,' she replied sadly, moving to the mirror. The contract at the gallery meant that they didn't get any sick leave, and were only paid for the hours they worked.

'You don't have to tell me what's going on if you don't want to.'

The reflection that greeted Kate was a mess. She pulled her long, fair hair out of its scrappy bun and let it tumble over her shoulders, before deciding that she hated it and wrapping it back up again, smoothing the last loose strands away from her forehead. Her face was round anyway, but now she was red and puffy to boot.

'No, it's OK. You're probably going to think it's stupid anyway.'

Kate told Renee about the pictures as they returned their bags to their lockers, and then started to make their way back upstairs.

'It's so stupid, getting so worked up about a Facebook post.'

'It's not stupid at all,' Renee replied. 'I completely get it.'

'I just thought if anyone was going to understand, that they would. They were my oldest friends. They weren't meant to give up on me so quickly. And then I thought, maybe it's not them, maybe it's me. I always tried really hard to keep up with them, so when I couldn't anymore, everything was bound to fall apart.'

'They don't sound like real friends, Kate.'

'Elise, the one who's getting married? She was my best friend back in school. It was never the same after university, after I made other friends, but I didn't think I was going to lose her. I thought we were stronger than that. We used to talk about what it would be like when we got married and we were each other's bridesmaids. I was with her when she met her husband. And you know when you call round with the good news? I was the first person she called! How did I go from being the first person she called to the person she doesn't even invite to her wedding?'

'So, how do we kill her?'

That made Kate laugh.

'I just can't help thinking that I've made a colossal mess of it. Out of everything. My career, my looks, my love life – none of it's right. And this just proves it.'

'You're doing fine, Kate.'

'But I'm not, though. I'm not where I want to be. With anything. Nothing's right.'

They reached the Central Hall, where they were due to split up so that they could go to their assigned rooms for the rest of the day.

'Sorry for being such a mess and ruining lunch,' Kate said.

'Please, don't worry about it. You're going through a rough patch. But you'll come through it. Let's talk more at the end of the day. Pub after work?'

'What about your hot date?'

'Claude can wait an extra hour for me. I'm going to buy you a drink first.'

It was a Saturday night, and the Rocking Horse was busy. Kate didn't like crowded pubs. She liked cosy booths, dark corners, soft lighting and places where bar staff actually looked you in the eye when they took your orders. But, as awful as the place was, it was also cheap, and surprisingly free of tourists for somewhere tucked between Trafalgar Square and Soho.

They found a spot at the back, right by a fire escape that had been propped open by a fire extinguisher, which Kate was thankful for as she hadn't brought anything to change into from her work uniform, and had to keep her big coat on so that people wouldn't know where she worked (the gallery had a strict policy on this matter, especially when it concerned being seen in places where alcohol was consumed). The winter breeze was oddly soothing and Kate angled her face towards it, eager for the relief from the busy heat.

'There we go!' Renee placed two gin and tonics down on the table and shucked her coat off to get comfy. Kate was conscious of the heads that turned to look at Renee in her little black dress, but Renee seemed oblivious. Men had never looked at Kate like that, no matter what she was wearing. But she didn't hate Renee for it; she hated the universe instead.

'Thanks,' Kate replied, taking a grateful sip.

'How are you feeling now?

'Better, I suppose. I haven't opened Facebook since.'

'You should delete it.'

'I think that would only panic my family. They're always checking up on me there.'

'They can call you if they're worried. Say your new year's resolution is spend less time on your phone, or that Zuckerberg has become too problematic or something.'

Kate thought about it.

'Or I could just delete Elise. And the others.'

'That would be a good start. Get rid of all that drama!'

Kate fished her phone out of her bag and fought the apprehension around switching it back on.

'Maybe I could make it up to them? Ring Elise, and take her out for drinks?

'No,' Renee was kind but firm. 'They're not your friends, Kate.'

'But they were once. Doesn't that count for something? Aren't the friendships you make in school meant to last forever?'

'Whoever said that was a nutcase. Friendships are just like any other relationship. Some run their course, and sometimes you have to learn to move on.'

'So, basically this is like a break-up.'

'Well, I guess it is. And you've survived all your other break-ups, you can survive this one too.'

'Well . . .' Kate swallowed hard. 'I've never been through a break-up, actually.'

'What do you mean, never?'

'I've never had a relationship. Not a proper long-term one, anyway.' Actually, never a relationship of any sort, but Kate wasn't about to lay all her cards on the table. She'd let Renee imagine passionate hook-ups, flings and holiday romances. No need to go into full humiliating detail.

'Oh, well, that's OK.' It seemed like Renee didn't know what to say.

Kate looked back down at her phone and searched for Elise's name in Facebook.

'That cow!'

'What is it?'

'She deleted me first!' Kate held up her phone, displaying an error message instead of a result.

'Perhaps you just don't have enough signal?'

Kate closed the app down, then opened it up again and put Elise's name in the search bar, but the results came up blank.

'Nope. She's deleted me, and maybe even blocked me?' Kate searched for India, then Georgina. 'They don't come up in searches any more. Instagram too. All blocked. Oh no, wait . . . Bella is still there, but it looks like she has a limited profile now. Is this what it's come to? Seriously?'

'They're not your friends,' Renee repeated as Kate felt her anxiety rising once more.

'But now I don't even get the satisfaction of unfriending them first! What the hell? Elise must have realised that I could see the photos. And then she went and blocked me? I suppose I should be grateful that she made a passing attempt at considering my feelings.'

'They're really not worth you getting upset over.' The gin and tonics were nearly finished.

'Let me get another round,' Renee offered.

'No, I'll get this one. Unless you have to go and meet Claude?'

'Oh, I messaged him when I was at the bar. He's on his way here instead.'

An exotic tantrum of a girl was serving at the bar, and Kate waited patiently as the guy next to her blatantly flirted and was rewarded for his efforts with a bored eyeroll. When it was finally her turn, Kate ordered another two gin and tonics, and then shifted her shoulders, feeling awkward in her big coat. She wondered what it must feel like to be genuinely flirted with and to have the luxury of brushing them off.

The barmaid was clearly not wearing a bra, so Kate turned away while the tonics were being poured, worried that anyone would think she was staring, and let her eyes fall on the cork noticeboard nearby.

ADULT VIRGINS ANONYMOUS
Are you still a virgin?
Want to talk about it in a safe space?
Meetings every other Tuesday.

You're not alone

Ha. Someone out there was having a laugh. Kate didn't imagine that she was the only grown-up virgin in the world – statistically she couldn't be – but the idea of anyone being willing to talk about it was ludicrous.

Then Kate noticed the address for the meet-up and raised her eyebrows when she realised that it was in one of her old university buildings in Bloomsbury. She remembered having tutorial group meetings there. That was it then: some student was doing research and wanted to develop some weird sociology experiment about the freakiest of the freaks. Not only was someone out there having giggle-fits about virgins, but they were planning on writing about them in some scientific paper, as if they were anomalies of nature. It was awful.

'Claude's nearly here!' Renee's smile was wide as Kate got back to their table, but her eyes betrayed her anxiety.

'Are you nervous?' Kate asked, placing the drink down in front of her.

'Yes. No. I'm not sure. It's not as if this is a blind date, but chatting after class and being drunk at a Christmas party is different from meeting up like this. There are expectations, you know? Sex adds a whole new layer on to things, and what if we don't click? Worse: what if we click too well and then we end up in a proper relationship?'

'You act as if that's a bad thing.'

'Let's just say that the whole boyfriend–girlfriend thing has never worked out for me before. Love isn't for me. It's like, when someone tells you not to think about an elephant, and then all you can do is think about an elephant. Tell me I can't have sex with anyone else, and then sex with other people is all I can think about.'

'But at least you'd still be having sex.'

'I just find it frustrating. Limiting. It makes me worry.'

Kate sipped her drink, wondering what it must be like to be frazzled over the idea of being in a committed relationship. Just getting one guy to like her enough to want to go to bed with her was such a big issue, she was finding it hard to empathise with worrying about all the sex she might be missing out on.

Claude arrived, and he was perfect. Just like his photos. Dark and Mediterranean almost to the point of cliché, and already gazing adoringly at Renee.

They stood to kiss each other on the cheek, and then when Claude leant in to do the same with Kate, she felt herself freeze, and then for some reason ended up giggling to cover her awkwardness.

'Sorry!' She hated herself for getting so flustered, all because a man was close and being friendly.

'You'll have to excuse Kate,' Renee laughed sympathetically, 'she's been having a bit of a day.'

Claude nodded, adjusting his Clark Kent-like glasses and taking a seat.

'Yes, I heard you had some bad news earlier?' he asked once he was settled, his accent thick and French. He was being sensitive, but Kate was on guard, wondering if he was being genuine or just trying to impress Renee.

'Not that bad,' Kate said, posture straight as she worked to portray herself more like an adult. 'I won't bore you with it. Just unexpected.'

'I understand,' he smiled back.

By the time the small talk started to dwindle, Kate's drink was finished too. She hugged Renee in close as she said goodbye, hoping that she'd understand from the pressure of it just how much of a good friend she had been, and how foolish Kate felt. Claude seemed to think he deserved a hug too, and opened his arms for her, but Kate found herself freaking out once again at the proximity of a real-life gorgeous boy who wanted to hug her, and sprang her hand up between them and into an awkward fist-bump instead.

When she had reached the bar, Kate turned back to see how the date was going now that she wasn't there to third-wheel it. Renee and Claude were close, their bodies angled into each other, their eyes fixed and curious. They were gorgeous together.

Still a bit of a romantic in there somewhere then, she thought, before wondering when the last of it would leave her and she'd become the withered old spinster she was sure she was destined to be.

Maybe it was the day's fraught panic. Maybe it was that vague sense of longing she felt as she watched Claude's fingers brush up Renee's bare forearm. Or maybe it was the two gin and tonics she'd had on an empty stomach, but without allowing herself the time to second-guess herself, Kate marched over to the cork board, pulled out her phone and took a quick snapshot of the pink card that hung there. Something had to change before it was too late. It was time.

5

Freddie recognised the building. He'd never had to come here for any academic reason, but it was right next to the Student Union, which he knew well. He rubbed at his neck, remembering the person he was back then, and how that compared to the person he was now.

Conscious that he might be starting to look strange, especially as there were actual students everywhere, Freddie stuffed his hands in his pockets, resisting the urge to find the nearest loos. University for Freddie had been a shock of opinions, of always feeling like you were wrong whatever opinion you happened to have, and the start of that creeping sensation of germ-infected self-hatred that would eventually become all-consuming in the years after graduation. Now, he found that some days were easier than others, and today he had purposely left the bottle of hand sanitiser at home, and the tiny travel toothpaste tube too, in the optimistic hope that he would be able to cope. He was an adult now, and he'd already been through the worst of it. He could manage his anxiety all on his own, just like any other ordinary person.

Work had finished at five thirty and he didn't have anywhere else to go before the meeting started at seven, so he'd arrived uncomfortably early. But there was a canteen on the ground floor of the Union building, and as his lunch had been a suboptimal tortilla wrap, Freddie decided to settle in and grab some food. While he waited for his hotdog and chunky fries, Freddie let himself wonder about the kind of people who would be at this meeting. He couldn't imagine that there'd be anyone like him; someone who could pass as being normal. He imagined train-spotter types wearing anoraks, or maybe a lonely old man who had saved himself for an unrequited sweetheart. God, this was going to be so horrible and embarrassing. Was it too late to back out? No one would know but him.

Freddie ate his food with a knife and fork. He noticed a couple of girls with messy hairdos and oversized glasses watching him curiously from a couple of tables away, but even eating chips with his hands meant getting them dirty and that meant having to wash them afterwards. And once he started washing, sometimes it wasn't easy to stop, especially if he was already anxious. If looking a little bit weird now was the price to pay to avoid getting very weird later, then so be it. He wasn't going to let the thousands of pounds his parents had paid in therapy bills go completely to waste.

He told himself that however uncomfortable he was feeling, however much he wanted to pretend that he'd never seen the noticeboard card, he was here now. He'd already emailed the organiser to confirm the details; they were expecting him.

The meeting room was on the third floor of the building, and it was slowly approaching seven, so Freddie decided that it was time to move.

As he waited for the lift, a girl came and stood by his side, but Freddie didn't dare look at her just in case she was going to the meeting. Or worse, she was *not* going to the meeting, but somehow knew about it anyway and therefore knew what he was and why he was there. As they stepped into the lift, he couldn't help but catch her eye. There was something familiar about her; she was too old to be a student, so possibly a lecturer or professor he'd crossed paths with at uni. She was clearly nervous like him though, and let out an awkward false laugh when their fingertips nearly met while both reaching for the button for the third floor.

The silence was unbearable. Did she know about the meeting? Did she know that was why Freddie was here? Was the word 'virgin' plastered in bright capital letters all over his now definitely perspiring forehead? He wished he had decided to bring the hand sanitiser out with him after all, but the truth was his nerves had put him far past the hand-sanitiser zone. He wanted to scour his hands with soap under a tap until they were red and sore. Only then would he know that he was really clean, and that nothing bad was going happen.

When the lift doors finally opened, the girl darted out ahead of him, leaving Freddie the time to gather himself as he checked the big wall sign to find the allocated room. It was at the end of a long corridor, one that reminded him less of his own time at this university and more of the various hospitals he'd visited in the years since he graduated. And then he was there, at the brink of the room, his one last chance to turn around without making an absolute fool of himself.

'Hello, come in!' someone called, a boyish girl or a girlish boy, it was hard for Freddie to tell. This only added to his anxiety as he didn't want to say the wrong thing and offend anyone unintentionally. 'Sorry about the heat. Last time it was freezing in here, so we asked maintenance to sort it out, and I guess they hate us or something because this time it's far too hot. We can open a window if people get too uncomfortable?'

He found himself in a steaming room (a radiator was on full blast) with high ceilings, wide windows and a circle of chairs arranged right in the middle. There were six other people in the room, apart from the one who was welcoming him in, and one of them was the girl from the lift. Freddie glanced at her for a moment, feeling that glimmer of recognition again, but she was clearly embarrassed herself and was staring down at her clasped hands.

'I'm Andy, by the way,' the host continued.

'Freddie,' Freddie muttered back.

'Ah Freddie, from the emails. Hi, take a seat, get comfy.'

Freddie resisted sitting next to the girl from the lift because for some reason he was scared that she hated him, so he took the seat almost directly opposite her in the circle instead. As he took his rucksack and coat off, he looked around at the rest of the assembled motley crew: a gentle-seeming middle-aged lady, another with the demeanour of a scared kitten, a gruff-looking guy who was barely out of his teens, and another woman about Freddie's age, with deep black skin, very stern eyebrows and long braids woven through with bright pink. Finally, there was a slightly older guy sitting just to his right, not in an anorak exactly, but definitely a coat that was waterproof, and with a face shape and hair colour that reminded him faintly of himself.

Freddie wasn't sure what to make of Andy. They had a girl's voice, and a thin, faintly curvy shape, but they weren't exactly feminine either. From their baggy shirt, buttoned up right through the collar, to their cropped, fair head shorn at the back and sides, Freddie wasn't convinced that he knew how to talk to them, or that he could talk to them without saying the wrong thing. Was Andy a girl? Or were they a boy? It shouldn't have mattered, Freddie realised, except that it was only adding to his war of nerves.

Aware of the silence, Andy spoke up again. 'So, most of you have met me before, although we have a couple of new faces this evening. For you two,' they looked at Freddie and the girl from the lift, 'let me introduce myself properly. I'm Andy and I'm a PhD student here at the university, studying sociology, and more specifically gender roles and gender discrimination. This group is a little project of mine that sprang up from some of my research last year, although I want to reassure you that nothing you say or do here will be documented in any way, and everything is strictly confidential. You don't have to disclose any personal details if you don't want to. Whatever you say in this room, stays in this room, understand?'

There were mumbled agreements from everyone.

'I also would like to make clear that this is a safe space, and that we should all feel free to express ourselves, to be ourselves, however we feel is necessary and right for us. I for one identify as a non-binary individual and my personal pronouns are they or them. If any of you have something similar you'd like to express, then please don't be shy about it. Let's be kind to each other, OK?'

Freddie had never met someone who identified as non-binary before, and felt the pressure grow even heavier, worried he was going to put his foot in it somehow.

'I would also like to get the ball rolling tonight, and maybe ease some of the tension, by being the first to say that I'm a virgin. Well, to be honest, I kind of have problems with the word virgin and what it means, and we can talk about that later if we like, but in the spirit of why we're all here, and in accordance with societal norms, then yes, I am a virgin. Perhaps one of the other regulars would like to introduce themselves next?'

Andy looked specifically over to the middle-aged lady, who had a kind face and eyes that seemed to be smiling even when the rest of her face wasn't quite there yet.

'Hello everyone,' she started. 'I'm Cathryn, and I met Andy through a survey they were doing here at the university, and they haven't really been able to shake me off since.'

She paused, readying herself, then continued: 'I was a nun until relatively recently. About three years ago, in fact. Never wore a habit or anything, not one of those nuns. But, as I started getting older, I realised it wasn't working any more. But that's a long, complicated story, for another time. So here I am. In my fifties, and no longer a nun. Everything's a bit of a mystery to me, you might say. Oh, and I'm also definitely gay.'

Something about the way she said it, so casually, but also as if she was remarking on something totally unimportant, like the weather, might have made Freddie chuckle if he hadn't been so tense with nerves.

'I never got to say stuff like that before, when I was younger, and doing all those nun things. I say it a fair bit now, to make up for lost time, if you will.'

'Thank you, Cathryn!' Andy said warmly. 'Lizzie? Want to go next?'

The woman next to Cathryn was perhaps the same age, maybe older, and seemed just as frightened as Freddie felt. She was small, and looked smaller still with her arms and legs folded in on herself.

'I'm Lizzie,' she offered a weak wave to the group. 'I've been coming here for a couple of months now, making friends. Getting out of the house. I'm an assistant at a veterinary clinic, which is nice because I really like the animals. Is there anything else you need me to say?'

'No, that's brilliant Lizzie, thank you,' Andy replied.

'Guess it's me next then, said the gruff-looking man.' He wasn't a kid; Freddie figured he was almost certainly in his early twenties, but there was something about him that made Freddie think of him as a kid anyway. Something about the way he was speaking now, about the angry tension that was surrounding him. 'I'm Mike. I'm a virgin. And I don't want to be, as soon as possible.'

'Is that all you want to say?' Andy asked, after it was clear he wasn't going to go any further.

'Oh, there's lots I'd like to say, but I'm trying to be on my best behaviour.' He emphasised the last couple of words by using his fingers to make air speech marks, before adding, a little guiltily: 'I don't want to upset anyone.'

'Why don't you introduce yourself next?' Andy was looking at the girl from the lift, who was playing with a long strand of fair hair, twisting it up and around her fingers, but then went to sit on her hands the moment she realised she was being looked at.

'Oh, OK. Um . . .' She swallowed, and Freddie wondered if she was about to cry. 'I'm Kate.'

'It's really nice to meet you Kate. We're glad you could be here. Anything else you'd like to share right now?' Andy asked.

'I guess we all know why I'm here,' Kate offered, with a nervous laugh. 'Do I really have to say it out loud?'

'Not if you don't want to,' Andy reassured.

'Well. Um, I suppose I'm just scared that life is passing me by, you know. Things haven't gone all that well for me lately. And I feel like, as I get older, it's all becoming a lot scarier.'

'I completely understand that!' Cathryn commented loudly. 'You try being a bride of Christ for more than thirty years and then realising there's a reason you never wanted to marry the nice chap from the next town who your parents thought was perfect for you. Or any other man, for that matter.'

'I just need to make a change, you know,' Kate said, looking at Cathryn with something like hope. 'But I have no idea what that change is meant to be. Or what I'm meant to do.'

'I had a man once,' Lizzie added, ignoring Kate. 'He was my everything. The perfect man. We were both nineteen when he left, and now there's nothing left.'

'Oh no!' Kate sounded genuinely startled, before Cathryn placed a hand on her shoulder and gently shook her head.

'I'm Hattie,' the girl with the braids said. 'I'm a post-doc here, and also a virgin, obviously, but I'm pretty OK with it because, to be honest, I don't even really want to have sex.'

Freddie spotted Mike roll his eyes.

'I just don't think sex is that important, and that people make too much of sexual attraction. Some of us just don't feel it, but we're made to feel bad or imperfect because of it. It's not fair. I try and talk about this on the outside, on my socials and stuff, but it's a battle, and everyone just won't stop going on about how great sex is; how I need to experience it before I know. But I think I know, and besides, turns out I don't really care. Anyway. I just want to talk about this stuff. Without people thinking I'm mad or something.'

'Thanks Hattie,' Andy said, giving her a thumbs up. 'Steve, you want to go next?'

'I'm Steve. I'm fifty-four. I'm a virgin. I'm a technical analyst for an engineering firm. I'm just curious about everybody else's opinions, and the group has really been helping me understand everything. Thank you.'

Freddie got the sense that he was used to being professional and didn't know how to communicate very well outside a work context. There was something almost robotic about the way he sounded, very careful and deliberate.

But now it was his turn. He'd made all this effort, the time had come.

'I'm Freddie.' He paused; his mouth felt parched. 'I'm a virgin, and I'm scared of what that means. So, yeah. Here I am.'

'Welcome to the group Freddie,' Andy said softly.

Freddie didn't say much during the meeting but he enjoyed listening to everybody else. Cathryn and Hattie seemed so spirited and passionate, and then, at the opposite end of the spectrum, there was Lizzie, who might have been in a world of her own, and Steve, whose expression was oddly blank for most of the session, except for when he decided that he agreed with something, or wanted to write down the name of an author of a book or article that they were talking about. He seemed to be very attentive to Lizzie, but Freddie didn't know if he was just imagining it. Lizzie seemed so delicate and worried by everything. Mike seemed quietly furious, his leg bobbing in front of him as he got more and more wound up, until Andy moderated and soothed him with some words of kindness. Freddie didn't feel like an intruder to this space, not exactly, yet he couldn't figure out how to interact properly either. Despite this, he still felt pleased with himself. He'd announced to a group of strangers that he was a virgin and the world hadn't come to an end immediately afterwards.

There was a point in the evening when his eyes fell on Kate. He wondered if she was as anxious as he was, whether she also felt the same vague thrill of relief after finally being able to say out loud what they'd been embarrassed about for so long. And then suddenly she was looking up and straight back at him, brow furrowed in thought, like she was trying to figure something out. Freddie smiled at her, a tense, quick smile, thinking that she'd catch herself staring and look away, but instead, he was surprised to find that she just smiled right back.

6

Well. This was turning out to be positively all right. Kate was relieved, and while not exactly relaxed, she had definitely eased into the situation.

'The thing is, as you get older, you learn to make peace with the anxiety of life passing you by too quickly,' Cathryn told her, referring back to what Kate had said when she had first introduced herself. 'Granted I've had a long time to think and get used to it all, but if you spend your time getting stressed about it, you end up missing out on the nice stuff that's out there in the world. Like getting to the bus stop at just the right time so that you're barely waiting a minute before the bus comes around the corner. Or watching Alexander Armstrong on *Pointless*. Because he's very nice.'

'Oh, he is nice!' Lizzie said, suddenly animated. 'He opened my cousin's village fete. They got a selfie together.'

'There we go then. Village fetes and wholesome TV presenters. Just remember that you can still allow yourself to be happy, even though things aren't necessarily going the way you want them to.'

Kate nodded appreciatively, trying and struggling to think of anything that had made her happy lately, before Andy chimed in, asking Cathryn how her dating adventures were going.

'Well, you know how last time I was showing you all the things I could do on my phone with those romance applications? Well, last week I actually went on a date!'

Kate turned to look around the room and saw Hattie's eyes widen with a distinct mix of admiration and horror. She liked Hattie instantly. She was the kind of person who seemed to wear every single emotion right there on her face for everyone else to see.

'It didn't work out or anything, but it was completely fascinating. She was one of the butch types, you know? Very stocky with short hair, but very pleasant nonetheless,' Cathryn continued, and Kate sensed Andy wincing at Cathryn's less than politically correct assessment of her date's aesthetic. 'And we talked about television, and politics, which was lovely. And then we talked about what it was like coming out. She'd been out for ever, but I could tell that she wasn't too impressed with me. I'm not out yet, you see,' she announced to Kate and Freddie. 'I mean, I'm out to you lot obviously, but I haven't told the wider world or anything. I figure the people at work just think I'm a merry divorcee or something similar – they don't even know I used to be a nun!

'So anyway, I'm on this date, and she's making a point of telling me that all her previous girlfriends had been out and proud, and that she didn't have too much patience for grown women still in the closet. Which is fair, I suppose, if you're at that stage of your life. But it put a dampener on things, so to speak. We didn't have much to talk about after that.'

'Did you tell her about your lack of experience? I've been scared to, in case it just shuts everything down,' Mike said.

'If it's the right person, then wouldn't they understand?' Hattie countered.

'I'd hope so, but how can you tell? I just imagine every girl laughing in my face when they find out. People expect so much of you, and it makes me angry. And I hate it. It's like there's no way out.'

'People think there's this magical spell thing when it comes to losing your virginity. Like that one experience is suddenly the most important experience you'll ever have,' Hattie added.

'Steve, what do you think?' Andy asked.

'I think . . .' Steve's face flushed deep red. 'I think it's important to wait for the right person.'

'All I'm saying is that the right person doesn't have to be someone you're deeply in love with. The right person might be a person you can be frank and honest with. A person you can trust, maybe have laugh with. It doesn't have to be a love thing.' Hattie's words resonated with Kate. She'd always felt herself swaying between the romantic ideal of true love, and the more practical desire to just get it done with anyone who was available, the latter always closely related to how much she'd been drinking. She hadn't considered the other option before, that it didn't have to be all fairy-tale romance, but it could still be trusting, maybe even a little fun.

'How do you write that in a dating profile, though?' Cathryn asked. 'How do you write "need someone to show me the ropes" without inviting trouble?'

'Or ridicule,' Mike added.

'People are so scared of virgins too,' Hattie said, this time with a little sadness in her voice. 'Like we're not real human beings. The number of times I've had to join in on sex jokes and conversations about sex, pretending that it's a part of my life, just to fit in and seem normal. It's exhausting.'

Kate thought about Renee's assumptions about her love life, about how whenever she discussed relationships with Lindsey, it felt like Lindsey was trying to be careful and gentle when talking about sex and romance, for fear of upsetting her. And then she thought about Elise and all the old school friends. Maybe they sensed it. Kate had barely had the courage to open Facebook on her phone in the week or so since discovering she hadn't been invited to Elise's hen. Every time her finger hovered over the phone screen, her stomach seemed to plummet, the anxiety rising in her with a hot flush. Did they know? Did they care? But then, even if they did, why did it have to matter so much?

Maybe I'm the one making too much of it, and that's what they pick up on, Kate thought.

'But you don't know though,' Lizzie said wistfully to Cathryn. 'If you never had the conversation with her, then how would you know? What if you gave up too easily?'

'I do wonder about that,' Cathryn said. 'I wonder if I was too picky and didn't give her a chance. But then don't I get a say too? It's all very well wondering and hoping that someone likes you, but really, the truth is, I didn't like her very much to begin with.'

'There's always porn,' Mike said. 'For learning stuff, I mean.'

'I don't think porn is very useful,' Hattie said with determination. 'Don't look at porn, Cathryn.'

'I wasn't planning to,' Cathryn laughed. 'Wouldn't even know where to begin!'

'People say it's not realistic,' Mike continued, 'but if you've got nothing to go on, nothing to compare it to, then it's got to be better than nothing. Right?'

'I think what Hattie is trying to say,' Andy said carefully, 'is that a lot of mainstream porn caters for the male gaze, and male pleasure. It's not the best place to learn about real sex.'

'Unless you're a man?' Mike offered, causing Steve to chuckle before he stopped abruptly and blushed an even deeper shade of scarlet.

'But sex isn't just about the man, about the man getting off. It's about everybody involved,' Hattie said emphatically.

'You don't even want sex, so what do you know?' Mike said. Kate thought she saw Hattie's eyes twitch with the need to retaliate.

'Remember, let's all be kind,' Andy soothed.

'I was only joking,' Mike said, a little half-heartedly.

'So, is porn OK?' Kate asked tentatively. It was the first time she had spoken in a while, and her voice sounded small and scared. 'I mean, I don't know. It's not like I've seen much, but is it bad?'

'It can be outrageously sexist,' Hattie replied instantly.

'It's dirty stuff, that,' Lizzie added quietly, arms crossed so tightly over her chest that her hands were tucked under her arms.

'It's not for everyone and there's some pretty dismal stuff out there,' Andy conceded. 'But if you know where to look and what you like – and as long as everybody involved has consented – then for many it can be a good option. I'm certainly not anti-pornography.'

'I'm not a prude, I don't think,' Kate said, feeling the need to clarify why she'd asked the question. 'I want to have sex. I know I do. I just haven't found anybody to have it with yet. And I don't know if it's bad luck, or if . . . it's just me. If there's something wrong with me.'

'There's nothing wrong with you,' Andy reassured.

'If there's one thing I know, it's that everybody is on their own course, and it doesn't help to constantly compare yourself to others,' Cathryn added.

'We've talked about it a lot in previous meetings,' Andy continued, 'so I don't want to dwell on it too much this time around, but I think it's worth saying that sex has many forms. Sometimes it's with another person, sometimes it's on your own. There are lots of different ways to express sexuality, and to have sex.'

While Andy and Hattie got into a terse conversation about whether you were still a virgin if you masturbated, Kate took the chance to look around the room again. Hattie, Mike and Cathryn were dominating the conversation, and between them were Lizzie, Steve and Freddie, who were all listening (well, to be honest, Kate wasn't too sure about Lizzie, who at times seemed to be drifting off into her own little world), but seemed too shy or scared to get involved.

'You've been very quiet, Freddie,' Andy said, after a time.

'Just listening to everyone,' he replied carefully. 'I'm not sure that I have anything to add right now.'

'Do you go out on dates?' Cathryn asked.

'No, but I want to,' he replied. 'I think. It's just hard. The talking thing. And the meeting girls thing. I'm scared I've left it too long, that there's too much stuff that I don't know about. And then there's finding someone who's all right with my inexperience. I guess I'm scared that I've left everything too late and it's all passed me by.'

Kate knew exactly what Freddie was saying, knew exactly where he was coming from. She watched him as he spoke: his eyes were cast down the whole time, his hands warring with themselves as if he were trying to wring water out of them. And then she started to feel some more of that relief, at realising she might not be completely alone after all; that there was at least one other person in the world who felt as lonely as she felt.

'Well, if it's too late for you, then there's no chance for me,' Cathryn laughed. 'But seriously though, I know that it's not exactly worked out for me yet. But you should maybe think about internet dating. Just to desensitise you to the whole "meeting girls" thing, or the talking thing, if that's the problem. That's what I'm doing it for, and if I end up meeting someone special, then that's a bonus!'

'Yeah?' Freddie asked, looking up to get the approval of the group.

'At the very least you end up with stories to tell. I know my story wasn't all that exciting, but let me tell you, it was better than anything that ever happened back at the convent.'

'I don't know. Maybe,' Freddie murmured.

'I should probably add here, for our newer members, that the point of this group isn't to try and get you to have sex,' said Andy. 'I don't want anyone to feel like we're pressuring them into doing something they don't want to do.'

'The sex would be nice though,' Mike said dryly.

'Sometimes I'm not sure that the sex even matters that much,' Kate found herself saying. 'But a relationship would be nice, I think.'

'And that's a fine thing to want,' Cathryn agreed.

'There are so many different kinds of relationship, though,' said Hattie. 'There's friends, and family, and people you live with, and colleagues. Romantic or sexual relationships don't even have to be that important. Some people get everything they need from all the other types, without the need for physical intimacy. I still think the world makes far too much out of all that stuff.'

But even so, a romantic or sexual relationship would still be nice, Kate thought but didn't say.

Kate was surprised to find that some of the attendees were going to the pub afterwards. They'd just spent nearly two hours cooped up together in a stuffy room talking about their most personal secrets, so extending the evening in a much more informal environment somehow felt a little strange.

'We try and leave all the sensitive stuff in the room,' Andy explained. 'Sometimes it's just nice to get a beer and vent afterwards.'

'My cats are on antibiotics,' was all Lizzie said by way of goodbye to the group before she hurried out.

'I'm going to head home too,' Cathryn said. 'Sorry to be a party pooper.'

'No worries!' Hattie said, reaching towards Cathryn for a hug.

'Have you all known each other long?' Kate asked as Cathryn put on her coat.

'Andy and I studied together,' Hattie explained, 'and then I met Cathryn through Andy's research. There are some others who come and go from the group, like Lizzie and Steve, and Mike's also pretty new, but we tend to be the core trio, don't we?'

'They're a godsend,' Cathryn said. 'I reckon I would have gone insane without them.'

'You pubbing?' Kate heard Steve ask Freddie, who was standing around looking a little lost.

'I don't know,' he admitted. 'This all feels kind of weird.'

'Aww, come on, it would be great to get to know you guys better,' Hattie encouraged.

Kate wondered if there was anything more to know about her – the sex thing was her deepest, darkest secret after all – but resolved that the pub could be fun, or at least a good way to decompress and feel more comfortable with everyone.

Andy led them around Bloomsbury to a pub settled into the corner of an old block of mansion flats, a rainbow flag draped proudly in one of the front windows. Kate was thankful to find that it was quiet inside, and free of any sign of students. The reason, she soon found, was because of the prices.

'You all right?' Kate asked Freddie, who was standing next to her at the bar. He didn't say anything at first, just kept looking at the counter, so that Kate wondered if he had heard her. 'Freddie, wasn't it?'

'Oh, yeah, hi.'

She took in his face, eyes that could be grey or green or hazel, she realised, depending on the light, and reddish-chestnut hair that he had run his hands through earlier, making it stick up at the front. He had a face she felt she had seen before; maybe he looked like someone she had seen on TV.

'We didn't just make gigantic fools of ourselves, did we?' Kate asked.

'You didn't,' Freddie conceded. 'I'm not so sure about me.'

'Let's just say we were both fine, and then try not to think too much more about it.'

'What are you having?' Freddie then asked, to her surprise.

'A small red,' Kate replied. 'But don't worry about it. I'll get it.'

'It's OK, really. I'm getting one for Steve too.'

'Oh, OK then.' She was a little worried about having to pitch in for a round later on, especially when her budget was tight and the drinks were so expensive, but figured that the evening was momentous enough that – if it ever came to that – she could allow herself the indulgence. Besides, Freddie seemed nice, and she didn't want him to think she was rude for turning down a friendly gesture.

'Want some help taking the drinks to the table?' she asked once they had been served.

Freddie nodded back at her appreciatively.

'We were just talking about you two,' Hattie said once they had both sat down and Freddie had delivered Steve's drink.

'What about us?' she asked tentatively.

'Turning up, being new. It was brave,' Hattie replied.

'I don't know if I'd say brave exactly,' Kate said, wishing that she had left her hair loose so that she could hide behind it. The half-up, half-down style she had gone for meant she only had a few wisps to wind nervously around her fingers.

'How did you guys find the meeting?' Andy asked them both.

'It was good,' Kate said, forcing a congenial smile.

'Yeah,' Freddie added, shy and noncommittal.

'We never really got the chance to talk about what you want to get out of it? Not that it matters, and we can talk about it at the next meeting if you'd prefer, but sometimes it's nice to know,' Andy said to both of them.

'Sex?' Kate said, a little too loudly, her voice a little too high, her attempt at a joke feeling lame and nonsensical even as she was saying it.

'I guess I just want a bit more confidence, so that maybe I can do something about the situation?' Freddie answered, more sensibly. 'And I can't afford a therapist or anything, so this makes sense?'

'You remind me of me,' Steve said to Freddie, whilst taking careful sips of his ale. 'I felt exactly the same way when I started coming here.'

'And now?' Freddie asked.

'Oh, I feel pretty much the same. But at least I have an event to put in my diary every two weeks.'

Kate saw Freddie give a weak chuckle as if he thought the comment was funny, but Kate wasn't sure it was meant to be taken that way.

'Well, if you want to try dating, to talk about your experiences on this journey, kind of like the way Cathryn is doing, then that's fine,' Andy said.

'I think you should go on a date before the next meeting,' Hattie dared, her tone sly but her eyes twinkling with delight.

'Hattie,' Andy scolded. 'That's not the point of any of this.'

'Just for fun, to test the waters. You know. Kate, you should try it too,' Hattie gave her a hard but playful stare.

'No, I don't do online dating,' Kate said, after taking a sip of her wine.

'A singles thing then? Or speed dating?'

Kate had always wondered about speed dating and had secretly always wanted to give it a try.

'I don't think so. I'm not ready.'

'You'll never know whether you're ready if you don't try. And what if you end up meeting someone? Just go and see what happens. Report back at the next meeting.'

Hattie folded her arms in front of her, looking very pleased with herself. Andy rested their head on their arm and sighed loudly, letting Hattie know that they didn't approve.

'What?' said Hattie defensively. 'We're not in the official group now. I'd never say this in group. This is the pub. And I think Kate and Freddie should try dating.'

A pause as Kate tried to work out what Hattie had meant.

'Not each other, obviously!' she added dramatically. 'We don't need any inter-group drama. There was enough of that when Steve asked Lizzie out.'

'Hattie!' Andy scolded.

'Oh, it's OK. I deserved it,' Steve sighed before he looked up at Kate and Freddie to explain: 'It was stupid. It was a while ago. I misinterpreted things.'

Kate had a vision then, of being stuck like she was for ever, of nothing ever changing. She'd decided to come to the group because she couldn't stand things the way they were, because she wanted more. That meant she had to challenge herself, to do things that she wouldn't ordinarily do to get out of her rut. And if these new, strange people and this group could help her do that, well, wasn't this what it was all for?

'OK,' Freddie said it first. 'I'll sign up for a dating app thing. I'll give it a go. Nothing to lose, I guess.'

'Yeah, same here,' Kate agreed, feeling light and hopeful.

7

So. This was happening. A date. An actual, real date. A date that Freddie was going on, with a real woman, in the real outside world. What could possibly go wrong?

It all happened terrifyingly quickly.

He had downloaded the app as soon as he got home after the pub because he knew that he would back out of the challenge if he slept on it, and uploaded the only three pictures of himself that he actually liked. One was a goofy selfie he had accidentally taken last November when he had dropped his phone and wanted to check that the camera still worked. He knew that it wasn't the most flattering of photos, but he liked it because he looked relaxed and carefree, feelings he so rarely actually felt. He didn't put that photo up first, though. For the profile shot he chose a picture from David and Stella's wedding, where he was suited and booted and came complete with a pink peony in his lapel. He hadn't been the best man – his brother had a retinue of friends all more qualified for the job than Freddie – but he had managed to make the cut for the wedding party, and had felt pretty great in a cravat and a suit jacket with tails. The final shot was from a comic book convention he had gone to the previous summer, where he had bought an opportunity for a posed photo with Richard Dean Anderson from *Stargate SG-1*, one of his favourite TV shows as a kid. He had decided to crop the photo, so that what was left was an image of Freddie looking pale, slightly hunched, one hand stuffed awkwardly in a pocket with the other one stretched away out of shot. He didn't look his best – he had been so overawed by meeting one of his heroes that he had been barely able to smile – but he looked like how he felt most of the time, so he thought it was honest.

There were no actual lies in his profile, but Freddie figured that a vague and gentle fudging was probably OK. He wasn't imagining anything going far enough for him to have to explain the truth. It was only a practice run, after all. Freddie had Hattie in his head, telling them that this was just one date; he didn't even have to really like the girl, he just had to get used to being relaxed around women. She had reassured him that no matter how scared he was, nobody could ever tell whether someone was a virgin or not, that he didn't have to say or do anything that he didn't want to, and that all they would do is casually chat, in just the same way that he had been doing with them that evening.

Then Freddie thought about Kate, and about whether she was going to go through with her side of the challenge. It might be nice to catch up next time and compare notes.

He had shown Damien the profile of the girl he was meeting once the date had been settled. Not because he wanted Damien's opinion per se, but because having an opinion, any opinion, felt important and validating. It meant it was really happening, meant that he had someone to hold him accountable should he try and back out.

'Well she seems . . . normal,' Damien had said, not quite sneering, but very nearly. He had just got home from work and was cleaning his coffee machine.

'But nice though, right?'

'Are you asking me for permission to see her or something?'

'No, I just . . . Nothing seems wrong about her?'

'So you think it might be a trap?'

'No, I—'

'She could be a raging Tory, I suppose, or even worse, a raging Communist. Either way is bad, I guess. As long as she's not an influencer, or a "YouTuber".'

'What would be so wrong with that?'

'She could ensnare you into appearing in her videos, or make you film her doing weird kooky things. Oh, don't look at me like that! I'm sure you'll be fine. I'm sure that she's perfectly normal. Exactly as her photo suggests.'

To be honest, Freddie thought Mia was pretty stunning. If anything, too stunning. He wondered if he should have picked someone who he didn't find so attractive for his first ever date. It might have made things easier.

Hattie had given him the impression that meeting up and chatting with someone you already kind of liked the look of would be easy somehow, but it definitely wasn't. Freddie would have been too intimidated to have even made eye contact with her if they had encountered each other for the first time in real life. But he had liked her photo, so swiped in the right direction, and then it transpired that she had done the same. Mia messaged first, asking how his day had been, and he had replied, until there was a pretty steady stream of messages. She was sweet, and funny, and they were in almost exactly the same place in a binge-watch of the US version of *The Office*. She had made a joke suggesting that Freddie might be the Jim to her Pam, and he had been so frightened by the prospect that he closed the dating app down immediately and didn't open it again for six hours. After which he decided that he was being stupid, that this was just some silly flirting on her part, and what would the point of any of this be if he didn't flirt a little back, and finally replied suggesting that they meet for a coffee.

So now here he was, a week later, in a coffee shop he had walked past countless times but had never allowed himself to go into because the drinks were too fancy to justify. Well, now he had a good reason.

Freddie found himself flicking back on to the dating app, checking up on Mia's profile just in case he had forgotten what she looked like. She seemed approachable, with big glasses over doe eyes made even bigger in one of her photos by some filter or another. Her hair was bobbed to just under her ears, and in each of her photos she seemed to be on an adventure: posing on a beach with arms outstretched here, peering out from behind a tree there.

'Hi, are you Freddie?'

He had been so busy looking at his phone that he hadn't spotted her come in. Like magic, there she was, looking exactly the same as her pictures, except for the big purple bobble hat on her head. God, it was cute.

'Hi, Mia?' Why was he asking? Of course she was Mia. Who else would she be?

'It's cold outside, right?' she commented, taking off her mittens.

'It might be getting colder. Could be snow at the end of the week,' Freddie commented, feeling pleased with himself. He was doing proper small talk like a proper adult!

'Have you ordered? Would you like me to get us something?' Mia asked.

Freddie wasn't sure what he should say. If this were a date, shouldn't he be the one ordering? Or was that a sexist presumption? He clasped his hands to his thighs to stop himself from wringing them together.

'A latte?' he asked, worried that his voice now sounded weird.

He watched Mia at the counter, waiting her turn to order the coffee. She seemed so sweet and sparkling.

She returned with two lattes, one for him and one for her.

'Can you believe how long this winter is lasting?' she commented. More small talk about the weather? That didn't seem like a good thing.

'Yeah . . .'

'I mean, I know that it's meant to be global warming, and it's only February, but it would be nice to get a little bit of warm sunshine, you know?'

Freddie tried to focus on keeping his hands steady as he spooned some sugar into his coffee. He didn't want Mia to see how nervous he was.

'So have you been on many online dates?' Mia asked.

'No, actually. This is the first.'

'Really? Just come out of a long relationship or something?'

'Or something,' Freddie conceded.

He suddenly had a memory of preparing to read something out loud for a school presentation, and of his dad coaching him on it the night before. It was probably Year Nine, possibly a book review of *Animal Farm* or *Lord of the Flies*. He could hear his dad's voice in his head, encouraging him to 'speak slowly' and 'make sure you look up when you're talking, and to make occasional eye contact'. It had been good advice, gentle and careful, but when he'd rehearsed in front of David later, his older brother had made fun of him for having Hannibal Lecter eyes. The next day, when he'd delivered his report in front of the class, he'd been too nervous to look up at anyone and was scored low for his presentation skills.

Now, as he stirred his coffee, he was struggling to work out how to look up and meet Mia's eyes without it seeming too overthought and creepy. So instead he stayed focused on the drink and chewed on his lower lip.

'I'm going on a lot of dates,' Mia told him. 'It's my new year's resolution, actually. I'm trying to go on at least one date a week. It's not easy either. Sometimes I'm busy, and sometimes there's nobody I want to meet up with, but so far so good.'

'So, you've been on six dates already this year?' Freddie asked.

'Seven actually. One week there were two.'

'Wow.' Freddie didn't know what to make of that. It had taken so much effort, so much courage, to do this one thing, and it was nothing to Mia. A drop in the ocean.

'Nothing's worked out yet, but it's still fun. It's more about just putting myself out there, you know?'

Freddie understood it, but realised then that he had been hoping that she was going to be just as nervous as him. That this could somehow be an adventure they could embark on together. He tried to smile through the disappointment.

'So you work in finance?' she asked.

Was she starting all of the conversations, or was he just imagining it?

'Yeah, well, actually,' he started, inwardly cursing himself for the tiny white lie on his profile, 'I work for a finance company. In the IT department.'

'Oh, well that's nice,' Mia replied.

'It's interesting. And I get to meet lots of people in the office. Plus I don't have to wear a suit or anything, which makes life easier.'

'I hate dressing up too. Much prefer the casual look. Luckily my place is very much a dress-down type of thing.'

He went to sip his coffee, which was still far too hot, but he drank it anyway, praying that he wasn't inadvertently burning his tongue.

'I work in fashion,' Mia continued, before Freddie realised that she had been waiting for him to ask.

'Really?'

'Well don't sound so surprised,' Mia joked.

'Oh no, I wasn't surprised! I guess . . . I thought that you maybe didn't look like a fashion type?'

Oh no . . . what am I saying?

'What, tall and skinny?'

'No!'

'Fashion isn't all glamazon models and designer labels, you know. Where I work is pretty low-key, high-street-type stuff. I do marketing.'

'I wasn't implying—'

'I'm sure you weren't.'

A beat of silence as Freddie took another painful sip.

'Oh come on, I was joking! You knew I was joking, right?'

'Oh, yeah, joking, of course!'

'I'm only teasing you,' Mia said, watching him closely as she took another sip of her drink. 'So, do you enjoy your job then?'

'It's all right. Pays the bills.'

'Well, that's good, I guess.'

Freddie spotted Mia sneaking a look at her watch before glancing up and around the shop lazily. Anywhere but at him. He imagined going to the next meeting, of being confronted with everyone, and telling them it was a disaster, and that it was all his fault. That he was a useless human who had no idea how to make conversation.

Freddie would be the last virgin left alive.

Unless he did something about it.

'Sorry,' he started, fighting a nervous stutter. He didn't dare look at Mia whilst he said it, didn't even know if she was paying him any attention. 'I'm not used to doing this. Any of this. I'm really nervous.'

'Oh, it's OK,' she replied, 'dating is tough.'

'I'm here on a bit of a challenge actually. I'm trying to get out of my shell a bit. I'm sorry if I'm coming across a bit weird or anything.'

'It's fine, really.' He noticed that she didn't contradict him about being weird. 'I mean, I've got a confession too. This whole "one date a week" thing? It's because I broke up with my boyfriend at the end of last year. Just before Christmas. And, well, this is one way of getting my revenge. But the truth is, I'm still really into him. Does that even make sense?'

After Freddie gave her a quizzical but curious look in response, Mia explained further: 'We had been together for just over three years, and I could tell that he was off at our three-year anniversary, but if anything, I thought he was being weird because he wanted to propose, not because he wanted to break up with me. Then he comes out and says this thing, this really horrid thing. He says that he thinks he can do better than me. Can you believe it?'

Freddie couldn't.

'So he says that he never actually imagined ending up with someone like me, even though his friends and family loved me; he just imagined being with someone different. He spends tons of time on Instagram, looking at "thirst pics" of girls with big arses at the gym. So he figured out that I wasn't what he wanted, and had to cut things off before they went too far.'

'Wasn't three years already too far?' Freddie asked.

'Well, exactly! He goes and he says all this – we were in public, if you can believe it, at a restaurant right around the corner from here. One of my favourites, which means that obviously I can never go to it ever again. Tosser. So this date-a-week thing was an idea of one of my other friends, to stop me getting depressed and to meet someone new really quickly.'

'It's certainly quite the idea . . .'

'I know,' she rolled her eyes. 'Sorry for wasting your time.'

Maybe it was because she had been so open with him, and because it was now absolutely clear that any chance of romance or sex was off the table, but Freddie relaxed. The pressure was off. He sat back in his chair and noticed that his hands had stopped shaking.

'You're not wasting my time. You're really not.'

'How long have you been single?' Mia asked.

'A long time,' Freddie replied with a sigh, and no intention of going into specifics.

'And this is your first online date?'

'It is.'

'How come?'

Freddie looked back at her, not sure that he understood the question.

'How come you haven't done online dating?' she tried again. 'It's refreshing to meet someone new to all of this, but trust me, it's rare too.'

'Oh,' Freddie said, before carefully adding, 'I have issues with anxiety.'

'That's OK,' Mia replied warmly. 'My sister has OCD.'

'She does?' Freddie was sceptical. He knew a lot of people liked to say they had OCD without really knowing what it meant.

'It's pretty mild, but she sees a therapist about it. I think she gets these obsessive bursts, like everything will be fine for ages, and then she'll be fixated on this one thing, and won't be able to stop until it's sorted. One time she stayed up all night taking apart a bookcase and then putting it all back together, because she couldn't get it out of her head that one of the shelves wasn't perfectly straight. Couldn't sleep until it was sorted out.'

'Actually,' Freddie took a pause, wondering when had been the last time he'd told someone new about all of this. 'I have OCD too. Mine's not like your sister's though.'

'Are you the washing hands and light switches type?'

'Never light switches for me, but hands, yeah. And germs in general. Teeth brushing. I used to have this thing about even numbers. When I was really bad, I counted my footsteps, and if I got anywhere I was going on an odd number of steps, I had to go back and start all over again. Got to the point where I couldn't even leave the house.'

'That sounds pretty intense.'

'I was hospitalised for it five years ago.'

'Oh my god, wow,' Mia said, using both hands to clasp on to her latte, staring at him in fascination.

'My dentist once had to tell me to stop brushing my teeth, if you can believe it. I was brushing too much and causing what he called "substantial gum damage". But I'm a lot better now. It's still there, but really, really far away in the background. Like a tiny, quiet voice I can usually ignore. Most of the time. It doesn't get in the way much any more.'

Wow, it felt good to talk. It felt good to not have that hot, pinched feeling between his shoulder-blades any more. It would come back, he was sure of it, but for the moment, it was gone.

'I should put you in touch with my sister. You'd have a lot to talk about.'

'Is she single?' Freddie joked, but even as he said it, cringed and felt terrible for it.

'She's married,' Mia said gently, with a kind smile. 'But honestly, should two people with OCD be together? Can you imagine?'

'Probably not a good idea, you're right.'

The silence hung for an awkward moment.

'So you've been single since then? Five years. Wow,' Mia ruminated. Freddie didn't correct her. There was no point, she didn't need to know. 'But if you're better now, then why has it taken you so long to get out there?'

'I don't know,' Freddie admitted. 'I guess, when I have a routine, I like sticking to it. I don't like to change things up much.'

'But you're trying now? You've been challenged to go on dates?'

'Something like that.'

'Well, I think all this is awesome. You should totally write about it or something, get one of those websites to do a thing. Or go on *This Morning*. You'd have a million girls falling at your feet in moments.'

'I don't know about that . . .' Just the mere thought of having any of this made public forced his fingers into tense fists.

'Why? Bet there are hundreds of girls who'd love a man like you.' He gave her a look in response. 'What's that actor – there's one you remind me of; he's lanky as well. Oh, I'll remember it once we're done here, I promise you.'

Then a hopeful thought, something that felt safe to say: 'We could hang out again maybe? Not like a date, but just to hang out?'

'Just friends?'

'Sure, why not?'

He hated himself after he said it, suddenly feeling like he was being too needy and strange.

'You're really nice Freddie . . .' Mia started.

'You're really nice too,' he said back.

'But that's not what I do this for. I don't think that's what you should be doing this for either.'

'Right.'

'You're sweet, but this is dating. For dates. Not for friends. You know?'

'Yeah. I know.'

'But thanks. And don't feel bad about asking. It was cool that you asked. You'll find the right girl, I'm certain of it.' She placed a hand on his arm, and held it there in a reassuring way.

'You shouldn't be letting yourself stay stuck on that other guy. He's an idiot,' Freddie said.

'You can't help who you love, even if they're deranged arseholes who think they deserve to be dating someone with a bum like a Kardashian,' she replied sadly. 'Speaking of which, you don't mind if we take a selfie together, do you? I won't tag you or anything, but I'm sort of blogging these dates on my Insta. He still follows me and I want him to see them. I promise to keep you anonymous?'

Somewhat startled, Freddie obliged, and then, once Mia had applied whatever filters she deemed necessary and written a comment about drinking the best coffee in London with a new friend, wink emoji, she said it was time to go. Freddie stood up with her and they battled through the awkward-hug thing. Then she put on her purple bobble hat and disappeared into the icy February air.

Well. That was it then. That was a date.

He walked home. It was freezing, and he had to wrap his scarf twice around his neck to keep out the bite of the cold, but he needed the walk. Freddie had long legs that were eager to pace and work away all the tension he felt after sitting nervously for so long. He had survived the date. It hadn't been a success exactly, but he was otherwise unscathed. And really, ultimately, it hadn't gone that badly? But the thought of having to do it all over again, maybe countless times until he found the one girl he liked enough, and who liked him enough back, still seemed like it might be exhausting. And what if she wasn't out there?

But at least he had made a start. He had taken action, and that felt like something.

8

There was a now familiar lurch in Kate's stomach as she turned into her parents' road.

'Are you sure?' Lindsey had asked, her face caught in a puzzle of static on her phone screen.

'Even if I did find someone else to rent your room, that doesn't escape the real issue. I can't afford it any more. I haven't been able to afford it for a while.'

'Oh Katie.'

'You're not mad?'

'Why would I be mad?'

'I don't know. Just if you needed to come back home suddenly, I thought you might want your old room.'

'I'd already figured it was the end of an era.'

'I know.' Maybe her flatmate leaving had been the excuse Kate needed to admit that it was time for her to leave too.

She had grown up in North London, and her parents, Cheryl and Jack, still lived in the same semi-detached house she had called home when she was growing up. A leafy street, the trees now bare with their branches clipped back, and not far from a Tube, but far enough for it to feel like countryside compared to what Kate had been used to for the last few years.

Her parents had been thrilled that she was visiting, which only made Kate's heart pang with guilt that she didn't pop over more often. The last time she'd seen them was over Christmas, but since Lindsey left in the new year, she'd been putting it off. Maybe because deep down, she knew she had this decision to make, that it was the only logical answer. Facing her parents would mean facing up to it. Now it was the middle of February, and the conversation that Kate had been avoiding felt ten times more significant than it ever should have done.

She let herself into the house and looked through the hallway to see her mother sitting at the island in the kitchen with her friend, Deirdre. Kate lingered in the entryway for a moment as she hung her coat over the stair banister and then quietly went to fuss over Cinnamon, the family labradoodle.

'Who's a good boy?' Kate cooed quietly, Cinnamon's tail fanning and thumping on the wooden floors as he rolled over to display his belly.

'Hello love,' Cheryl Mundy said, once Kate had finally decided to brave the kitchen, her fingers laced around a mug of tea, in her eyes a conspiratorial warning.

'Katie!' Deirdre's voice burst out of her with an unexpected shrillness. 'Well, don't you look healthy!'

'Thank you,' Kate replied with a forced smile, knowing full well that Deirdre meant fat.

Her eyes flickered over the kitchen island, and to the Valentine's Day cards standing proudly. A card from Kate's father to her mother, featuring two cuddly cartoon bears snuggling, and its partner, from her mother to her father, depicting a similarly cute scene, of two dogs kissing noses within a pink heart. Kate had never received a Valentine, at least not a proper one. Her dad used to get her silly ones when she was very little, and there was once a boy in Year Eight who decided to write a card to every single girl in the class, but she didn't think that counted.

She frowned as the cards made her think of her plans for that evening, a Valentine's-themed speed-dating event in Holborn. It felt like such a ludicrous idea now.

'Deirdre was just telling me about Xanthe and Natalia,' her mother said dryly, bringing her thoughts back into the room.

'Xanthe is expecting her second – can you believe it? And Natalia just got engaged,' Deirdre beamed.

'Congratulations,' Kate said, trying her best to sound enthusiastic. She still pictured Xanthe and Natalia as they were in primary school, tiny with wide foreheads and knobbly knees. It was hard to believe they were both coupled up and having babies of their own.

'And how are you doing?' Deirdre asked. 'Still at the gallery?'

'Yes, still at the gallery,' Kate replied, her voice coming out higher pitched than planned.

'Boyfriend?' Deirdre added.

'Nope, not right now!'

'It's OK, Cheryl,' she turned to Kate's mother, 'there's still time. A year ago Natalia and Alec hadn't even met, and now look at them. You never know what's going to happen just around the corner.'

Kate met her mother's gaze briefly as Deidre hunted through her phone for pictures, allowing time for a mutual eyeroll.

'When's the wedding?' Kate asked, the need to be polite almost painful.

'Oh, not for another year yet, because the venue they want is so popular, they have to wait. You wait, Cheryl, when it's your turn you're going to know all about this.'

Kate felt instantly sad that she hadn't been able to give her mother everything that Deirdre had, before Cheryl decided to speak up herself.

'You don't find it tiring?' she asked. 'All the catering stuff, choosing the band? '

'But it's worth it,' Deirdre assured her. 'Think of the photos, the memories.'

'Well, if our Katie got married, it wouldn't half mess up mine and Jack's plans to sort out that loft conversion,' Cheryl smiled.

Kate loved her mum. She'd never pushed Kate into doing anything or being like anyone.

Kate bore Deirdre's gaze for a moment, a disbelieving kind of pity, before she looked at her mother again and tried to stifle a giggle.

'Well, I guess I'd better be going then,' Deirdre announced just as Cinnamon ambled into the kitchen for a drink of water. He managed to get right under Deirdre's feet as she tried to back out of the kitchen. Kate knew she wasn't a dog person.

'Oh no, what a shame,' Kate commented, hoping that she didn't sound too sarcastic. 'Do send my love to Xanthe and Natalia.'

'Of course. They're always asking after you!'

No they aren't, Kate thought. They had probably forgotten she even existed.

'You'll call me when you know the date?' Cheryl asked, seeing Deirdre to the door.

'That woman,' she said, taking her spot again at the kitchen island.

'I have no idea why you're still friends with her,' Kate remarked.

'Oh, her heart's in the right place really, she's just excited. But anyway, my darling, how are you? How's Lindsey doing in Hong Kong? Tell me everything.'

'I'm good, Lindsey's good. You should message her. She'd love to hear from you. But where's Dad? We need to chat.'

'Good chat or bad chat?'

'Chat chat.'

'That doesn't sound ominous at all. Oh, and I saw your friend Elise's wedding is coming up soon. Why didn't you tell me? I would have sent her parents a card.'

Crap. Kate had forgotten that her mother was on Facebook, and 'friends' with the mothers of her ex-friends. Suddenly she felt sick. Suddenly coming here felt like a very bad idea.

'Oh, you know, we don't really hang out any more.' Saying it out loud wasn't easy.

'That's a shame. I thought you were always so close?'

So did I, Kate thought, but to her mother she just shrugged.

Her father came into the kitchen then, heading straight for the fridge without even noticing that Kate was there.

'Jack!' Cheryl exclaimed. 'Say hello to your daughter!'

'Hello to your daughter,' Jack murmured half-heartedly, nearly tripping over the dog. 'Where's that chicken from yesterday?'

'You finished it.'

'There was another portion. I was going to have it today for lunch.'

'You finished it last night.'

'When?'

'You wanted a sandwich, remember? You were hungry after dinner and wanted a sandwich. You finished the chicken then.'

'Oh.'

Jack Mundy begrudged every moment of making his sandwich – with cheese instead of chicken – but once he was settled and happily munching, Kate started: 'So can we chat?'

'You're not pregnant, are you?' her father asked.

'No.'

'Thank goodness for that. Can't be dealing with babies. Too noisy.'

'No, but this is about me.'

'Are you OK? Is it your health?'

'My health is fine, but it's about the flat.' She waited for her parents to say something, hoping that they'd somehow infer what she wanted to say and stop her from having to say it. They didn't.

Kate took a deep breath. 'You've been helping me out for a while now, but I think the time has come to face reality. I didn't think it would be so difficult to find a new position that paid the same as the last one. I'm nearly out of my savings, and I can't ask you to put any more money into helping me pay my bills. So, I've made a decision, but I have no idea what you're going to think about it.'

'Whatever it is, Katie, we'll work through it together,' her mother reassured.

'Well,' she paused, 'I think it's time for me to move back here. Just for a bit, until I get back to where I was. It's not what I really want, and I'm sure it's not what you would want either, but I don't see any other way right now.'

Silence. Kate couldn't even look at her parents' faces. She felt so ashamed, like she had let everybody down.

'We'd love to have you back here,' Cheryl said after a brief pause. 'Wouldn't we, Jack?'

'I don't see the issue. We haven't got around to converting your room yet. You might want to sort it out a bit, though.'

'Really? I wouldn't be a burden or anything?'

'Do me a favour – a burden? There were a million far worse things you could have come to chat with us about, but this would be a pleasure. You know we love having you around.'

'It's not going to be easy . . .'

'Well, you're earning enough to contribute to the shopping and the bills, but we wouldn't ask you for rent,' Cheryl said.

'We wouldn't?' her husband asked.

'No, we wouldn't. Katie can put all her spare funds back into her savings and that will make it easier for her to get back on her feet.'

'So, this is OK? With both of you?' Kate bit her lip, anxious for her parents' reassurance.

'If you pay for the Netflix, then it's all fine with me,' Jack said, chomping down on his sandwich, a stray piece of cheese falling to the table.

'So how soon will this be happening?' her mum asked.

'I guess that I'll have to give my landlord some notice,' Kate said. 'Another month? I suppose I could start moving my stuff sooner.'

'We'll help with all of that,' her father assured her.

Kate felt a rush of love for her kind, solid, supportive parents, and resolved right there to keep one of her famous spreadsheets tallying up every single penny they had helped her with, so that she could pay them back one day. She'd do it with interest.

'Come here love,' Cheryl said, pulling her daughter in close and holding her tight for a moment. Once she let go, her father offered all the physical affection he could manage, a reassuring and firm hand on her shoulder.

'We'll be all right,' Jack sighed finally, taking his empty plate over to the sink to wash up. 'It won't be for long anyway, I'm sure.'

But what if it was?

What if the housing crisis became a housing apocalypse?

What if, as well as being a washed-up old virgin, she ended up a washed-up old virgin who lived with her parents?

Before she left she went up to her room, ostensibly to check how much work needed to be done clearing the old stuff out so that her current stuff could be moved back in, but also in an attempt to cement her decision, to make it real.

There was her bed, the mattress slightly depressed from years of use, and next to it her bedside table, where her lamp, the base covered in stupid stickers of hearts and teddy bears, still stood proudly. She'd decided the colour of the walls when she was twelve, a hot orange she'd thought would be cool when all her friends were still obsessed with soft pinks, purples and baby blues. She'd been that kind of girl once, the kind who could see what everybody else was doing and who'd decide to march in completely the opposite direction. And then at some point in her teens, being like everybody else became the most important thing.

Folded away behind her door was the easel her parents had bought for her when she started studying A level art. It had barely been used since then. At its base a toolbox filled with dried-out tubes of cheap paint, and brushes, their ends frayed and brittle. She couldn't remember the last time she'd even picked up a pencil to sketch, but here, on the walls, her parents had left her old doodles pinned up. Some silly watercolours, caricatures of teachers, the odd serious practice piece in acrylic that she'd attempted before she'd got scared of how much work she'd have to do to get better and given up.

As Kate took another turn, taking it all in, finally she found her reflection in the full-length mirror, propped up against a wall and draped with a scarf she last wore a decade ago. There was an adult body, rounder than she would have liked it to be, but healthy, and above it a face that she had never really much liked, but could sometimes reluctantly admit was pretty. She'd never highlighted her hair and yet it gleamed blonde in the light that found its way into the room, as her dark eyes glazed with the threat of tears.

There were worse places she could be, Kate realised.

She hadn't told her parents about the speed-dating event she was going to that evening, mostly because she was almost certain that she wasn't going to go through with it. As she headed back into town on the Tube, she wondered what the hell she had been thinking, and whether there was some way she could possibly get her money back. The terms and conditions on the event website had said that tickets were non-refundable, and twenty-five pounds was not something to be sniffed at, especially for someone in her situation.

She found herself thinking about Freddie, and whether he had gone through with his side of the challenge. She wished she had his number, so that they could share stories of their respective misadventures. Online dating might have been easier in some respects, but Kate had been there before. She had signed up for apps, spent forever searching and swiping and sifting through sexist and icky messages, and in the end was left vaguely traumatised. But now, feeling as low as she did, she wondered why she had ever thought that speed dating was a better alternative.

Kate had popped back to her flat, her lovely, precious-but-half-empty flat, to get changed before leaving for the bar. She chose a black dress that had buttons all the way up the front, even though the ticket encouraged people to wear red or pink for St Valentine, and hoped that it was flattering enough (she had nothing pink in her wardrobe, and the only red was a big fluffy jumper). She wore her heeled black boots, even though they were uncomfortable, and left her hair loose. It was comforting to feel it around her face. When she was younger she used to twist strands in her fingers and chew on it, and on the Tube now, whilst she low-key panicked about everything she was potentially going to lose in the near future, she found herself reaching for a twist of hair again, but refrained from chewing only for the sake of her lipstick (bright red and given to her by Renee).

The bar was hip and dark and just around the corner from Holborn station, and she was one of the first people there.

'I'm here for the thing?' Kate said tentatively to one of the organisers, a chipper guy who couldn't have been more than twenty years old, and who Kate thought might have preferred organising a university bar crawl to a singles event for late twenty/early thirty somethings. But he was kind, kinder than he needed to be, and gave Kate a name sticker with hearts all over it, and told her to enjoy her free drink at the bar whilst they waited for everyone else to arrive.

In all there were forty of them, twenty girls and twenty boys. And once they were all assembled, Kate realised that she was very much out of her depth.

Initially the thought of speed dating had been wonderful. She could just sit there, nice and comfortable, whilst a parade of men were brought before her. She could make a choice, and had the security of knowing that if the connection was bad, then she would only have to talk to them for two minutes max. What Kate hadn't thought about was that, even though it was the men doing all the moving around, they made choices too, and out of the twenty girls, she saw herself as the worst option. There was a strange upside to online dating, Kate thought, in that you never knew what you were up against.

She wasn't like the other girls, in their flirty dresses and calamitous heels. She couldn't see how any of these men would ever choose her, given the options. She didn't feel beautiful, didn't feel intelligent, didn't feel as if she had anything to offer. This was going to be a disaster.

The chipper guy from the door, accompanied by an equally chipper girl of about the same age, wearing a similar T-shirt emblazoned with the logo of the company organising the dating experience, appeared before them to say that the games were about to begin.

'Don't be nervous,' the girl said, coming over to Kate and leading her to one of the carefully positioned tables and chairs around the room. 'They smell fear, you know. And you look terrified!'

'Ha-ha,' Kate laughed, a little overexuberantly. She *was* terrified.

She let herself have an initial scan of the guys in the room, and nobody jumped out at her.

Too muscly.

Too beardy.

Too tattooed.

But then, initial attraction had never been Kate's strong point. She marvelled at people who were able to spot each other from afar and attract the other like sexually charged magnets.

Each man seemed like a strange alien, too much of an unknown entity. She couldn't imagine herself with any of them. It didn't help that some were clearly already making their moves on some of the women. Kate supposed it was possible that if she liked one of them, she could win him over with her dazzling charm, make a genuine connection over a shared interest, but with only two minutes to play with? There was no hope.

Before the first man reached her table, she stood up.

'Everything all right?' the hostess asked. 'We're about to start the first round.'

'I have to go,' Kate said. Her heart was thudding in her chest.

'But you'll make the numbers uneven,' the girl said, all the playfulness gone from her voice.

'I'm sorry,' Kate flustered. 'But I can't be here, and I really have to go.'

'Don't expect to get your money back or anything,' the girl called as Kate hurried on her coat.

The panic attack hit fully once she was outside. She managed to walk a distance away before she found herself desperate to sit down – to lie down if she could – but found enough energy to lean on a nearby building, its smooth marbled exterior soothing despite the cold. Gradually her breathing calmed, and the sweat on her forehead subsided and evaporated. She was left with the intense need to have a cup of tea and a good cry.

9

'A date? Our Freddie went on a date?' Baz was more incredulous than Freddie would have liked, despite the validity of his disbelief. 'How? When? Who?'

'Her name was Mia. And it was nice, but it was also nothing,' Freddie replied.

They were in a bar not far from the university building, close enough that Freddie could walk there easily for the group meeting later.

'Still, that's the first time I've heard you talk about a girl since, what was her name? In university? Carnation?'

'Camellia.'

'Camellia! Never seen anyone so lovesick. What happened there anyway? Did you ever tell me, or did I just forget?'

'You forgot,' Freddie mumbled. There had, of course, been nothing to tell. But Baz didn't need to know that. The months after graduation were a rush of job and house-hunting, with Baz moving back to the Midlands for a bit before he managed to find and land the graduate placement he wanted. Anything could have happened during that time, and Freddie had let him believe that anything did.

'So what was with this Mia then? Why did that happen?'

'It was just a dating app thing I was trying out. She was cute but not over her ex and it clearly wasn't going anywhere.'

'Well, good on you mate.'

'Thanks.'

Baz put his beer back down on the table and, leaning across, kept his voice quiet: 'You know you can talk to me, if you need it?'

The tone caught Freddie off guard, uncertain about what he was referring to. Baz had been there when his life had gone a little off the rails five years ago, but that was in the past. He'd moved on. He was fine now. Very nearly perfectly fine.

'Oh, yeah. I know. Thank you, I will.'

'No listen Freddie, before Wayne arrives and lowers the tone. You know I worry about you sometimes.'

'Why? There's nothing to worry about.'

'I think that after Camellia,' the way Baz said her name made Freddie wince, 'and then when everything went downhill not long after . . . I think sometimes that we never really got the chance to catch up. I don't know if I was a good friend to you. Or, at least, as good a friend as I could have been.'

'You were great, Baz, you were always there.'

'Freddie, look, I got lucky with Laura. But that doesn't mean that I don't understand, and that you can't talk to me if you need to.'

Freddie's started playing with the foil of an empty packet of salted peanuts, pulling it into thin strips.

'You're getting all intense,' he tried to laugh, his voice sounding throttled and fake. 'Chill out, I'm fine.'

'Right,' Baz paused. His gaze was intense. 'It's just—'

'Wa-hey!' Wayne bounded up to their table, smile almost as wide as his arms.

'Wayne!' Freddie said, overjoyed at the interruption. He stood up and gave his friend a hug. 'Pleased to see you before I head off.'

'You're off? Already? Can't even get one in with us?'

'Oh, I've been hanging out with Baz for a while, and I have this thing. Sorry to rush off.'

'Aw mate! What's up? Not a date, is it?'

'Something like that.' Freddie caught Baz's gaze as he said it. 'I'll catch you properly next time though, yeah?'

'Absolutely.'

There was a brisk goodbye with Baz and then Freddie was out of the pub and down the road as quickly as he could make it. He didn't know what Baz had been referring to exactly, but it was almost certainly too personal and overwhelming to be sprung on him so suddenly. Was it possible that Baz had noticed the lack of women in his life, and extrapolated Freddie's biggest secret? He didn't think that Baz would make fun of him, he definitely wasn't like that, but even so, it was a conversation he absolutely did not want to have. He wanted to be normal, one of the guys. And having his virginity out there and acknowledged by his closest friends was just too much. At least when he was in the group with strangers he was anonymous, and could run away into obscurity if he ever needed to. Facing up to things in real life? Too much. Far too much.

Saved by the Wayne, he thought.

He saw Kate waiting for the lift in lobby of the Union building, and briefly pondered hiding away for a minute so that he didn't have to interact with her. Not that he had anything against her personally – she did seem nice, after all – but the thought of having to make small talk, when he knew nothing about her other than that she was as sexually inexperienced as him, was just too excruciating.

Unfortunately, she turned as he approached, smiling weakly when she saw him. Freddie knew it would now be far more embarrassing to avoid her than it would be to go over and join her in the lift.

'We really should stop meeting like this,' she said.

Freddie didn't really know what to say, so offered a sympathetic smile in response, then made sure that he was closest to the buttons as they got into the lift so that they couldn't both reach for them at the same time again.

'You know, I used to go here,' Kate said.

Ah, she's a talker, Freddie thought first, before he heard what she said.

'You went to this university?' he asked. 'Me too.'

'No way! When did you graduate?'

'Twenty eleven.'

'Same here. What did you study?'

'Computer Science.'

'I did English and History. You know, I thought I recognised you. How many times do you think we passed each other in the corridors? Funny how things turn out, I guess.'

Freddie didn't know what to say to that, but fortunately the lift doors opened just at the right time and they walked the rest of the way in silence to their assigned room. He was trying to work out if it was an uncomfortable silence, if he was being friendly enough, but then he was also nervous and just wanted to get to the room so that he could say what he wanted to say, and get the advice he needed.

Cathryn, Hattie, Steve and Andy were already there, chatting happily, but Lizzie and Mike hadn't arrived yet.

'Ah, we were wondering if you'd make it back,' Andy said warmly.

'So, did you date?' Hattie was practically bursting out of her seat with excitement. Then, seeing Cathryn's bemused face, explained: 'We dared Kate and Freddie to go out and meet people.'

'*You* dared them,' Andy clarified.

'So, spill. Did you go on a date?' Hattie asked Freddie, looking him dead in the eye.

Freddie thought about saying no. Not because he wanted to lie or was ashamed or embarrassed, but because it was so much easier than saying yes. But that wasn't what he was here for, and not how he wanted to be any more.

'Yes,' he finally murmured shyly.

'And?' Cathryn asked.

'And . . .' Freddie didn't know what to say. Didn't know how to explain it. That it was perfectly fine, but that it didn't feel in any way romantic either.

'Who was she?' Hattie prompted.

'Her name was Mia.'

'And where did you meet?'

'At a coffee place not far from where I live.'

'And then what happened?'

'Perhaps we should give Freddie some space?' Andy suggested. 'We haven't even started the meeting properly yet.'

Freddie had started picking at the cuticle of his thumb. It wasn't the most helpful of distractions, especially when it started to bleed. He used his other thumb to press at the tiny wound, and then felt worried. The cut was minuscule, barely even noticeable, but what if it got infected? What if he got septicaemia? What if he died?

'Freddie?' Andy asked. 'Are you all right?'

'What?' Freddie looked up, aware that people were looking at him. Aware that Kate was looking at him.

'You don't have to talk about it if you don't want to,' Andy said.

'But I do want to,' he heard himself saying. 'I came here to talk. It's just, it's not easy.'

The door creaked as Lizzie came in, and she sat on her hands when she took her seat. 'Sorry I'm late.'

Andy took the cue to formally start the meeting, going through the same spiel as the last time, making sure that everyone knew the space was safe, and that they shouldn't feel scared to say how they really felt.

'So, Freddie, do you want to tell us more about your date, or should we move on?' Andy asked him gently. Freddie could tell that he could back out if he wanted to, that Andy was giving him the room to be shy if he needed it. But he also knew that he wanted to talk. At least, he wanted to be able to talk.

'We drank coffee. She was hung up on her ex. That's about it, really.'

'What did you talk about?' Cathryn asked, encouraging.

'Umm ... some mental health things, her ex-boyfriend, our jobs.'

'That sounds pretty decent, like you made a connection, even if it wasn't a romantic one?' Hattie offered.

'I guess. But I think I wanted to feel something more. If anything, not feeling anything romance-wise made it easier to get on and talk, but that's not really what I wanted from it.'

'It's early days,' said Cathryn. 'You can't expect to find everything you want from the first date.'

'I had those feelings once – for a girl, I mean – and to be honest, it was pretty terrible. What if I can't feel them any more? What if my brain has managed to switch all that off?'

'It's possible you've locked up that part of you,' Andy said carefully. 'Psychologically speaking, you may be protecting yourself from allowing a deeper connection. But it won't have gone for ever. If something is switched off, then I can assure you it's capable of being switched on again. Coming here might have been the start, and maybe meeting Mia was another part of that process.'

'Are you going to try again?' Hattie asked.

'I feel like maybe I should, but I'm in no rush.'

'That's fair,' Cathryn said.

'What about you, Kate?' Hattie challenged.

'Hang on, what have I missed?' Lizzie asked. 'Did Kate and Freddie date each other? I'm confused.'

Freddie blanched at the suggestion and, when he dared glance up at Kate, noticed that she had flushed scarlet. Her reaction eased some of the discomfort he felt. She caught his eye and he smiled.

'No!' Hattie hissed. 'I suggested they go out and meet people. Which I know isn't in the group rules – sorry Andy – but we're just catching up on how they did. *Separately*.'

'I signed up for a speed-dating event,' Kate revealed, her blush still evident.

'Oh, I've always wanted to try that,' Cathryn said enthusiastically.

'I just didn't stay for it,' Kate finished.

'Ah.'

'What happened?' Andy asked.

'I don't know. Maybe I just realised that I hated myself and that meant everybody else would hate me too?' She was trying to make light of it, to make the situation seem funny and out of her control. It was a defence mechanism that Freddie recognised and understood keenly.

'Do you really hate yourself?' Hattie asked, concerned. Kate just shrugged in reply.

'What scared you?' Andy asked.

'Scared me?' Kate was resisting. Her arms were folded across her chest now, and her legs crossed underneath her chair. Freddie saw it all, and felt the kinship strengthen.

'I'd be terrified of a speed-dating thing. Sounds like my worst nightmare,' Hattie said, trying to be supportive. 'Just a meat market. Sell yourself in two minutes: go! On to the next one. Go! Like you can understand all the important stuff in two minutes.'

'Maybe it's not about the important stuff,' Lizzie said. 'Maybe it's about the first impression. You can learn a lot in a first impression.'

'Honestly, I think it's just a lust thing,' said Hattie, ignoring her. 'I mean yes, so maybe first impressions are important. I get it. You need to look sharp sometimes, have the aesthetic on point for people to take you seriously. Job interviews and all that. That's great, but when we're talking about speed dating? First impressions in those situations basically amount to "do I want to sleep with you"?'

'What if some people want those things?' Andy put to the group. 'What's so wrong with taking someone's appearance at face value, deciding if we like it, if they're *hot or not*, if you will, and then just having sex and enjoying ourselves?'

'Because some of us aren't hot,' Kate said plainly. She wasn't joking now. 'Some of us will never be hot.'

'Beauty is in the eye of the beholder,' said Lizzie, her voice high and wistful.

'But I'm not sure that really means anything,' said Kate. 'Nobody notices me. If I'd hung around at that speed-dating thing, I know I wouldn't have ended up with any dates, because I saw the other options. I can't see how I'd have anything to offer, compared to the other girls there.'

'I don't think that's true,' said Cathryn. Freddie agreed, but didn't say anything.

'I'm not fishing for compliments. It's how I really feel.' Kate paused, composing herself. 'Sorry, it's been tough for me lately.'

'You're doing fine, lovely.' Cathryn leaned over to place a hand on Kate's shoulder.

'I decided to move back in with my parents because I can't afford the place I've been living in for the past few years any more. My best friend and flatmate got the job of her dreams, except that it's on the other side of the world, and my career trajectory has flatlined. I just don't know what to do. I know that a lot of people have things a lot worse, but that doesn't stop me feeling really insecure about everything. About myself too. Sometimes I wonder, if I were beautiful, not in that inner sense, but if I were objectively hot, then I wouldn't be in this mess. That life would be ten times easier. It sounds stupid, I know. Maybe I'd be married by now. I'd have a house and babies. Like everyone else.'

'Not everyone is married with babies; in fact, statistically fewer people your age are married with babies than ever,' Hattie said.

'But it feels that way to me,' Kate replied.

'Do you even want to be married?' Andy asked.

'That's the thing. I really don't. Not now, anyway. Not any time soon. I just wonder if life would be easier if it had all worked out that way. Instead of this way. Which, frankly, sucks. Wouldn't I be happier if I was married?'

'Marriage doesn't make you happy,' Hattie said.

'I don't know,' Lizzie countered. 'I think I understand what Kate is saying. I thought I would be married too. I thought that I had found my one true love and that I wouldn't have to worry about anything else after that. But then he wasn't there any more, and I haven't been the same since. Nothing has been right.'

Cathryn reached over to Lizzie and put a sympathetic hand on her arm. Freddie looked around and noticed Steve shifting in his seat, pained and uncomfortable. He'd been so quiet through the whole session, it was easy to forget that he was even there.

'I know you think that, but who says that finding your perfect partner is the one key to making you happy?' Cathryn said. 'There are lots of things that could make you happy. You can't spend your whole life like Miss Havisham. You've got to go out, find new ways to make yourself happy, be active in creating happiness.'

Freddie was playing with his fingers again, picking at another uneven cuticle. He was hearing what Cathryn was saying, and it made sense. But there was still a part of him that thought that if he had a girlfriend, maybe if Camellia had been available and waiting for him that night at the Leavers' Ball, things would have turned out differently. He wouldn't be the way he was now.

'How do you know that finding the right person isn't the key to happiness? What if it is?' he asked.

'So what about the people who have lots of partners? Or choose to have no partner? Are they doomed to be unhappy for ever?' Hattie was sceptical, a single eyebrow arched.

'Maybe it's different for everyone. But what if it's true for some people?' Freddie wondered out loud.

'I don't think it's wise to fixate on another person being the answer to all your problems,' Andy said gently.

'There's no such thing as a happily ever after,' Hattie agreed. 'Let's say you meet your soul mate, if soul mates even exist . . . and then what? You could still lose your job. You could still have financial problems. Accidents and diseases and everything else. Being in love doesn't stop any of that from happening.'

'But what if it makes those things easier to handle?' Freddie asked.

'That's not sex and romance and marriage. That's friendship and family,' Hattie answered. The quiet that followed suggested that everyone there agreed with her.

'Is there anything else you want to tell us about the speed dating?' Andy asked Kate after they let themselves sit in the silence for a moment.

'I don't know. I went into the bar, I sat down and looked around at all these hot people and felt like I didn't belong there. So I left. I'm tired, and I'm sad.'

'I think you might be angry too,' Andy said.

'Probably.'

'I'm angry for you,' Hattie leaned back in her chair and let her hands fly wide. 'The fact that society has taught you to think that the only way you can be happy is if you fit this picture-perfect image. That's patriarchy for you.'

Freddie looked at Kate with a strange sense of wonder. He had thought that he was alone when he wasn't. He thought girls had it so easy, but they didn't. There were a million things on their minds that he hadn't even considered. But he understood it. He understood the pressure, the expectations.

The meeting wrapped up after nearly an hour and a half, during which time Hattie told a story about getting into an argument with a men's rights activist on Twitter, and then nearly got into a very similar argument with Steve, who wasn't a men's rights activist, as it eventually turned out, but just completely clueless as to what Hattie meant and somehow thought that playing devil's advocate was the best way to handle the discussion.

Andy called for the pub as they were putting their chairs away, and this time Freddie felt eager to go. He liked listening to these people, he realised, liked being with them.

'I see a lot of myself in you,' Steve said, matching his stride as they walked through Bloomsbury.

'Right,' Freddie replied, unsure of what Steve meant.

'I know we talk a lot in this group about it not being too late, and not holding ourselves up to this perfect image of what we could be, but I really do think I've left it too late.'

'Surely not,' Freddie looked over at Steve, a man half a foot shorter than him, and significantly balder, but otherwise fairly similar in face and body shape. They had the same pale skin, the same hard concentration of a jaw. Anyone looking at them now might think they were cousins, perhaps even brothers with an age gap between them.

'I pretend like I still have hope,' Steve revealed. 'But I don't really. I still like to listen to everyone else, though.'

'There must be something that gives you some hope?'

'I used to think that maybe there was a chance for me and Lizzie. When I first met her, but I don't know. She's still very hung up on that fella of hers. You know, I don't think she's seen him in over thirty years, but she's still convinced they'll end up together. It makes it hard to say anything.'

'Wait, he's still alive? I presumed he had died when they were young?'

'She likes people to think that. She thinks being a widow is far more romantic than being, well, I guess she was dumped.'

'Wow. I had no idea.'

'I've been coming to this group for a while. She'll tell that story again eventually, and then we'll all help her tell the truth, the real story.'

'Right.'

'And then I'll get the crazy idea that maybe I can save her. That, at least, I should say something to her. Let her know that I care.'

'Maybe you should?'

'Tried to go down that road once before. It was pretty brutal. Don't think I have it in me to try again,' Steve patted Freddie on the arm. 'You're young, and you're tall too. You've still got a chance.'

'I, umm . . .' Freddie wasn't sure what the right thing to say was, but he tried anyway: 'I don't think you should give up.'

They were at the pub now. Steve gave Freddie a sad, thin-lipped smile, and then waved a hurried goodbye before continuing towards the Tube station.

'That was weird,' Freddie revealed when they all sat down with their drinks.

'What was?' Hattie asked.

'Steve. He just admitted to me that he still likes Lizzie.'

'Well, isn't that sweet,' Cathryn smiled.

'This again,' Hattie sighed. 'Maybe it wouldn't be such a bad thing to try and get them together?'

'Absolutely not,' Andy said firmly. 'The group is a safe space, remember? What if it doesn't work out? We don't want to make things awkward for them if they both turn up for some sense of sanctuary.'

'But what if it does work out?' Kate asked.

'Well, if they both want it to happen, then it should happen on their own terms. We shouldn't force it. Let it happen naturally, if it's going to happen at all. We can't be involved in it.'

'Spoilsport,' Hattie moaned.

'Look, I'd love it if they found each other. But Lizzie wasn't interested before, why would she be interested now? Plus she's awfully stuck in her past,' said Andy.

While the group debated the pros and cons of matchmaking within the group, Freddie thought a little more about what Steve had said to him, specifically the fact that he reminded Steve of a younger version of himself. It was worrying, the thought of being that lonely and quiet all those years in the future. He didn't want to get to Steve's age and still be in the same place. He wanted to be someone who took risks and told people how he really felt. He wanted to be so much more than he was now.

'Freddie, are you all right?' Kate was looking at him.

'Yeah,' he replied, 'I'm getting there.'

IO

'Well, what about doing something completely different?' Renee asked. They were sitting together in the staff room on their lunch break, Kate staring at her phone whilst Renee worked on a sketch.

'Different how?'

'Well, you keep looking for the same type of job you did before, right? Why not try something else?'

'I don't know about that.'

'It's not as if you have millions of choices right now.'

Kate glanced over at Renee's sketchbook. It was just an idle doodle, something to keep her hands busy whilst they waited out their lunch hour, but Renee was talented. A wolf-ish beast with human-like eyes was slowly emerging on the page as if it were the easiest thing in the world. Watching her, Kate yearned to draw again, but she knew she was nowhere near as good. She'd considered going to art school back when she was studying for her GCSEs and A levels, but the career opportunities further down the line had seemed so limited. A joke, considering the situation she was in now. There was every chance she would have been better off, and even if she wasn't, the thought that she might have been happier anyway created a sting of sadness.

Before she'd ended up at the gallery, Kate had been a project coordinator for a high-end chain of department stores. She had started out as a marketing assistant, her first big job after graduation, and over the years had spent time in various teams across head office. She had been allowed to be creative, until the purse strings started getting tighter. She had been brave enough to raise her voice in big meetings once in a while, until the big meetings had started to be less about exciting new ideas and more about drastic and austere rescue efforts. When the bottom finally fell out of the share price in 2017, Kate hadn't been surprised when she found herself up for redundancy. Even through she'd only been there six years, her salary was too high and her role too nebulous to be considered indispensable. She wasn't the only one to go either. Stores were closing across the country, and many of her head-office colleagues had jumped ship in the preceding months. The redundancy package had been pretty good, but it hadn't lasted long.

Kate knew she didn't want to work in retail marketing again, but besides that, she had little idea what she was good for. Everything she entered into the job search website returned results that were bleak and uninspiring.

'What do you think I should do?' Kate asked her friend, genuinely curious.

'What did you want to be when you were little?'

'Honestly? I never really got that figured out. But my mum always wanted me to be a teacher.'

'Urgh, teenagers though,' Renee said.

'Exactly,' Kate agreed.

'What subject would you do? If you decided to go that way?'

'I guess it would have to be English or History. I did a joint honours degree.'

'Oh, you should definitely do English. You can do loads of rousing speeches about great works of literature, and then all the kids would worship you like in *Dead Poets Society*.'

'I think you have to just stick to the curriculum nowadays.'

'Well, that sucks. But still, teaching. It could work?'

'Do you honestly think I'm a rousing speeches kind of person?' Kate looked at Renee.

'You could learn to be?' Renee grimaced and shrugged.

The sound of Renee's pencil gently scraping on paper was soothing, and for a moment Kate pined that her pay wasn't better so that she could just keep doing this job for ever. She idly tapped her way to the gallery website and clicked through to the Jobs pages.

'There's something going in the Learning and Development department here,' Kate announced. 'It's a temporary placement. Do you think they'd let me do it but keep my current job for when the contract ends?'

'Are you kidding me? Of course they would! This place is always looking for people, and the fact that you know where all the emergency exits are is seriously in your favour.'

'I should probably ask our manager first though. Do you think she'd be happy with me going for it?'

Renee shuffled over so that she could look at Kate's phone screen with her.

'Definitely ask her first, but apply regardless of what she says,' she advised.

The galleries were quiet. Nowhere near empty – they never were – but quiet enough to allow Kate to drift a little, absorb the atmosphere of the paintings, and watch the people as they did the same. She was feeling optimistic. The group had helped with this, she knew that. And the support of her parents. After months and months of feeling like the world was against her, discovering that she had the power to make choices was like having a pressure valve released. Granted, the choices weren't ideal (however wonderful her parents were being, Kate would still have preferred to not have to move back in with them), but they were choices nonetheless. Small but positive steps.

There was still one step she thought would make all the difference, though. Despite what they had been talking about in the group sessions, and knowing that her virginity didn't make or break her as a person, it was still something she couldn't stop thinking about. She didn't want it to be so important. She wanted to be like Hattie, confident and vibrant and completely self-assured. But she also wanted to be able to gossip with Renee, and not feel like she was lying somehow. She didn't want to be left out. She still wanted to have sex – badly – and to know for herself.

If life had worked out a different way, Kate suspected that she would have had at least three sexual partners by now. They wouldn't necessarily have all been boyfriends, but they might have been. And those were just the ones she knew about. She hoped there might have been others too, and that she had just been oblivious, too caught up in her own insecurities to notice. Plus, it wasn't as if she made a habit of putting herself out there. She cringed when she thought about the one time she did: that drunken last-ditch effort at the university Leavers' Ball that had left her stupefied with embarrassment when she had recalled it the following morning.

There had been sweet, immature crushes before, but Nathan was the first boy she had really, genuinely liked. He had approached her at a party she had gone to with Elise and the other girls one weekend, after they had done their schoolgirlish job of not-so-subtly revealing to his friend that Kate liked him. Kate had watched as Nathan was cornered by his friend (a few moments after said friend had been cornered by Elise and Georgie), and their heads had bobbed in her direction. They were talking about her. Nathan was new to the sixth form – it was attached to their high school, but there were some students who'd joined having done their GCSEs elsewhere. When Nathan had first walked through the swinging doors of the common room, hair spiked with too much gel and collar of his polo shirt popped, Kate had been instantly smitten. Her crushes, and other weird teenage fascinations, had never been like this. Nathan was different. He was Orlando Bloom, Jesse Bradford and Shane West all rolled into one.

Kate had expected him to run a mile the moment that he found out about her crush. She was deathly embarrassed by it. She hated that she somehow knew his timetable, knew where he'd be when their free periods matched up. She hated that she paid attention to *Match of the Day* now, so that she could know what was going on with his favourite football team. She would sign in and out of MSN Messenger, hoping that he'd notice her name ping on his contact list, know who she was, and maybe say hello. It was excruciating. And Elise hadn't made it easier for her either.

'I'm going to tell him,' she had said, giggling one lunch break.

'Please don't. He'll hate me,' Kate had replied.

'He won't hate you. He's cool. My cousin's friend knows him from before. He's a nice one. I promise you.'

'But what if he doesn't like me back?'

'What if he does?'

It finally went down at a house party, where Kate was too scared to drink anything alcoholic, and India teased her mercilessly for it.

'It's not going to kill you!' she'd said, more annoyed than she should have been, Kate had always thought.

'I don't want to drink, leave it out,' she'd replied.

'Honestly, you're so frigid sometimes,' India said, looking over her shoulder at Elise and Georgie to spread the gossip. 'You honestly think you're ready for a guy like that?' she'd asked Kate.

Nathan hadn't balked when he'd heard the news. But he didn't come over to Kate straight away either. He took his time, working the room until he got around to her.

'Hi,' he said. He was drinking a Corona, which seemed oddly sophisticated to Kate, compared to all the people frantically downing shots or chugging back bright blue WKDs and Bacardi Breezers.

'Hi,' Kate replied, her voice a feeble squeak. She couldn't look at him, couldn't bear to. He knew she liked him. *He knew.*

They had chatted. It hadn't been for long, and it was awful, mostly because of the pumping garage music and the fact that someone threw up in the kitchen sink and all the girls had started screaming. But they had chatted. And Kate hadn't died from it.

'So, what are you doing tomorrow?' Nathan had asked.

'Oh, I have this huge thing to do for Art. It's project work for a piece that counts towards my final mark. Art takes up so much time, you know? It's basically like doing two A levels, not one.'

'Is it going to take all day?'

'Probably. Well, I'll do some of that English reading in the morning, but yeah, most of the afternoon will be spent on Art. Then I usually spend time with my parents later on. We used to have "family days" on Sundays, but it's kind of fallen apart since I started studying so hard. We try and do something, though. Usually it's something lame like a board game, or catching up on the telly we've missed during the week. Stupid stuff.'

Stop talking, she had told herself. *Just stop talking!*

'Yeah, parents can be so annoying.'

'Yeah.'

'But you don't study that hard every weekend? You do other stuff too, right, like being out tonight?'

'Yeah, no, totally. I mean, not really, but totally.' She dared herself to look him directly in the eyes, and then found the task impossible. 'I tend to study really hard. I really want to go to Warwick or UCL, so I have to work a lot.'

'I know what you mean. My brother is at Bristol. He went nuts when it came to final year of A levels.'

'Oh wow, Bristol. That's so impressive!'

'It's all right. I went to visit him once, seemed a bit tame to be honest.'

'Tame?'

'Yeah. I think I'd prefer the vibe at Leeds or Nottingham. Maybe Newcastle. Good clubs, good parties.'

'Oh yeah, absolutely,' Kate remembered, trying to seem cool. Praying that Nathan didn't think she was lame.

'But you're really into revising and stuff, yeah?'

'I just think if I work hard now, it'll probably pay off later.' She was feeling the moment slipping away from her. Remembered noticing him looking around the room.

'Work hard party harder, I reckon,' Nathan said nonchalantly, taking a long swig of the Corona.

Kate nodded. 'Sure, it's all about the balance,' she remembered trying hard to sound convincingly cool.

Nathan stared at his empty bottle. 'I'm going to get another drink,' he said finally, and it was only after he had walked away that Kate realised he hadn't offered to get her one too.

Later on, Kate peeked into a study and saw Nathan kissing India. She couldn't tell it was her at first. The room was dark and India's hair was almost jet black with it, but as their bodies turned she couldn't mistake India's thin boho headband, and Nathan's fingers trying to move it out of the way. She called her dad and said that things at the house party were winding down and she wanted to come home.

'You idiot,' Bella had said to her in school on Monday. 'He was asking you out.'

'No, he wasn't,' Kate protested.

'He definitely was. Jonny told me,' Elise confirmed. She was going out with Jonny at the time.

'But he ended up with India,' Kate replied. Just saying her name stung.

'For God's sake,' India had moaned at her later. 'You really think I was interested in him? He was just there. I didn't think it would be a big deal, as you clearly didn't want him.'

But India had known, Kate thought. She'd been with her earlier in the evening when Kate had admitted to her that she was scared she'd mess it up.

Elise and the others didn't seem to think India had done anything wrong, and encouraged Kate to try again. They suggested that she let herself get drunk as it would give her more confidence, but she didn't feel the same about Nathan having watched him get off with someone else (especially someone like India). With a distinct lack of anyone else eligible in the sixth-form common room, Kate told herself again that the payoff would be later, that there would be amazing boys at university who wouldn't just be obsessed with partying and distracted by the first drunk girl who walked by.

First year passed without a romantic incident – but that was OK, Kate told herself, because she was finding her feet and making friends. It was during the summer holiday between first and second years when she felt like her life was finally really beginning. His name was Marcus.

Kate had been on holiday with her parents and was finding it unbearable. They were staying at a resort in Spain, nothing too tacky, and nothing too noisy, but Kate was bored. She'd read two paperbacks already and was hungry for something to do. The nearby town was nothing but sleepy whitewashed houses and a small church that had been interesting for half an hour. So, during the hottest hours, when her parents retired to their room to nap after lunch, Kate had drifted down to the hotel bar. It was practically empty during the day, but had these deep sofas for lounging, so Kate had taken to sitting back with either a book or her sketchbook and watching hotel guests and staff drift through the lobby. She tried to sketch the figures as they went, attempting to capture their gait or posture. She was failing miserably. After getting a high mark in her Art A level, she'd barely put pencil to paper during her entire first year at UCL.

'What are you doing?' He was Spanish, fair-haired, and looming over her, blocking her light.

'Nothing,' Kate said, at first nervous that she was trespassing, even though she was a guest.

'You're good,' the man had commented. He couldn't have been much older than her. She'd seen him around. He worked behind the bar in the evenings, and sometimes at the outside bar and food station by the pool during the day.

It turned out he was just as eager to have someone to talk to as she was. He was also bored; the bar only picked up in the evenings, and if he sat a certain way on the arm of her sofa, a tiny notepad and pen at the ready, then to anyone passing through he looked like he was taking an order and not just casually chatting. They chatted a lot. His English wasn't perfect, but he was trying to get better. He wanted to come to London to study once he had saved up enough money. Marcus would tell her how frustrating it was, coming from such a small town and working down the road at the resort. He wanted to meet people and see the world. And Kate would tell him that her first year of university was not turning out to be the exciting whirlwind she thought it was meant to be – she was discovering that she was miserable and anxious whenever she got drunk.

'But there are nice boys for you?' Marcus said, and Kate blushed.

No, there had been no nice boys for her.

Marcus listened (Kate wasn't sure that he actually understood everything) and then they started flirting. He'd touch her unnecessarily – a pat on the arm, a squeeze on the shoulder – and when he looked at her she couldn't help but smile. They were friends, but they were something else too. Maybe it was the forbidden thing, because staff weren't meant to fraternise with guests, but Kate was excited.

Finally, one quiet afternoon, when the horizon was fuzzy with heat, and the cicadas sounded even louder than usual, he'd caught her arm as she stood up and pulled her in to a gentle kiss. For Kate it had a wondrous, magical quality. She couldn't move at first, frightened to get it wrong, even more frightened that Marcus would notice how frightened she was, but after a moment, when she had allowed herself to relax, she drank in the kiss like she was never going to get the chance to kiss him again.

Which she wouldn't. Later that day, as she passed the bar on the way to dinner, she spied him talking with another man in quick, heightened Spanish. Finally, his face red with anger and his voice loud, Marcus ended the conversation by swiping his arm across the bar and shoving a load of just-cleaned champagne flutes to the tiled floor. They sparkled as they shattered.

Kate never saw Marcus again, and she spent the last few days of the holiday pining while reclining on a sun lounger, wondering if she'd imagined the whole thing.

Potential boyfriend number three had been a friend of Pippa's. After university they'd all lived together in a terrible house-share in Hackney: terrible not just because there was a constant influx of mice and the boiler rarely worked, but because Pippa turned out to be a terrible person to live with. She'd been wild during their undergrad years, but who hadn't been a little wild? Lindsey had shared with her in student accommodation and would send Kate frequent panicked, exasperated messages about how she had never been this bad back then, or that she thought Pippa would have grown out of her bad habits by now, but just over a year out, things hit breaking point.

Pippa had decided to throw a house party, and then also decided that she didn't need to tell Lindsey and Kate about it.

'I put it up on Facebook,' she said, as the house crowded with people. 'Didn't you see?'

Lindsey and Kate spent much of the evening holed in Lindsey's room working through *Orange Is the New Black* on Netflix, trying to ignore the thump of the music and the smell of weed that was starting to drift under the door.

'Are we lame?' Lindsey had asked, snuggled in close to Kate.

'Absolutely,' Kate had replied.

Things got quieter at around 2 a.m., so Kate peeled herself out from under a sleeping Lindsey and took herself back to her room. Pippa was strung out on the sofa but called out when she saw Kate pass by.

'I told Nikesh he could crash in your room,' she mumbled.

'What the . . .? Why would you do that?' Kate asked. She was exhausted. She wanted to wake up from whatever nightmare this was.

'He needed somewhere to sleep. He missed the last Tube.'

'Where am I going to sleep?'

But Pippa was already out cold again.

Kate resolved to get what she needed from her room and then skulk back to Lindsey's for the rest of the night. She wasn't expecting Nikesh to be awake, propped up on her bed and laughing at videos on his phone.

'Oh, I'm sorry,' she said, before remembering it should have been him who was apologising.

'This your room? Pippa said I could crash.' Kate's face, even in the barely there light, must have said it all. 'Right. Pippa didn't ask you. Sorry.'

'Why are you sorry? She's my housemate.'

'I can go, I don't have to stay. It's your room.' He made to get up.

'Pippa said you'd missed the last Tube?'

'Yeah.'

'So where would you go?'

'I honestly have no idea.'

He was cute. Still a little dopey from his high, but not wasted like Pippa was.

'No, you stay here. I'll crash with my other housemate. Just don't touch anything.'

She went to a drawer to pull out some fresh pyjamas and some clothes for the following morning, so that she didn't have to come back in and disturb him. It wasn't his fault that Pippa was being a nightmare, she reasoned. She'd wait till she got back from work the next day, and liaise with Lindsey about a course of action, before letting Pippa know how she really felt. At that moment she was tired, and there was no point causing trouble when Pippa would barely remember it.

'What are you watching?' Kate asked as Nikesh sniggered.

'Oh, it's stupid.'

But now Kate was intrigued. Nikesh shuffled over so that she could lean closer and watch his screen. It was just a video of a cat pushing items off shelves, the clips edited together with exceptional comic timing. Soon they were talking about cats, and after that they were talking about everything else.

When Kate woke up in the morning she was still in her clothes, on top of the covers, neck sore from being propped up awkwardly. Nikesh was already gone. Had she imagined a connection? A level of instant comfort she rarely felt with anyone? You didn't share a bed with someone you didn't like, did you?

The row with Pippa the following evening had been apocalyptic, and she'd moved out soon after. It was this shift that had prompted Kate and Lindsey to find the new flat, just the two of them together, the one she was now leaving behind.

She had thought about asking Pippa for Nikesh's number as Pippa was packing to leave, but it didn't seem appropriate somehow. Battle lines were being drawn, and any contact with her was charged with the potential for new, even more bitter arguments. If Nikesh had asked about her, she reckoned Pippa was likely to have blocked the connection.

My first night sleeping with a boy and I have nothing to show for it, Kate thought as she decided that if it was meant to be one day, then she had to let it be. Then, a couple of years later, she managed to track him down online and found the pictures from his wedding.

She wished she had been bolder. At school, at university, and after, it seemed like every single opportunity had been blown by her own hesitancy. And after that there hadn't really seemed to be any more opportunities. She had been under the impression that once she had settled into adulthood, then she would feel more comfortable with herself, that all her insecurities would be washed away by the wisdom of years. But lately Kate had just found the confidence she had draining away instead.

Kate found Beth, her line manager, towards the end of her shift and pulled her to one side.

'Would you be annoyed if I went for it?' she asked after telling her about the job opening.

'You know, I thought about you when I saw that one,' Beth replied. 'I can write you a recommendation letter if you like?'

Kate struggled to maintain her composure, wanting to make sure that Beth knew how grateful she was without overdoing it with bubbly enthusiasm, but as soon as she was out of eyeline and earshot, she allowed herself to take a moment to feel her heart racing, and smiled.

She caught the figure in her peripheral vision first, a strange blur of movement far too fast for the gentle pace of the gallery. Kate had had to warn bored teenagers to stop running around or playing hide and seek before, but the figure had seemed too tall to be a kid. Aware now that someone had darted behind a pillar to avoid her for some reason, her hand went to the radio clipped to her waist, ready to alert security if she needed.

'Excuse me, can I help you?' Kate started as she approached, before cocking her head with recognition.

The man who had been trying and failing to hide from her was Freddie.

II

Freddie was having a disaster of a day.

His mum had been trying to arrange a good time to chat for the last couple of weeks, but Freddie had been putting it off. Christine Weir often sent her son a gentle text message first thing in the morning, and Freddie would reply in an optimistic way that would make it sound as if he was content and that no further intervention was necessary: a bright, *Looks like it's going to be a lovely day today!* or a just a simple, *I'm good, how's Dad doing?* But he knew he was putting off the inevitable, that he had to talk to his mum at some point. Freddie loved his mum dearly, but that didn't always mean that he wanted to share his feelings with her.

How is everything? she had asked.

Freddie missed the text message. He was in the shower, and hadn't thought to look at his phone once he was back in his bedroom.

Freddie? His mum had typed again. When this one came in, he had been in the kitchen munching on some toast.

She decided to ring just as he was tying the laces of his sneakers and getting ready to head out.

'Is everything OK?' Freddie had asked. Already he was calculating the effect this would have on his usually perfectly timed commute.

'I'm fine!' Christine chirped. 'Are you OK?'

'I'm good, Mum. What's up? Why are you ringing?'

'You didn't answer me.'

Freddie brought his phone away from his face so that he could flick to his messages. He saw two alerts and rubbed at his forehead.

'I was getting ready for work,' Freddie explained.

'Usually you reply much more quickly. I was concerned.'

Freddie knew that wasn't true. He remembered one time he'd left it until lunchtime to text his mum back. But he also knew that arguing would just delay the inevitable.

'I was concerned,' Christine insisted. 'But now that I've caught you . . .' There it was.

'Mum, I've got to go to work. Can this wait?'

'It'll only take a minute.'

Freddie glanced up at the clock on his wall. He was running two minutes early, and if he didn't resist, he might just get through the conversation with enough time to catch his usual train.

'It's just, at Lacey's birthday party, you seemed stressed?'

'You know how parties stress me out.'

'But it wasn't a party really, it was family.'

'Family stresses me out too.'

He could hear his mother thinking across the phone line, trying to choose her words carefully.

'Mum, I've really got to get going.'

'You know I get worried about you, that's all. We haven't had a proper catch-up in ages – don't think I don't know that you're putting off my calls – and your father said to just leave you be, but you know I can't do that.'

'You don't have to worry about me, Mum, I promise.'

'You're taking your medication?'

'I'm fine, I promise.'

'We don't want a repeat of last time. I just need to know you're all right.'

'I'm good. I'm going to be late for work, but I'm good.'

'Right then. I'll leave you to it. I know I annoy you sometimes.'

'It's fine, Mum.'

'And I hear that you're going round to your brother's for dinner soon? Is that right?'

Freddie had forgotten he'd arranged that. Stella had invited him around for a meal and he'd absent-mindedly agreed without thinking it through. One of the items on the agenda was discussing the plans for his parents' anniversary party, but he had wondered afterwards if there was an alternative agenda he should be thinking about and planning for. Now that his mother was aware of the arrangement, he wouldn't be able to back out without raising more questions and worries. And more than anything, Freddie didn't want them to worry about him.

'Looking forward to Stella's cooking,' Freddie joked.

'Don't be mean, she's improved,' his mother laughed. 'But seriously, I'm pleased that you're getting on better with David. You know how much I'd love you to be closer.'

'He doesn't make it easy, Mum,' he started rubbing at his forehead again.

'You know how stressful his work is. How much time he puts in. He's always needed a vent for that energy.'

He could find kinder ways to vent his frustration, Freddie had thought to himself.

'There was no other reason for the call? Everything good with you and Dad?'

'We're swell. Don't worry about us.'

'Then don't worry about me either.'

'You know we have to, darling.'

Once he put the phone down, Freddie let himself take in a deep breath, then exhaled it in a loud sigh.

It had been years, but they wouldn't let him forget what had happened, nor how bad it had been. He wished he could go and scrub the episode from everyone's memories, make sure they knew that he was in control now and that he wasn't prepared to let the intrusive thoughts get that bad ever again. The medication helped, but so did the stability of his job. It wasn't a particularly hard or stressful one, although it had its moments, but it was enough. And anything more intense had the potential for dire consequences. It was about control, having mastery over himself, and not letting himself get into situations where outside stress could overwhelm him and make him forget all the hard work he had done.

He walked quickly to the station, but just caught sight of his usual train as it left the platform. His favourite seat was taken when the next train arrived, so he had to stand. Standing in itself was fine, it was the proximity to other people he couldn't bear. Plus having to hold on to a rail. When he had been ill, just the thought of touching a railing or door handle was enough to send him into a spiral of loud thinking, the if/then mechanism of his brain overloading and running through a million consequences, none of them good. The only way to avoid those terrible consequences? Avoid doing the thing. Until his avoidance tactics made it nearly impossible to leave the house.

His family admitted him to a private hospital, Freddie only agreeing to go because the path of least resistance also seemed like the fastest way to get back out again. His plan involved playing along for a couple of days, then working an angle where he presented as 'cured'. It would be hard work, pure method acting whilst his brain fried from the pressure, but worth it to get his family off his back. It wasn't that he wanted to stay ill, but more to do with the fact that at the time he hadn't seen much point in getting better. He'd been in a dark place. He didn't intend on going back there.

The rest of the day was a scramble to get back into his usual routine. His rituals took time, required specific processes that were frustratingly invisible to his teammates, who seemed to always demand easy spontaneity from him.

Just being a single minute off caused his stress to heighten exponentially.

At lunch time he got a text from Baz. *Fancy pub after work?*

Freddie thought about the last time they were together, about the conversation they were on the brink of having, the truths that seemed on the cusp of being revealed.

Busy tonight, Freddie texted back.

Tomorrow then?

It wasn't that Freddie was scared of revealing he was a virgin. He'd done that already, and it turned out not to be that bad. He'd found people who understood him, who listened to him, and that helped to ease the pressure.

But that wasn't the same as talking to Baz. His oldest friend, the man who had women falling at his feet at university, and who'd found his perfect partner and got married so soon after. What could he possibly understand about what Freddie was going through? And besides that, there was also the fact that all those years ago Freddie had lied to him. Did Baz know? Was that what he wanted to talk about? It might be a good thing to get it all out in the open eventually, but Freddie wasn't ready. Not yet.

Lots going on right now, Freddie messaged, before turning his phone on silent.

It wasn't as if failing to get together with Camellia was the moment that led to the breakdown, but it hadn't helped. He'd invested so much into that, so many emotions, that to have all hope ripped away so suddenly felt diabolical. But he'd not been well long before it. Nobody knew, but it hadn't been easy to hide. He had started drinking a lot, which helped to disguise the behaviour, as well as to dampen some of the compulsive impulses and worries that were popping up – with sometimes startling volume and insistence – inside his head.

Drunkenness helped him pretend that his fingers didn't itch with all the billions of germs that accumulated with every single thing that he touched, that furry mould wasn't growing on his gums, thicker with every hour that passed between brushing his teeth. Freddie didn't even consider himself to be that bad back then, and yet he had been wrapping his hands in toilet paper just to pull the chain to flush and counting his steps from one place to another, finding solace every time he landed on an even number, a dark sense of dread every time it was odd. There were germs everywhere, and every movement he chose to make had the potential to trigger a parasitic thought in his brain that would latch on and not let go, until it grew into something he could only forget with increasingly large quantities of alcohol.

He'd seen Camellia around before they officially met, and a lot of people knew who she was. She was one of those girls who had managed to arrive on campus a ready-made celebrity, fully formed with her punky, pin-up aesthetic and complete with fan following. It helped that she was beautiful, of course. Nobody had locked down their privacy settings on their Facebook profiles back then; besides which, everyone wanted to be open and easily findable, and it turned out that she was a mere two degrees of separation away from Freddie. She was in a tutorial group with the housemate of someone he knew from rowing club (Freddie signed up in Freshers' Week, was fawned over for his lean height for a couple of weeks before everyone realised that he was an uncoordinated mess). There were nights when he couldn't settle the persistent thoughts in his head for long enough to fall asleep, so he'd find himself browsing through Facebook on his clunky laptop, then finding a tagged photo of her on her page. It wasn't like how it was now, with social media and endless selfies filtered and Photoshopped to high heaven. Nobody had smart phones back then. But inevitably someone would bring a digital camera on a night out, and Camellia's perfection was duly documented.

This was how he saw her, more often than he saw her in real life, at least until final year. Alongside the comic book girls and the sci-fi princesses, for Freddie Camellia existed more perfectly on a screen than in reality.

So when suddenly she was right there, he was hopeless.

She was on a fancy-dress bar crawl, dressed as Lara Croft via Angelina Jolie, because of course she was. A fake ponytail was attached to her tautly pulled-back hair, a water pistol secured to her thigh with a holster made of duct tape. They were at the bar, and Freddie remembered not caring that she was being served first, despite the fact he'd got there before her. Freddie watched her flirt, his own drunkenness allowing him to get away with unabashed gazing, as if she wasn't there at all, just some computer projection generated for his own pleasure. She didn't seem to care that he was staring at her. Maybe she was used to it.

And then, as she was scrambling for change in her purse, a sprinkling of coins fell to the floor. His body on autopilot, Freddie reached down to pick them up.

'Aww, thank you!' Her voice sounded harsher than he expected it to be, heavy with a Lancashire accent. Or was it Yorkshire? Freddie had never been able to tell which was which.

'It's OK,' Freddie mumbled back, letting her pick the remaining coins out of his palm.

When she was done, and just before she deployed an impressive four-pint-carrying manoeuvre, Camellia stood up on the tips of her toes (enclosed in some stocky – but somehow on her, sexy – hiking boots) and planted a light kiss on Freddie's cheek.

A few weeks later she came over to sit with him in the library as he revised. He was stunned. It was too early for his first drink, and he felt panicked at having to negotiate this encounter without his usual crutch.

'You remember me, right?' she had asked. 'I was Lara Croft? You were my hero?'

'Sure,' Freddie replied, bashful.

'I'm Camellia,' she said, and it took all his strength to not reply 'I know'. 'What are you studying?'

'Computer Science.'

'You're one of those tech guys then?'

He nodded. He felt pathetic.

'I'm studying Law. I don't know why. I thought it would be a good idea a few years ago, but I guess it's too late now to change it up.'

They became library pals. It was slow-going. Some days Freddie found it too intense; her confident sense of style, and tendency to say exactly what she was thinking, was overwhelming, but it was also endearing. He learned a lot about her. She cared about big issues, she wanted to do well but often felt stupid, she got riled up by Tories and the Scientologists who would stand outside their building on Tottenham Court Road inviting people in for what she was certain were bog-standard lie-detector tests.

Camellia rarely asked about Freddie, but he didn't mind because he didn't think he really had anything special or important to say. He much preferred listening to her, helping her through any problem she was having. He felt the connection and was sure that she did too. He went to the vending machine and bought her a Yorkie.

He'd kissed girls before. There had been a couple of clumsy fumbles in secondary school: one with a girl who later pretended they'd never met; another who had just given him a startled, insecure blush whenever they encountered each other in the corridors afterwards. There was that one who'd caught him off guard at a club night in the Student Union and somehow latched on to his face, vaguely squid-like. He'd never found out who she was, but didn't remember much of anything else from the rest of that evening anyway. There had also been the few times Baz had tried to set him up with the best friend of whatever girl he happened to be dating, and would confidently sing Freddie's praises, hoping for the opportunity of a double date. It had never happened.

But he had never felt as he felt for Camellia. Adoration mixed with awe mixed with longing. He looked forward to seeing her every day. Loved the way she smiled, the way she dressed, and the way she would get so enthusiastic about whatever was bothering her.

She became a part of his routine. In the weeks that led up to exams, he'd only let himself look up at her on the even minutes, never the odd. He saved her a space and they'd both pretend that it was coincidence that there was always one free right next to him.

Camellia wasn't the only fixed point in his life that had disappeared after the Leavers' Ball. Many, many other things dropped off too. Struggling to find work straight away, he'd moved back from student accommodation into his parents' house. Not only did he find it hard to fit into their routines, the only routines he had that were his own revolved around the regularity of the TV schedule. Job interviews left him frazzled and tired. Worse of all, there was no Baz to pull him out of his funk, to force him out to pubs and clubs and just generally be his best champion. Everything he had that was solid had disappeared. Camellia had been an important facet of that; his emotions felt meaningless without her around to adore.

Freddie didn't want to go straight home after work. He'd been off-key all day, distracted and bad-tempered, fizzing with pent-up energy. So he decided to do what he always did in situations like this, what his hours and hours of in-patient therapy had taught him. He reached into his mental health toolkit and decided to go for a walk.

There was no planned route, no time limit. He'd just pick a direction and go. When he hit a crossroads, he'd look for signs: if the green man was showing he'd continue onwards, if not, he'd take a turn. If he liked the look of a building, he aimed for it; if a shop-front caught his eye, that was next. There weren't any rules when Freddie was walking. He went on instinct, following whatever his gut said to him in the moment, free from habits and compulsions. It was intensely relaxing.

He stopped outside the Central Art Gallery, realising that he'd not gone inside in years. He'd been here on school trips when he was younger, and then again a handful of times to see an exhibition or just to wander. Right now, there was something in his mind that was almost like a lightbulb switched on, a recognition that made him wonder if someone had mentioned it recently, or if he'd seen a poster on the Tube advertising it.

The gallery was having a late opening, but there weren't many people around. As he paced through the rooms, taking a moment here and there to pause and let a painting wash over him, enjoying the feeling and fragrance of the rich, varnished hardwood beneath his feet, the sense of familiarity intensified. Who was it that he'd heard talking about this place? Like an important word teetering on the tip of his tongue it annoyed him.

Then he saw her and realised. She must have mentioned it at a meeting. This was where Kate worked.

He thought about rushing away in the opposite direction, but then worried that the sudden movement would attract too much attention. She was talking to someone in a suit who looked important, and he didn't want to distract her. He didn't want her to notice him at all. So instead he sauntered to the side, hoping that a pillar would do enough work to hide him.

'Excuse me . . .' Damn it. He'd been spotted. 'Oh, it's you.'

12

He looked so out of place in this gallery she knew so well. Kate felt as if she was at sea, trying to keep her footing as the ship rocked around her.

'What are you doing here?' she asked, trying to sound breezy and cool when actually she was worrying if her manager was far enough away, or if Renee was going to appear suddenly around a corner and ask to be introduced. Kate wouldn't have been able to bear that.

'I didn't know you worked here, I swear! At least, I only realised when I came in and saw you,' Freddie replied. He did not sound breezy and cool.

'But why did you come?'

'I was walking. I was thinking and walking and then I was outside and it was open. I'm sorry. I can go, I can disappear. I don't want this to be weird.'

It's already weird, Kate thought.

She liked Freddie, had felt keenly for him whenever he had shared his experiences in group, had enjoyed his company in the pub afterwards, but they barely knew each other. Certainly not enough for him to just turn up at her workplace.

'Are you OK?' she asked him.

She considered him, his shoulders sloping as though he wanted to make himself three feet shorter, the shine on his forehead causing strands of hair to darken and stick, the aura of sorrow that seemed to cloud him sometimes.

'Oh, I'm fine. Totally fine.'

She'd watched him enough in group, how his posture would change when he was talking about his anxiety and his fears.

'I don't believe you,' she said. He didn't argue with her.

'I should go. You're working.'

Kate could have let him go. She could have waved him off, then wandered over to the next room she was meant to be patrolling. She didn't have to care about him, and yet . . . He just seemed so sad. She didn't need to know why, but the least she could do was offer her company.

'I finish in twenty minutes. And look around, the place is empty. But if someone who works here comes along, just pretend you're asking me directions to the gift shop or something.'

'I don't want to disturb you.'

'From what, all the art thieves?'

'No, but . . . I don't know.'

'You're fine, Freddie. Don't worry. At least, don't *add* to your worrying.'

Kate noticed that Freddie kept his hands tense in his pockets as they slowly walked, moving to stand in front of a painting of a naked bathing nymph.

'So, you just walk around? Keeping an eye on things?' he asked, his voice still nervous.

'Oh, it's much more than that. There's floor-plan logistics, the sociology of crowd control, expert levels of art history knowledge, gift shop economics.' Freddie was staring at her, baffled. 'But mostly, yeah. I just walk around, keeping an eye on things.'

He seemed reluctant to smile at the joke.

'Do you ever get bored?'

'Not really. Some people do, but I find things to think about. It can be quite a nice mindfulness exercise sometimes. Doesn't matter what's going on outside, this place is like a bubble. Nothing can bother me here. All I have to do is think about what's going on inside these walls. The people, the paintings. The rest of the world can wait.'

'That sounds nice.'

'Look at that couple there,' Kate gave Freddie a gentle nudge, indicating two people just in front of them. A woman in a sleek black coat was standing, eyes focused on the painting before her, next to a man in oversized trousers who was looking anywhere but. 'I reckon they're on the verge of divorce. Or, if they're not married, at least breaking up. She's dragged him here on a date night, maybe they're going to dinner later, and she thought a trip to a gallery would be romantic. Maybe they had their first date here, and they're trying to rekindle something. But he's squirming. He hates it. He's doing the absolute minimum to get away with making her happy . . . except she's not happy. She wants him to be different. He's trying to do what she wants, but it's not going to work.'

'You can tell all that just from staring at their backs?'

'No, but I can imagine it. They might not even know each other. It's one of the games I play to keep my mind busy. Imagine tragic or romantic backstories for visitors.'

Sure enough, the couple parted and started walking in opposite directions, paying each other barely any attention. They were strangers after all. Kate sighed.

'Can I play the game?' Freddie asked.

'Go for it.'

She looked up at him as he scanned the gallery, one of the larger rooms, but at this late hour with barely a soul in it.

'There,' he indicated with a nod of the head to a young man, just out of his teens, sitting cross-legged on the floor with a sketchbook in front of a portrait of a woman in a headwrap. 'He got rejected from art school, so comes here every evening to work on his skills. He sits, and he studies, but his friends and family all laugh at him because really, he's not very good. He wants to be, but no matter how hard he tries, he just can't get it right.'

Kate thought about this for a moment, thought about how sad it was, and how that was the very first story to spring into his mind.

'Shall we go and have a look?' she whispered to him.

They slowly wandered over, trying not to look as though they were deliberately heading in that direction. Kate half hoped that the sketches were bad but, as it turned out, the drawing was brilliant. It was a level of skill Kate had never been close to attaining, and she felt the familiar tiny twinge of jealousy.

'Damn, he was good,' Freddie said excitedly once they had moved out of earshot.

'There are so many amazing artists here. You see them all the time, studying the composition of famous paintings, the tone. Sometimes people come in with these travel easels and actually paint.'

'Really? Don't they get embarrassed that people come and watch what they're doing? I'd get so nervous.'

'They only do it if they're already good. I think some of them enjoy showing off.'

'If I was as good as that kid, I would show off all the time.'

They wandered through one room, and then another, Freddie taking moments to stop and investigate a painting, Kate noticing how his brow furrowed with concentration as he tried to make sense of it all.

'You like art then?' Kate asked.

'Not usually this kind of stuff. Graphic novels, comics. Art that tells stories.'

'That sounds cool. I've never read a comic.'

'I was just thinking,' Freddie continued, 'that this gallery is basically one huge comic book. It's hard to make sense of the narrative, but you could imagine one painting leading into another, like a sequence. There's whole multi-strand epics in just one room, if you think about it.'

'I can see that. You know, there's a whole bunch of characters in the portrait room that I like to think might have known each other back in their time. Now I'm going to be imagining them with speech bubbles coming out of the frames,' she grinned.

'I could lend you some books if you like,' Freddie said. 'If you want to try reading comics? I have loads, all different types of stories. I bet I could find something you liked.'

'That would be nice,' she replied, genuinely thinking it would be. Then she looked at her watch. 'Well, that's me done. Shift's over.'

Freddie just stood there, a little uncomfortable, clearly not knowing what he was meant to say or do next. And again, Kate felt that pang of recognition for his unhappiness, and that desire to want to help cheer him up.

'Hey, have you eaten? Do you want to grab some food?' she asked. If their positions were reversed, if she needed company but didn't know how to articulate it, she hoped that someone would do the same for her.

'Sure,' Freddie replied.

Kate didn't think he'd be there when she got out, but sure enough, Freddie was standing just outside the staff door, leaning on a railing and playing with his phone. In that moment before he noticed her looking, she found herself admiring his stance, line of his shoulders and the tilt of his head. There was something about the intensity of him, even though he was just looking at his phone, that made him seem cool and a little exciting. A mystery box in human form.

'Is that him?' Renee asked, nodding her head in Freddie's direction, and shaking Kate out of her brief reverie.

'He's just a friend,' Kate hissed in reply.

'Sure. OK, whatever. I'll see you tomorrow.' Renee smiled as she hugged Kate goodbye. Then, as she was walking away, she turned and yelled: 'Nice to meet you, Freddie!'

Kate cringed as she watched Freddie's confusion.

'Who was that?' he asked.

'Renee. A friend of mine. She thinks she's being funny. Sorry, I hope that didn't make you uncomfortable or anything?'

'Oh, no. It's fine.' Then, after a beat, 'What food do you fancy?'

This made Kate nervous. She couldn't afford much, but all the cheap places around the gallery were supremely tacky and tourist-orientated. But then again, she'd been the one to invite him out, which implied that she should make the decision of where to go.

'I don't know. I'm not fussy,' she replied, hoping that he'd choose for her.

'Well, what food do you like?'

'Honestly I'm happy with anything.'

'Well then, how about McDonald's?' he suggested.

'I haven't been in a McDonald's in years! Maybe not since uni?'

'Shall we go?'

'Yes! There's one right around the corner.'

The delight she felt in that moment almost inspired her to take his hand and run. Almost.

There was a quaintness in sitting in a booth, a childlike glee she felt slurping on a strawberry milkshake, the texture of her chips glazed in nostalgia. Freddie seemed just as happy. His shoulders didn't have that solemn hunched quality any more, and his eyes were bright under the sharp white lights. Today they were blue, Kate noticed, but she wanted to check again once they were back outside to see if they'd changed.

'This was such a good idea,' Freddie said.

'It was your idea!' Kate laughed.

'Well, it was a good idea, even if I do say so myself then,' he laughed.

'You know, my dad used to sneak me out to McDonald's sometimes.' Kate told him. 'My mum hates this kind of food, so my dad used to say that I was accompanying him on errands on weekends, and we'd go to the drive-through not far from our house. We had to keep it a secret and then clean the car out afterwards, spray it with air freshener so Mum wouldn't know – although I suspect she always did. But it was so much fun. It felt illicit and dangerous.'

'Do you get on with your parents?' Freddie asked.

'I do. I'm lucky. Don't think I could cope moving back in with them if I didn't.'

'I forgot about that. I don't think I could do it. Move back in with my parents, I mean. I did it once, after university, and it wasn't great for me.'

'Don't you get on with them?'

'I do . . . it's fine, it's just hard. I put them through a lot, and sometimes I feel like they don't let me forget it. But they love me. It's my brother I have a bigger issue with.'

'What's he like?'

'David is . . . David's perfect. I used to be jealous of him a lot when I was younger, but now, not so much. We're just different people. And I don't think he understands me. He tries to help sometimes, but he never seems to get that the way he wants to help can just make things worse. Sometimes, not often but sometimes, it just feels mean.'

'That's relatable.'

'It is?'

'Sure. I bet he doesn't even know when he's coming over as mean. Some people are like that.' For some reason, India came to mind in her head. 'It can't be easy, but at least you don't have to see him all the time.'

'I'm going round to dinner with them this weekend. Nothing fancy. David and my sister-in-law, Stella, they want to meet up to organise something for my parents' anniversary. It's a big one.'

'That's nice!'

'Last time I saw Stella, she said something weird to me though.'

'What?'

'I haven't even said this in group, because it feels so silly.'

'I won't tell anyone. Scout's honour,' Kate offered up her pinkie finger as a promise. It took Freddie a moment to realise what she was doing, but he slowly entwined his finger with hers.

'Stella thinks I'm gay. She had this whole speech about how she thinks I should come out, and how she wants my niece to grow up knowing.'

'Wow, really?' Kate's jaw dropped in disbelief, and she placed her milkshake firmly back down on the table. 'Did you correct her?'

'Not really.'

'You didn't say anything?'

'I didn't really know what to say. She seemed so sure of herself, and I'm always so unsure.'

'Freddie. This is about *you*. *You* have to be the most certain person when it comes to *yourself*. Is that why you've been moping around and wandering into art galleries?'

'Not just that.'

'You don't have to talk about it if you don't want to.'

'It's nothing specific. I just worry sometimes.' Kate watched Freddie as he gathered himself. *Let him have all the time he needed*, she thought. 'It's not just Stella. It's my whole family, my job, the group . . . sometimes it just gets to me. Some days just feel more fragile than others.'

'That's understandable. If it helps at all, I'm glad you found me.'

'You are?'

'Sure. We're friends. Of course I'll help whenever I can. Anyone in the group would.'

Kate added the last part just to make sure Freddie didn't get the wrong idea. She didn't know what the right one was exactly, but it seemed like an important clarification nonetheless. Freddie smiled anyway. His smile was quiet, just the corners of his mouth crooking up against his will, but Kate felt proud that she had been the one to make it happen.

'You finished?' she asked, after slurping the last of dregs of her milkshake.

He nodded, piling the napkins and wrappers on his tray to make it easier to carry over to the trash. To Kate's surprise, when he stood up, he took her tray with him too. She watched him as he walked away, then tipped everything into the bin. She liked the way he looked, she realised. She had never been drawn to anyone who was as quiet as him, tended to like guys who had a bit more of a presence, but even so, there was something about Freddie, something like encountering a secret ghost only she could see, that made her like him, despite herself.

Like as a friend, the voice in Kate's head insisted, and repeated several times.

'You didn't have to do that.' she said when he came back to the table. He shrugged in reply, like it was nothing.

'Look, do you mind,' he said, massaging the back of his neck with his hand. 'I don't normally eat food with my fingers . . . do you mind if I go and wash my hands?'

'Of course not.'

'I'll be back soon.'

She waited for him, and when he came back they went out to the street. Kate could smell the soap on his hands. It was dark, the rush-hour crowd all having scarpered home, making way for the sociable crowd looking for fun. It created an energy, a buzz that promised adventure and laughter.

'I might just walk home,' he said. Kate felt disappointed but didn't quite understand why.

'Where do you live? Do you have far to go?'

'Umm, from here, about four miles?'

'Four miles! I can't remember when I last walked that far.'

'It'll only take an hour.'

'I'm heading the same way. I'll walk with you for a bit.'

They walked through Soho and then north towards Euston.

'You know, when I caught you earlier, I'd just finished talking to my manager about endorsing me for a new job at the gallery,' Kate told him.

'That's cool.'

'Yeah, she was pretty enthusiastic, but I'm scared to be hopeful.'

'Why?'

'Because I've tried so many times already. So many jobs. I feel like I used to be someone, or at least on my way to becoming someone, and then it all stopped. And because of that, I don't think I come across well in interviews. I panic that I'm a big old imposter and don't know anything about what I'm talking about. I don't know if I'm explaining it right, but I won't let myself get my hopes up.'

'I think you're being too hard on yourself,' Freddie said.

'Sorry for offloading. We're not even in group.'

'It's OK. If it helps at all, I feel that way a lot too. Not just about work stuff, but about everything. My flatmate, my family . . . You at least thought you were going to be someone. I've never felt that way.'

Kate didn't think it was the right time to offer reassurance, didn't think that it was what Freddie wanted. The fact that they both seemed to understand each other, and could talk openly, seemed to be enough for now.

'Oh my God, look!' she said as they passed an alleyway, narrow and grimy, the dead space between two otherwise boring buildings, but all lit up with neon strips that painted an iridescent rainbow. 'We need to walk down it!'

'Why?' Freddie asked.

'Because it's pretty! Come on!'

She resisted the sudden urge to just take his hand and drag him down the alley, but made her bold move forward and hoped that Freddie would follow. He did.

The lights shifted and flowed through the spectrum, casting strange-hued shadows and impossible sunbeams, one moment violet, the next buttercup yellow. Kate loved stuff like this, tiny parts of the city coming alive with random street art. And there was nobody else around, no one else to ruin the moment with selfie-sticks. Her very own night-rainbow.

When she looked at Freddie and at his blank confusion, she realised that it wasn't that he was unimpressed, but because he had no idea what to do.

'Come on,' she said to him, laughing. 'Just walk through it, enjoy the colours!'

'It's very pretty,' Freddie conceded, looking around with the same seriousness that he'd shown back in the gallery.

'Doesn't it make you feel happy?' She walked to the end of the alleyway, and turned back to see Freddie's face bathed in red. The way the light caught his angles, picking up the natural reddish highlights in his brown hair, suddenly sparked in Kate a jolt of something like recognition, but that didn't make sense. They already knew each other, so why would she just recognise him now? Déjà vu then, except that wasn't quite right either. As the light shifted to sea-green, Kate realised that her heart was thumping loudly, that she felt nervous, and that she needed to get out of the rainbow alley right away.

'Let's go then,' she said, trying to sound like it didn't matter, that something hadn't just happened inside her.

They walked as far as King's Cross station. Kate could get home from here by Tube.

'Thanks for tonight,' Freddie told her. 'And sorry for turning up like a weird stalker at the gallery.'

'It's OK,' Kate replied. 'I'm just glad I could be there. And sorry that you were feeling so glum.'

'Tonight helped. It was nice,' he said, and there was that tiny, secret smile again.

'Well, that's what friends are for . . .'

After a moment of silence, Kate said, 'Want to swap numbers?' at the same time as Freddie said, 'We should hang out again.'

'We can be each other's support animal,' she laughed. 'If you get in trouble or want to vent or get lost walking or something, you can text me.'

'Yeah, support animal,' he said. 'I wish I could offer you interview advice or something, but I'm pretty bad at that kind of stuff too. But, if you need to vent or want to walk somewhere . . .' He paused. 'Swapping numbers would be cool.'

'I think so too.'

They swapped numbers.

'I'll see you at the next group?' he asked as she moved to leave.

'Not if I see you first!' She couldn't believe she'd said that – what was she, ten years old? – and she squirmed with embarrassment as she walked away.

13

Hope the dinner isn't too bad!

The text from Kate came in as he was on the train to his brother's house, causing Freddie to marvel a little at how nice it was to have someone thinking about him, someone new on his side.

His evening with Kate had been a revelation, a tiny island of peace in a world that sometimes felt too frantic and lonely. Over the next couple of days, he had found himself smiling unknowingly, realising that he felt lighter than he had in ages.

They had been messaging. Just a tiny trickle of them at first, but lately he realised she was sounding like herself, as if the words on his phone screen reflected the cadence of her real voice: honest and fun. He hoped that he sounded like himself too, but then worried that it meant he would come across as dull and too shy.

But Kate seemed far away now as he headed to his brother's house. Freddie couldn't remember the last time he'd casually hung out with his brother and his family. He and David moved in different circles and never really shared any interests growing up. While Freddie was introverted and spent most of his time indoors, David was outgoing, always involved in some rugby tournament or another, always outside having adventures. He wondered if David felt the dissonance as keenly as he always had.

Their house looked like an immaculate show home, the fake lawn lit up under tiny spotlights in the evening dusk.

Freddie wondered at the three cars parked directly outside the house, in addition to David's Mercedes and Stella's Land Rover, but maybe there was a party next door and there was nowhere else for the cars to go.

'Freddie!' Stella greeted him with a kiss on each cheek when she opened the front door, wearing an apron, an oven glove still attached to one hand. 'David is just upstairs getting Lacey to sleep. He'll be down in a bit. Come in, come in!'

The house smelt of expensive candles and flowery perfume. From the lounge the muted tones of dinner jazz drifted towards him. It seemed a little much for an informal dinner.

'What's happening? I thought this was a casual thing?' Freddie asked, taking in the dimmed lighting, the aura of candlelight that was coming from the dining room, and then, wafting from the kitchen behind Stella, the smell of minted lamb. Stella looked immaculate too. While he had turned up in his favourite slacks and a T-shirt under a casual checked shirt, beneath her apron Stella was in a flowing dark dress, full make-up and large, jewelled earrings.

'Oh well,' Stella started, 'I thought that if I was making something for you, then I might as well make something a little bigger. Still a casual thing, but now a bit more of a get-together. Come on, there are some people I would love you to meet!'

'I thought we were going to discuss our parents' anniversary party?' Freddie asked as David came down the stairs.

'This was Stella's idea, not mine,' David replied.

'Oh come on,' Stella said after clocking Freddie's concern. 'If I had warned you then you never would have come. And I've been so excited about doing this for you!'

Freddie started to wonder what exactly was being done for him.

Too uncertain to do or say anything else, he followed Stella into the lounge, where he was introduced to Jemima and Paul, a couple David worked with at the bank, and then to

Evie and Amos, a couple Stella worked with at her PR consultancy. And then, finally, she handed him a large glass of wine and drew him towards the fireplace where she introduced him to Kevin.

'I just think you two are going to get along famously,' Stella said, switching her gaze as if observing a tennis match, looking keenly into each of their faces before clasping her hands together (one still attached to the oven gloves) and trotting back to the kitchen to check on the lamb, her high heels clicking on the wooden floor.

Kevin was a handsome guy, frighteningly so. They were about the same height, maybe Freddie was a touch taller, but Kevin was filled out in a way that implied a commitment to good nutrition and exercise. His shoulders were so packed out that Freddie wondered if his arms still had full rotation. His chest was broad and shielded behind a pale grey jumper over a patterned shirt.

'So, Stella tells me that you work with computers?' Kevin asked.

'I work in the IT department for a finance company,' Freddie said, 'mostly help-desk stuff. What about you?'

'I work with Stella. We're on different teams, though. I'm in accounts whereas Stella is more on the creative side, but I've known her for a few years now. She's been talking about you a lot.'

Oh. Oh God. Freddie fought the heat as it crept up the back of his neck. Was this a set-up? If it wasn't for the wine glass he was holding, Freddie would have been wringing his hands together. Instead, he stuffed the free one into his trouser pocket, and scrunched it up so hard that he could feel it going red then white.

No, he reasoned. Stella wouldn't do that to him. Not like this.

'Do you like your job?' Freddie asked as he took a gulp of his wine.

'It's fine. Been there a while. I'd like to have my own company one day, though, be my own boss. How about you?'

'Oh, you know,' Freddie replied, not wanting to go much further into it.

'Stella says that you like reading?'

Reading?

'Um . . .'

'What kind of stuff do you read?'

'Comics, mostly,' Freddie admitted.

'Oh yeah? What are you into right now?' Kevin seemed genuinely interested, which was a welcome surprise.

'Actually, I'm rereading the *Starboy Sequence* by Brian Teller at the moment.'

'No way! I was at a signing of his, a while back. That man is an absolute *legend*.'

'Really? At Ben Day Comics?'

'That's it!'

'Oh wow, I was there too. I have the entire first run of single issues, so I got him to sign all of them. I'm rereading them all now before I put them away for safe-keeping.'

OK, Freddie thought with relief. This isn't a dating thing. This is a friends thing. Stella had found someone for him to talk to about comics.

'My little brother not boring your brains out about comics, I hope?' David slapped Freddie on the back as he came to stand next to him, nearly causing Freddie to tip out the contents of his wine glass.

'Not at all,' Kevin replied smoothly, 'Do you realise that a rare Brian Teller drawing sold for over ten thousand at Christie's last year?'

'Come off it. Really?' David scoffed.

'I mean, he's probably the finest graphic artist and writer living right now. Your brother has good taste.'

'Stop being nice to him, he doesn't deserve it!' David laughed and reached over to Freddie in an attempt to gently ruffle his hair. He probably hoped that it would come off as affectionate, but it wasn't a gesture Freddie appreciated and he ducked out quickly.

He reached into his pocket for his phone as David beckoned for everyone to make their way into the dining room.

This is a proper dinner party, he messaged Kate. *I'm being forced to mingle!*

Nooooooo, she replied almost straight away. Then there was a run of texts in quick succession:

You've been ambushed.

Are you OK?

Do you need rescuing?

I think this is OK, Freddie messaged back. *People seem nice.*

He noticed that Stella had made little place cards showing where they were all to sit, meaning he was placed directly between the hostess and Kevin. As they sat down, David gave his brother a thumbs up, along with a wide grin. Freddie gave him an awkward thumbs up back.

After a moment had passed, Freddie leaned over to him to ask: 'When are we going to chat about Mum and Dad, and all the anniversary stuff?'

'Oh, plenty of time for all that. Besides, Stella's nearly finished organising it. We've hired out the restaurant at the golf club. Thought we'd do a drinks, buffet and dance thing, invite all their friends.'

'I didn't realise you'd already organised something,' Freddie said, wondering how long ago they had planned it, and how he was going to afford his share.

'Don't you worry your pretty little head about it, baby bro,' David added, noticing the worry on his face. 'Stells and I have it covered. Just get yourself there on time and we'll say that you contributed.'

'But I haven't.'

David leaned in closer, over Stella's empty chair, so that it was harder for everybody else to hear them. 'We know how things are for you, Fred. You'll get some money in the bank one day. Who knows, play your cards right, and maybe you'll be able to cater their fortieth?'

It might have been the candlelight messing with his eyes, but Freddie could have sworn that he saw David gesture towards Kevin.

Brother is behaving weird, he texted Kate under the table.

How?

Don't know. Something's up.

You're being paranormal.

Freddie stared at the screen. *Paranormal?*

DAMN AUTOCORRECT, Kate typed quickly. *PARANOID. PARANOIDDDDDD.*

I don't know, I think I like paranormal better.

Freddie shoved his phone away when Stella came in to serve the food, after which Kevin leaned over towards him.

'You know, I'd never been to Ben Day Comics before,' he said. 'Seems like a really cool place.'

'It's nice,' Freddie said, swallowing his lamb hurriedly.

'I'm surprised I've never really seen it, as it's just around the corner from this club I go to a lot. The Rabbit Hole. You been there?'

'No. I don't, uh, I don't really go to clubs.'

'The Rabbit Hole is cool, though. Late at night it gets pretty hot and heavy, if you know what I mean, but they have a nice chilled-out lounge area for earlier on. And great shows too. Miss Ella Waters performed there the other week.'

'Miss Ella Waters!' Stella cried out suddenly. Freddie hadn't even realised she'd been listening in. 'You know her name is a play on micellar water? Like make-up remover, right? Oh my God, she's so hilarious!'

'Who is Miss Ella Waters?' Freddie asked.

'She's a legendary drag queen,' Stella explained. 'Was on this American TV show, got to the final, but was totally robbed after Phoebe B. Beebe death-dropped off a sparkly shipping container. I love her! Kevin, why didn't you tell me you were going to that? You should have taken me!'

Kevin laughed and sipped on his wine. The way he did it made Freddie wonder just exactly how close friends they really were.

'We could go some time?' he offered to Freddie quietly, once he saw that Stella was deep in discussion with Evie and Amos.

'Go where?' Freddie asked nervously.

'The Rabbit Hole. I could take you, introduce you, if you like?'

'Umm, no. No, it's OK,' sighed Freddie. 'Not my thing, really.'

Kevin paused, and made a thoughtful face. 'You know your brother and sister-in-law are jerks of the highest order, right?' he finally chuckled.

'Excuse me?' Freddie looked around to check whether anyone had heard them. They hadn't. Kevin's voice was low, like a rumble.

'Stella has you all wrong. Trying to set us up like this. You're not gay, are you?'

'Sorry, no. Afraid not.' So it *had* been a set-up. 'I think she means well, and you are very handsome, but no. I'm not gay.'

'Oh boy, isn't this a pickle.'

Freddie didn't know how to respond to that, so just kept eating.

'I mean, why would they just assume something like that?' Kevin continued.

'I'm sorry. Stella's just trying to help, I think.' Freddie paused, but then, by way of explanation, added: 'I don't talk about my love life much. It's complicated, and I keep it private. I think they just made assumptions. Maybe I should have been clearer with them.'

'You don't have anything to be sorry for. It's your sister-in-law I'm annoyed with.'

'You're not going to say anything, are you?'

'I think I should.'

'Please don't, it'll just cause more drama.'

'Well, exactly.'

Freddie was worried, but the conversation paused as dessert was served. Again, he felt through his pocket and brought his phone up under the table.

This was a set-up, he messaged Kate, hesitating before sending it.

Need more details.

My SIL tried to set me up with someone.Whole point of dinner I think.

Freddie watched the three dots appear and disappear, then appear once again.

Is she nice?

He!!!

Oh,WOW! Is he nice????

'Who are you talking to?' Freddie didn't realise Kevin had been looking over his shoulder.

'Nobody,' he replied too quickly, like a kid caught stealing.

Kevin peered again at the phone. 'Kate? Who's Kate?'

'Nobody. A friend.'

'Do your family know about her?'

'No, she's . . . she's just a friend.'

'Oh sure. I believe you.' Freddie was sure that Kevin almost certainly did not believe him.

'So, how are you lovely boys getting along?' Stella asked as she brought out a board laden with grapes and cheese.

'Your charming brother-in-law was just telling me about his girlfriend,' Kevin announced loudly, causing Freddie to sit bolt upright, meerkat-like.

What? What was he saying?

'Girlfriend?' David asked, peering around Stella, a sceptical look on his face.

Freddie stared directly at Kevin, who gave him a cheeky wink in return.

'What are you doing?' Freddie hissed.

'If you're not going to sort out your problems yourself, then maybe you need a little helping hand,' Kevin said under his breath.

'Is Kevin right, Freddie? Do you have a girlfriend?' Stella asked in a way that made Freddie think she was disappointed.

'Oh, it's nothing,' Freddie replied. 'Really, it's actually nothing.'

'No, go on then. Tell us,' David urged.

Freddie looked around the table at the other couples he had barely even had a chance to chat to. He wasn't even sure if he remembered their names.

'Just a girl. It's new. It's not serious or anything.'

It didn't feel good, implying that Kate was more than she really was, but if it meant Stella would stop trying to matchmake, then maybe it would be worth it.

'Where did you meet her?' asked David.

'Online,' Freddie said, not daring to look his brother in the face. He was certain that David could tell when he was lying.

'What's her name?' pressed Stella.

'Kate,' Freddie admitted. He turned to look back at Kevin, who was looking at him happily. The bastard.

'What's she like?' Jemima asked, joining in. Freddie wanted the ground to swallow him up.

'Nice. Tall, not as tall as me. Blonde. But a dark kind of blonde? She's nice.'

'Come on Fred,' David laughed. 'Sounds like you've conjured this woman from thin air.'

'She works at an art gallery.'

'Oh, like a curator or a conservator?' Evie asked.

'No, nothing like that.' Freddie's face was so hot now, and he was sweating so much that he could feel it pooling at his lower back.

'Well, why don't you bring her to your parents' anniversary party? I'm sure they'd love to meet her,' Stella suggested.

Oh, no. No, no no.

Freddie looked at Kevin, hoping he would provide some sort of escape plan. Kevin looked as if he was enjoying himself far too much to do or say anything helpful.

'Oh, I don't think that's a good idea,' Freddie attempted. 'It's still pretty new and everything.'

'Worried that we'll scare her off?' said David.

Yes actually, Freddie wanted to scream. Then he realised David thought he was lying.

Don't think this is weird, Freddie messaged Kate later as everybody was getting ready to leave. *But I was caught texting you and now my family know about you.*

Not weird!

No, you don't understand. He sent the message too quickly, and then didn't know what to say next. Again the three dots as Kate attempted a reply. They appeared and disappeared several times.

Is everything OK? she asked.

Don't worry about it. I'll tell you later. It's funny, actually!

Freddie shoved his phone away again, feeling strange, but he wasn't exactly sure why.

'So, you're definitely not gay then?' Stella asked once nearly everyone had left. The table was empty apart from them.

'No,' said Freddie, looking down at his sneakers.

'Why didn't you say something?'

'I didn't think I had to.'

'Well, that was the whole problem. You let me assume. You let everybody assume. And now I look like an absolute fool in front of my colleagues.'

'I don't think . . .' he started, before David came over.

'You should bring this Kate,' he said. Then, when Freddie looked confused, he added: 'To the anniversary party.'

'I really shouldn't,' Freddie replied.

'No, please do. It would make Mum and Dad so happy to see you with a girl. Make that your gift to them?'

This wasn't a request, Freddie realised. But a challenge.

'Kate might be busy.'

'Well, I'm sure she has enough time to sort her schedule out.' He paused, thoughtfully. 'You know, if Kevin isn't your type, you could just say.'

'He's not my type. He is *very much* not my type. I like girls.'

'In which case, we'll see you and Kate together at the party then.'

After they'd gone to the kitchen to start tidying up, Kevin came back into the dining room to say goodbye.

'Just wanted to check in with you before I left. No hard feelings, right?'

'It's fine. I didn't want them to know about her, but it's out there now.'

'Listen, Freddie, did you ever stop to think that maybe you wouldn't be in this mess if you were more open about everything?'

'I wasn't ready, and it's more complicated than you think. We're not even dating. And now I've lied to my family about it.'

'Oh please, I can't remember the last time I told the truth to my family. You'll be fine.'

'I don't like presuming,' Freddie said, trying to explain. 'I don't want to jinx it.'

'Wait a second, you really like this girl, don't you?'

'It's not like that.'

'But you want it to be?'

'I don't know.'

Kevin squinted thoughtfully at Freddie before continuing. 'Can I offer you some advice? Be honest. With yourself and with your family. It makes everything much easier. Trust me.'

'OK.'

'I'm being serious here. You're a good guy and I'm sorry I got you into that mess, but seriously, just be honest. With everyone. They're going to walk all over you otherwise.'

'I know.'

Kevin placed a firm hand on Freddie's shoulder. 'I'll see you around at Ben Day Comics, right?'

'Sure,' Freddie smiled.

'Good. And maybe I'll get to meet Kate some time too?'

'Sure.' This time he sighed.

After a final goodbye to David and Stella, during which time they both emphasised how much they were looking forward to meeting Kate, Freddie went out into the night. Once at the station he checked his phone for the timetable, before absently drifting over to his messages. He read through everything that had passed between them. He thought about messaging her again, of telling her how much fun it had been to have her there in his pocket as he had endured the evening, but decided that it would just be too weird. He didn't want to imply anything beyond their agreement to be just friends. Each other's support animals.

Except, when he let himself consider the idea of her being his girlfriend, of presenting her to his parents and family as if she was, he felt an odd warm pang close to his heart. It was the opposite of unpleasant.

She'd never agree to it, he told himself, but as he waited for his train, he decided to let himself dream.

14

'Hey Kate!'

She turned from the counter to see Hattie, her hair out of the long braids and now styled so that it twisted up into a cloud of tight black curls on top of her head, like a crown.

'Hey!' she replied, pleased to see her. 'I got here early so I'm just grabbing coffee.'

They were in the Student Union building. The café area was busier than Kate had remembered it being the last two times she was here, but she figured that had something to do with the sound system that was currently being tested in the larger adjoining event space.

'Great idea. I'll join you,' Hattie said, smiling. She had her phone in her hand and seemed to be in the middle of something important, so Kate indicated that she was going to find a table for them to sit at whilst Hattie ordered her drink.

'Sorry,' Hattie said, once she'd come and sat down. 'I've just got a million emails to look at and sort out. Just when I think I'm on top of it, everything goes crazy again.'

'What is it that you do exactly?'

'Other than my research here, I'm involved with a lobby group that advocates for abuse victims, I run a spoken-word night at a local club where we aim to highlight diverse and under-represented voices, and I'm trying to get some writing stuff sorted out too.'

Hattie looked tired in that moment. As if she'd only just now realised exactly how much she was doing. Kate looked at the myriad studs and tiny hoops that decorated her ears, the layered necklaces around her neck, and then the collection of rings that adorned her fingers, chunky and esoteric. Hattie was playing with one of the rings now, twirling it with her fingers, a beautiful fidget toy.

'Wait, so you're literally a social justice warrior?' she asked.

'Ha!' Hattie bellowed. But then her brows knitted closely together as she thought about the best way to respond. 'I don't want to be flippant,' she explained. 'We all live in a society, you know? I just want it to be as fair as possible.'

'That's all pretty amazing work you do.'

'Back at school I was a trouble-maker. Loud-mouthed, always talking back to teachers. The amount of times my mum was called in, I really put her through it. I thought my personality was a curse, you know? But then I realised that I could use my voice. That I could be loud and also help other people be louder.'

'Is that why you're so keen to see me and Freddie try out dating?' Kate realised that she wanted to be careful how she put it, so added: 'Dating other people, I mean.'

If there was any awkwardness to her phrasing, it didn't seem as if Hattie noticed it. Even so, Kate found herself getting hotter, feeling the same kind of belly tension she did when a panic attack was on the horizon. Just saying Freddie's name.

'Look, just tell me if all of that was too much. Andy doesn't like to do that type of stuff in the group. They don't think it's right to tell people what to do, anything like that. The group is for listening, for advice, yes, but not anything *firmer* than advice. But I don't know, I think Andy can play it too safe sometimes. I just think when you see someone who needs help, who can't see what's right in front of them, option wise, then it can be a good thing to make that a little clearer for them. To give them a little push.'

'Well, I appreciate the push . . .' Kate started, unsure of how to continue.

'But too much?'

'Maybe, but mostly too soon.'

'I get that,' Hattie agreed. She drank her coffee, and Kate did the same, hoping that she hadn't offended Hattie, wondering what she was thinking now. 'Except,' Hattie continued, setting her cup down.

'Except what?'

'I don't know. Ignore me.'

'You just said "except". I can't really ignore that!' Kate laughed.

'I'm going to get myself in trouble for saying something, I know it. I don't want you to hate me.'

'Just say it.'

'Right then. Here's the thing, what I've been hearing in the last couple of group meetings: that you think that sex has to be the ultimate romantic expression. And the truth is, that it's not. It can be, for some people, but if you don't want to be a virgin any more, if you've decided that you really want to have sex, to get it over with or whatever it means to you, then you might have to put the romantic stuff to the side. You can just do it. Pick someone, someone you find attractive, someone you get on with, and just do it.'

'As easy as that?' Kate was very aware of the people around them. Nobody was close enough to overhear, and Hattie wasn't being very loud anyway, but to speak so openly without the protection of the walls of the classroom upstairs made Kate feel exposed.

The sound system next door wailed with feedback for a few seconds before it was abruptly cut off and someone yelled an apology.

'Just a thought,' Hattie said. 'You're putting a lot of pressure on it. But sex can be transactional too. It might even be better for it.'

'You're asexual. You don't even want to have sex,' Kate said, keeping her voice low and hiding her mouth with her hand, embarrassed.

'That just means I'm able to be objective on the matter. I don't have stakes in it, and see it for what it is.' Hattie paused, catching Kate's concern. 'I'm not saying to just go and have sex with the next person you see. It's not like that. I know that's not the kind of person you are. All I'm saying is, it doesn't have to be as tied up in perfection as you think it has to be. If anything, it might just be more disappointing if you tie it up with perfection, because what's perfect?'

'Well, thanks for the input,' Kate paused. 'I guess a first time can be pretty awkward and uncomfortable, even if it's with the love of your life.'

'I'm not saying that it can't be more emotionally gratifying if it's with someone you care deeply about, and who cares about you back. Trust is big, definitely. I just get annoyed at the fairy-tale fantasy, you know? You want to hold out for the fairy tale, fine by me. But if you want to lose your virginity, it might be worth thinking a little outside the box. As it were. Also, what if you found that perfect person but then realised you didn't connect sexually? That can happen too.'

Kate chewed the inside of her cheek, almost annoyed at how much sense Hattie was making.

'We should probably go upstairs,' she said.

'I haven't upset you, have I?' Hattie asked as they stood up from the table.

'No, not at all. I'm just thinking about it.'

'I thought it might help.'

'Yeah, I get that, and I really appreciate it,' Kate replied.

Hattie suggested they swap phone numbers as they took the lift up to the meeting room, and Kate enjoyed the giddy feeling she got at the thought of a new friendship starting. As they headed down the corridor, she considered Hattie's advice, wondering if she might be right. Perhaps she could solve the most urgent of her problems by loosening up a bit, by considering that things didn't have to be perfect, and that it didn't have to be the big deal she always thought it was.

She could just have sex. She could just pick a guy, someone she liked to be around and who liked to be around her, they could have a conversation as adults, and agree to do it. It didn't have to be romance and roses and intense emotions. It could be much, much easier than that. And then she could move on.

Freddie was already in the room when she and Hattie walked in, and Kate offered him a friendly wave and smile as she went to sit down. She liked the way he smiled back at her, before he ducked his head down again shyly.

'So how are we all doing?' Andy asked, looking around the group.

Everyone was there, Cathryn, Lizzie, Steve and Mike, plus of course Hattie, who was still busy with her phone.

'Sorry, I'll put it away.' She held her hands up when Andy gave her a severe look.

'I'm not so good,' Lizzie said after everyone else had gone around the room briefly mentioning anything that had happened over the past week.

Kate noticed that Freddie didn't say anything about his walk to her gallery, nor their impromptu dinner. She didn't say anything either. It would have felt strange to mention it here, to invite the others in on something that Kate felt had been private. There was an unspoken camaraderie that was heart-warming, that made Kate feel like she could trust him.

'What's been happening, Lizzie?' Andy asked.

'I had this dream the other night, about you-know-who.'

Kate heard Cathryn sigh next to her. It was sympathetic, but Kate also felt that it was the sigh of someone who'd been here before.

'And what happened in the dream?'

'Well, I told him that I was saving myself for him, that I've always been waiting for him, and he just disappeared into dust. And then I woke up crying.'

'That sounds very sad,' Andy said gently.

Lizzie looked to Kate and then to Freddie.

'We were nineteen and promised to each other,' she explained to them. 'He was meant to be there for ever, and then he wasn't. I've been lost without him.'

'He's not dead, Lizzie,' Steve said.

Kate had almost forgotten what Steve's voice sounded like. He was usually so quiet. The other sessions he'd barely moved much either, save for the odd shift in his seat. He was a patient man, Kate could tell, and one who seemed to like just being there and listening. His words now, while not exactly said in a forceful manner, felt forceful anyway because he was so often quiet.

'Steve,' Andy warned softly.

'Nobody else is saying it, but we all know,' Steve continued. Kate glanced at Lizzie, who looked as if she might be about to cry. 'I'm sorry if I have to be abrupt about it, and I know we've been here before, but Freddie said something to me last time and I just can't get it out of my head.'

Kate looked at Freddie, who had blanched so pale with shock and horror that Kate almost wanted to laugh.

'Freddie said to me,' Steve continued, 'he said that it wasn't too late. That sometimes our pasts hold us back. After last time, I'd given up – given up on you, Lizzie – but I've realised since that giving up is a stupid thing to do. Especially if there's a chance. You cling on to the past like it's a real thing. But it's not. And I've always been here. We can go around in circles again, but you need to know that I'm waiting for you just like you've been waiting for him. When I get frustrated with you, I realise that really it's me I'm frustrated with.'

Steve stopped, as if he was suddenly aware of the room around him and hadn't been before.

'I'm sorry,' he said, before picking his coat up from the back of his chair and making to leave.

When he opened the door, the muffled, consistent thud of the speaker system somewhere below was an unexpected exclamation point, the silence again after he'd closed it behind him uncomfortable and strange.

'I should go too, I'm so embarrassed,' Lizzie said eventually. Kate thought she looked even smaller than she normally did.

'Don't feel embarrassed,' Cathryn said warmly.

'He died to me,' Lizzie explained. 'Even if he didn't actually die – and I know that, I do – it still felt like he died. I mourned. I'm still mourning. Why can't other people see that?'

'Do you wonder though,' Kate could see that Cathryn was picking her words very carefully, 'that maybe you don't have to mourn? Or that, if you do, if the grief is like that for you – and who are any of us to say that it isn't? – but that maybe you don't have to let it take over everything?'

A single tear fell down Lizzie's cheek, and her chin quivered.

'We're all here, and it's a safe space to say how we feel. Steve should have thought a little more about how his words impacted you, but we're all trying to help,' Andy said.

'It sounds like he really cares about you,' Hattie added.

'I just feel so guilty,' Lizzie said sadly.

'I made a promise a long time ago,' said Cathryn. 'And when I realised that the promise wasn't working for me, I felt guilty about it. I felt guilty for a long, long time, but I stuck at the promise. I lost a huge chunk of my life to that promise. They weren't bad years by any means, but I still wonder what I could have had if I had been braver. And then, one day, I decided to be brave. It was the scariest thing I've ever done, but I'm so glad I did it and broke free.'

'Do you still feel guilty?' Lizzie asked.

'Every single day,' Cathryn replied sadly. 'But I also feel guilty for me. For denying myself what I really needed to make myself happy.'

Lizzie thought for a moment and took in a deep breath in an attempt to stop herself from crying any more.

'I'm going to go,' she then announced. 'I need to go and be on my own for a bit.'

'We understand,' Andy said.

The group was quiet as Lizzie gathered her things and left. Once again, the background thud from the party below permeated the room when the door was opened and quieted again after it was closed.

'Way to go, Freddie,' Mike said sarcastically. 'You obviously got to old man Steve-o!'

'I didn't mean to upset him,' said Freddie.

At the pub afterwards, Kate was studying Freddie. She was watching his face, his form, the way he moved, the way he talked (which wasn't often). She was thinking about how his body might look without clothes on, how it would feel.

He'd be sensitive, she knew this. But she would have to be sensitive to him too. She'd have to think about how his mind worked, and what made him stressed. It wasn't an impossible task by any means. And he was nice-looking. He had a kind face, focus in his eyes, hair that was easily ruffled.

'What are you thinking about?' Hattie asked when they were at the bar together. 'You look like you're trying to speak common sense to a politician.'

'I'm thinking about what we were discussing about earlier,' Kate said.

'What specifically?'

'About how sex could be transactional. That I might have been overthinking it.'

'And now it looks like you're overthinking the overthinking,' Hattie laughed, then paid the bartender and went back to the table.

A little later, and they were down to three – herself, Freddie and Andy. Kate was staying later than she would usually have done, and she wondered if Freddie was too.

'Do you think Lizzie is going to be all right?' Kate asked Andy.

'Steve too? Should someone check in on him?' Freddie added.

'I'll drop them both an email in the morning,' Andy said. 'I don't want to get too intrusive. It may be that they decide not to come back again, and ultimately they've got to be the ones who decide that.'

'Does it get stressful, running the group?' Kate asked.

'Not often . . . It started out as more of a curiosity for myself. Not just for my research. I think I wanted people to talk to, and when I realised that such a forum didn't exist, Hattie helped me realise that I should make it. But it's been going for about a year now, and I really think that it's helping people. It's helped me certainly. I think it's going to help Lizzie and Steve too, though maybe not straight away.'

'It's helped me,' Freddie revealed, his voice quiet.

'It has?' Andy asked. 'I was worried we were going to scare you off at some point.'

'I don't know that I can explain it properly, but definitely, yeah. It's helped.'

'Me too,' Kate added supportively, 'it's still helping.'

'Well, that's good to hear. Thanks guys,' Andy sighed, and pressed two fingers to the bridge of their nose. 'Would you mind if I made a move? Got a bit of a headache coming on I think.'

Freddie moved out of the way so that Andy could squeeze by him, and when he sat down again Kate felt suddenly overwhelmed by how close they were, how *alone* they were. She was embarrassed by the thoughts she'd been having earlier in the evening, ashamed of sullying their just burgeoning friendship, but then here he was, right in front of her, and something felt incredibly right about that.

Kate had had enough wine by now to be tipsy. Not enough that she considered herself drunk, but enough that she felt loose, playful and, more than anything, brave.

'Hey,' she said to Freddie, who then eyed her suspiciously.

'Hey,' he replied.

'If I suggested something extremely crazy right now, would you indulge me?'

'Okay,' he said, his brow immediately furrowing in trepidation.

'Because it's definitely a crazy idea. Ridiculous even.'

'What is it?'

'I just think that we're two people, and this world is a big world, and sometimes two people have a problem, and it turns out they could be the best ones to help each other out. With that problem.'

'I'm really not following.'

Of course he wasn't.

'What I'm trying to say, Freddie, is that maybe we could help each other out.'

'Help each other . . .' he started, swallowing as a look of utter panic started to spread across his face.

'Out,' Kate finished, nodding suggestively.

'As in?' he looked suggestively back at her, to indicate that he followed.

'Told you it was ridiculous.'

'No, I mean. I think . . . I don't know.'

Kate dared herself to look up at Freddie. He was cute when he was thinking, she realised. His Adam's apple moved in his throat with each careful swallow, a faint but insistent blush working its way across his face.

They both took long, sustained sips of their drinks, and then allowed the moment of intense silence to go on for far too long. Kate noticed how stuffy the pub had got. When did it get so stuffy? It was cold enough to snow outside and yet the pub suddenly felt like a sauna on overdrive.

'So, we could just get it over with. Together. As friends.'

'As friends,' he repeated cautiously. 'Like, friends with benefits?'

'I guess. We could make it more business-like, if that makes it easier? Set some ground rules?'

'Like a contract?'

'It sounds silly. I know it sounds silly. I shouldn't have said anything,' Kate buried her face in her hands, embarrassed.

'No, I don't think it's silly.'

'You don't?' she asked, looking up at him again.

Freddie was looking back at her with these wide, sincere eyes. He was leaning over the table, posture mirroring her own, his hands balled up in front of him, thoughtful creases lining his forehead.

Is he drunk? she wondered. *Will he even remember this conversation tomorrow?*

'You could do that?' he asked, almost hopeful. 'You could have sex with someone without . . . everything else?'

'I don't know,' she admitted. But she wanted to try. 'Could you?'

'I need to think about it,' he said.

Kate wondered if the conversation was over. That she'd made a huge mistake and ruined whatever burgeoning real friendship they had. This was his way of shutting everything down. He had been polite before, she thought, but now he was calmly bringing things to a close. She finished her wine and thought about getting ready to go.

'We're friends, right?' Freddie then said unexpectedly. Kate just looked at him, wondering. 'We haven't spent a lot of time together, admittedly, but we already know each other's biggest secret. I mean, you probably know more about me than anybody else on the planet right now. But we're not good enough friends that if this all turns out to be a huge mistake, it would ruin all this history or anything. I mean, if this happens, if we do this, and it's awful, and we're both so embarrassed that we can't even look at each other again, then we could easily just walk away from each other and everything would be fine. Couldn't we?'

Kate's heart started to race in quiet panic. 'I guess,' she said.

'OK then.'

Kate couldn't tell if he was terrified or exhilarated. She was feeling both.

'We're really going to do this? You want to have sex with me? We're going to have sex?' he asked, looking right at her again.

'Why not?' she said, smiling.

15

It was the stupidest idea he'd ever heard.

It was the best idea he'd ever heard.

The way Kate had looked at him, her eyes bright, almost playful. Not many people had looked at him that way. Like they needed him.

And they were on the same page, sort of. Maybe. She hadn't been joking, he trusted that, but she had been drunk. And he had been too. There was every chance she'd wake up in the morning and regret everything. There was every chance he'd regret everything as well. Freddie worked to remember exactly what he'd said, and the precise way that he'd said it, in case something came back to bite him later. He felt like he'd been swept up in the moment, caught off guard by her, willing to do anything she wanted.

He tapped his foot as he waited for his bus.

They'd agreed on waiting a week or so.

'There's no rush,' Kate had said. 'Is there?'

'Absolutely no rush,' Freddie had agreed.

'Gives us both enough time to think it all through. To prepare.'

'What do you need to prepare?' He had been genuinely curious. It was the first time he'd ever been able to talk to a girl about things like this.

'Oh, you know. Stuff. Girls have to think about this kind of thing.'

'They do?'

He could tell that Kate was too shy to say anything else, but between them they'd decided that a week on Friday would be the perfect time. Neither had to get up for work the following morning and it gave both of them a chance to mentally prepare.

'Do you want to meet between now and then?' Freddie had asked, tentatively. 'Maybe dinner before or something?'

'Do you think we should? I don't want to complicate things,' Kate had replied. Freddie was a little disappointed. 'This arrangement,' She further explained. 'I don't want things to get confusing between us. I think, if we went out to dinner, that it might feel like dating?'

'You're right,' he had said.

'The whole point of this is that we have a distance from each other. That we can do this without getting swept up in our emotions. It's perfect really. How we are now, how we're talking right now. It should be like this. This would be fine.'

Freddie had nodded, unable to counter her logic, but now he wasn't so sure.

He could do it. He could have sex with her. It made a lot of sense. It was what other people did all the time, for the entirety of history. Two people met, got on, and decided to sleep with each other. Why should they be any different? Why should it be any harder for them?

Except it was harder. Because Freddie was liking becoming Kate's friend, and the one thing he risked by sleeping with her was that friendship. What if everything went wrong, if they both ended up completely embarrassed and never saw each other again?

He remembered the rainbow alley. He hadn't known how to behave, how to show her that he was enjoying himself too, but he had liked being with her there, and watching her be happy. He remembered her now with the rose light on her face, smiling at him with those big brown eyes. He didn't want to lose that.

Do I like her? He asked himself. The obvious answer was yes. She was the person he most wanted to be around right now.

Do I like *like her?* He didn't know. He'd tumbled down that rabbit hole before and look where that had left him. *But*, he reasoned, *if I keep a safe distance, if I deal with this like a scientist, like a contractual obligation, then we both get what we want without any of the messy stuff. Without anybody's feelings getting hurt.*

It made sense in his head, but then the bus arrived, and as soon as he sat down on the top deck his head scrambled and he was left confused and unsure once again.

Freddie was a little concerned when he got home and saw the light on. Their flat was on the fourth floor, with the living room looking out on to the street. Damien should have left for work hours ago. He was fastidious about saving energy and keeping bills down; it wasn't like him to leave a light on before he left. Which suggested that he might be home. This concerned Freddie too – it was an unusual break in the routine. Damien always worked on Tuesday nights, and if he was home, it might mean that he was sick. Freddie wasn't great with sick people. His imagination ran riot worrying about germs and viruses, and his obsessive compulsions tended to run riot accordingly.

After he unlocked the front door, he stood in the hallway for a moment, listening out for any Damien-like sounds. When he heard nothing, he moved to the living room, looking around for any clues. Freddie switched the light off and went to the kitchen to grab a drink of water.

There was a sound. Like something falling in another room. With no sign that Damien was there, and an intruder being unlikely considering the front door seemed normal, Freddie's mind instantly went to rodents. He wasn't scared of rats, but he was scared of the bugs they might carry.

Freddie picked up a saucepan and went back out into the hallway. The flat was tiny, the hallway itself barely larger than a closet, a tiny rectangular box from which all the other rooms sprouted, but nevertheless Freddie moved slowly and carefully. He put an ear to Damien's bedroom door. There was definitely a noise in there. Something was moving.

'Damien?' Freddie called, just in case. No reply.

He could honestly say that he'd never gone into Damien's room without express invitation. And he'd only ever had the invitation a handful of times. It was his flatmate's private den, and Freddie expected the same level of privacy in return. He felt terrible about opening the door, but was also determined that it was the best thing to do given the circumstances.

He was not ready for what was on the other side. Damien was indeed home, and he was not alone.

'What the hell!' Damien cried.

As soon as Freddie realised that Damien was naked, he turned away and covered his face with the saucepan.

'I called out,' Freddie replied, voice muffled behind the cookware. 'I heard a noise and I called out to see if it was you and nobody replied so I thought I needed to check!'

'I didn't agree to a party,' the woman in Damien's bed said. She didn't sound scared or embarrassed. If anything, she seemed vaguely bored.

'There's no party,' Damien said to her.

When Freddie dared to move the saucepan away from his face, he saw that the woman was practically naked. Freddie marvelled at her long black hair, glossy and rather vampiric, as she got out of the bed and arranged one of Damien's dressing gowns around herself.

'I needed the loo anyway,' she said, before moving past Freddie to get to the bathroom. Once in there, he heard her lock the door from the other side.

'Didn't you hear me call out?' Freddie asked his flatmate in a loud whisper.

'I was a bit busy,' Damien puffed, his face a peculiar shade of puce. He was sitting on the end of his bed, boxers on now, and scooping up some errant clothes from the floor.

'I'm so sorry Damien,' Freddie tried. 'I'll go to my room and won't come out until morning. You won't even know I'm here.'

The toilet flushed and the bathroom door unlocked. The woman reappeared. Damien and Freddie both froze as she framed herself in Damien's doorway, looked at them and sighed dramatically.

'I'm really sorry,' Freddie said to her.

'Oh don't be silly, it happens,' she replied before turning to Damien. 'You ready to try again?'

Freddie just caught Damien's dazzled face as his bedroom door closed in front of him.

Damien was standing over his coffee machine in the morning.

'Hey,' Freddie mumbled as he reached for his favourite bowl and the cornflakes.

Damien just mumbled in return.

'She seemed nice?' Freddie said.

Damien ignored him in a way Freddie felt was very deliberate.

'Again, I am so sorry,' he tried. 'I honestly had no idea. If I had known, I don't know, I might have found a way to let you have the place for the night. I didn't have to be here at all.'

'It's OK,' Damien grumbled.

'It's just that this has never happened before. I didn't even think—'

'Seriously Freddie, relax. So it didn't go as smoothly as I would have liked, but it wasn't a big deal in the end.'

'What was her name?' Freddie asked, putting a pause on eating his cornflakes so that he could listen.

'Veronica.'

'Am I likely to be seeing her again?'

'I guess that's up to her.'

'I thought she was OK, after my interruption. She seemed fine?'

'She was fine. Me, less so.'

'Oh.'

'It happens. I could have warned you. For that I apologise. It won't happen that way again.'

Even Damien is having sex, Freddie thought as he resumed his breakfast.

He wondered if that was a spiteful thing to think. If it was cruel to think about Damien being a generally sexless person. He was only a year or two older than Freddie, but behaved with all the seriousness of someone in their forties. Freddie realised that until that point he'd always fancied himself the 'cool' one in the flat. At a push, the more good-looking one. It stung to realise that Damien was capable of making more headway with a sex life, even if it had been interrupted by his virgin flatmate.

He thought about Kate again. About her offer, and about agreeing to her offer. He could get it over with. He didn't have to feel like a loser any more, could finally gain access to that special club that every single other adult on the planet already had unlimited membership to. It could be easy. Afterwards, he wouldn't be a virgin any more. And if he could get that one aspect of his life sorted out, then maybe everything else could be sorted out after?

He could do this.

He had to do it.

'Damien,' Freddie started. 'Can I ask you something?'

His flatmate just looked at him, and took another loud sip of his coffee.

'Say you're about to sleep with a girl. It's all consensual and great and you like each other, but it's your first time together. How do you . . . prepare?'

'What exactly are you asking me?'

'I'm just curious,' Freddie explained hurriedly. 'It's been a while for me, and it's never gone well in the past, but I don't know, it feels like things are looking up. I suppose what I'm asking is, what do girls expect nowadays?'

'That's a big question.'

'I know.'

'Depends on the girl.'

'I know that too.'

'Have you discussed protection methods?' he said it with the seriousness of a tax collector.

'Not yet.'

'Well, if you don't have the chance to ask first, then maybe buy a selection? Something you'd like, something you think she'd like. Scented, flavoured, textured . . .'

'Right,' Freddie mumbled, blushing now. He wished that he hadn't asked.

'You might want to see documentation too.'

'Documentation?'

'Blood test results, letters from the doctor.' When Freddie looked confused, Damien continued: 'STIs. Diseases. You don't want to get caught out.'

'I'm not sure that's going to be an issue for us.'

'It's an issue for everyone, Freddie,' Damien warned.

'I was thinking more, y'know, in the bedroom. What do girls like?'

'Have you asked her?'

'No, but I will. I definitely will. But your insight might be good too?' This was the longest and friendliest conversation he'd had with Damien for ages, and it seemed a shame to shut it down when the information might be so useful.

'Well, you have your standards: missionary, cowgirl, reverse cowgirl . . .'

This was OK. Freddie knew what those were.

'And then there are your more . . . unconventional positions. The frog, the teacup, the handbag.'

'You're making those up.'

'Am I, Freddie? Am I?'

Damien tipped his espresso cup all the way back and afterwards made a loud, gratified sound.

'What's her name?' Damien asked.

'Kate,' Freddie said.

'Well, just give me warning if she's going to be over. We both know what happens if you don't.'

Freddie saluted as Damien left the kitchen and went back to his room, then he quickly washed up his bowl and spoon and got ready to leave for work.

There was a couple sitting opposite Freddie on the train. They both seemed tired; she had her head rested on his shoulder while he was looking down at his phone. Then, at one point, he tilted his head so that he could see her, and she reached up and kissed him. It was a tender moment and one that gave Freddie an odd fluttery feeling in his chest. He imagined being in his place, with an affectionate partner he was happy to kiss whenever the opportunity arose. He wanted that, he realised.

Kate had made it clear that it wasn't what she wanted though; at least, not with him. But he was starting to hope that this would be what made their arrangement easier. His mind trailed back to his date with Mia, how much better he had felt being around her once he realised that romance was off the table. He'd been able to relax. The pressure had been lifted.

Freddie tried to imagine that this was a similar situation. That because he and Kate had discussed what they wanted to happen and formally agreed that it wasn't a romantic thing, that the pressure should be off here too.

But he still felt the pressure regardless.

He looked at the couple sitting across from him on the train and starting daydreaming that the girl who sat next to him, with her head on his shoulder, had long blonde hair.

16

'So he's coming over? Tonight?' Lindsey's eyes were big on Kate's phone screen.

'You're going to try and talk me out of it, aren't you?'

'You think I'm going to talk you out of inviting round a guy you like? Who seems to like you back? To sleep with?'

'But we're not a couple. It's not romantic. Isn't that weird?'

'Let's try that again. Do I think that two people who like each other having consensual sex is weird? Really Kate?' Lindsey was trying not to laugh.

'Don't make fun of me!' Kate said, trying not to laugh with her.

'Look,' Lindsey's face changed then, thoughtful. Kate wished that she was in the room with her so that she could better read her friend's body language, pick up on the signals. She hated having such an intimate discussion when they were separated by thousands of miles. 'Do I wish you were in a loving relationship? Of course, I do. Do I wish that things had worked out differently for you, that your path had been clearer, or easier maybe, up to this point? Sure. But this is where we are. I just want the best for you. I want you to be happy.'

'Now you're sounding soppy.'

'Seriously, Kate. I have no problem with you doing this tonight, if that's what you want. I'm just wondering if it is what you want. Because I've known you for a long time. Don't do this because you think that you have to, because you've arranged it and don't want to back out. Do it because it feels right – for both of you.'

Kate could feel tears springing to her eyes and hoped that her phone camera wasn't good enough for Lindsey to notice.

'I like Freddie. He's kind, he's cute and it's easy to be with him, plus he seems to like me back.'

'In which case, I'm confused. Why isn't this romantic? Because it sounds like you get along better than I did with at least two previous boyfriends.'

'I guess that love is scarier than sex right now,' Kate admitted. She watched as Lindsey waited for her to continue. 'Things have been changing so much lately. You went away, I have one week left in this flat, and then discovering that my old friends had dumped me. It's scary, Linds.'

'I didn't want to upset you,' Lindsey said. 'I want you to have a good time with Freddie tonight. Now, do I have to do the safety talk?'

'No.'

'I'm giving you the three Cs.'

'*No.*'

'CLEANLINESS. CONSENT. CONDOMS.'

Kate buried her phone into her chest as she groaned. When she brought it back up in front of her, Lindsey was smiling.

'I think my neighbours heard that, so hopefully their English isn't great,' she said.

'I love you, Lindsey.'

'Look after yourself tonight. Remember you can say no at any point.'

'I've got it. I'll be fine.'

'In which case, love you too.'

'Hi.'

'Hi.'

An hour later, and there was a boy. Here in her flat.

Lindsey had brought guys over before – a few who had overstayed their welcome, in fact – but Kate never had. Not in this context, anyway. It felt naughty, like she was going to get caught and admonished at any moment.

'So, should we get naked?' Freddie asked.

There he was, in her room, sitting on her bed, asking about whether they should be getting naked. It was almost too much for Kate to handle.

'Do you *want* to get naked?' Kate challenged.

She heard Freddie swallow, a gulp of reticence that would have been comedic if she didn't feel it too.

Kate finished her glass of wine. She regretted the final sip as soon as she had taken it, because she had promised herself that she was not going to get drunk tonight. She didn't want anything muddying the experience, or for there to be any question about whether she wanted to do this. She wanted it. She had wanted it for so long. This was what everything had been about, and she didn't want to ruin it by being clumsy or saying the wrong thing, or forgetting herself. All things she was liable to do after the right (or wrong) amount of wine.

'I think that probably we *should* get naked?' Freddie said finally, although the way he said it, with that hint of an upward inflection at the end, made Kate wonder if he meant it. God, she wished she knew what he was thinking.

'I'm scared that you're not going to like what I look like,' Kate admitted.

'Is there anything I can tell you to make you not think that?' Freddie asked, his voice soft.

'I don't think so,' Kate replied.

'Does it help if I tell you that I feel the same way?'

'How can you feel the same? You look fine.' Kate squirmed her toes and fought the blush.

'But don't girls like guys to be beefcakes?'

'Beefcakes?'

'You know, all that Thor and Captain America stuff, with their abs out and their arms flexed?'

'I don't want that,' Kate said. 'I mean, sure it's nice to look at, like statues are nice to look at, but rock-hard abs and biceps have always made me feel a little queasy. It doesn't look remotely comfortable.'

Freddie put his wine glass down on the bedside table and lifted up his T-shirt to reveal his paper-white stomach. 'But look, it goes concave when I breathe in. I'd want a six-pack over protruding ribs any day.'

She stole a glance. Yes, he was a skinny guy. But he wasn't nearly as bad as he was making out. When he relaxed, when he didn't make a big show of breathing in deep, his belly was soft and flat. You could even see the outline of his muscles. They were underdeveloped, but they were there. The shadow-line of abs, hint of the elusive 'v' that crept under the waist of his jeans.

Kate felt bold. She lifted up her top, revealing her own tummy. She was wearing her most flattering jeans, but there was no escaping the roundness of her.

'Don't guys want flat tummies?' she asked.

Freddie leaned over and gave her a playful poke right by her belly button and smiled. It was the first time he had touched her that evening.

'You're soft,' he remarked. 'I think it's nice that you're soft.'

He took a deep breath and continued. 'I know that being naked is a huge deal to you, probably more of a huge deal than it is for me, but hear me out. You're fine. I think you're fine. I don't think that you believe me, but for the purposes of what we're trying to do, you might just have to pretend to believe me, all right?'

Kate had never heard him be quite so assertive. He usually seemed so meek and frightened.

'And I'm nervous too, by the way. There's a lot of pressure. And this is difficult. But before I met you, I honestly thought I would be dying a virgin and now I'm probably not, so I'm grateful. I'm actually really grateful. And I'm trying. So, maybe, just for tonight, we can both get over the fact we don't have perfect bodies, whatever that means?'

Kate noticed Freddie wringing his hands together so tightly that they were going red. She wanted to grab them, to separate them and hold them in hers, but she worried that it was too intimate. Or was it? He was in her room, on her bed. If she couldn't even hold his hands, then what hope was there for the rest of the night?

He breathed in sharply as she found a way to wind her own fingers between his until they were completely intertwined. Kate was surprised at how hot they were, and clammy.

'I'm sweating,' Freddie admitted apologetically.

'It's OK,' Kate said, surprised at herself for how OK it was.

'Wait a minute.' He broke up the grip and crossed his arms over his chest to take his T-shirt completely off. He threw it across the room and then went back to holding Kate's hand again.

She took in the line of his shoulders, the gentle ridge of his clavicle. Kate wondered if it would be OK to stroke him, right there, where the hair was so light that she could only just see it.

'Your turn then.' Freddie's voice shook.

Kate took in a deep breath, knowing that there was no way round this. This time it was her turn to break up the hand-holding, as she reached over herself to take her top all the way off. She hoped that he liked the bra. She'd thought about going out and getting something new, but bras were expensive, so she'd found her favourite one instead, the one she usually saved for nights out, slightly plunging and edged in black lace.

'What?' she asked, when she looked up again at his face. His expression was almost pained. 'What is it?'

'Nothing.'

'No, really – what is it? Are you all right? You're looking at me weirdly.'

'No, I'm . . .' Freddie avoided finishing the sentence to reach over to the bedside table to grab some more wine.

Kate waited, nervous.

'I was just thinking that you look great, actually.'

Kate felt a rush inside her, a rush that felt empowering.

She saw how he was shifting on the bed and tried not to think of all the things about men she didn't really have personal experience of yet.

'I know we haven't really talked about it specifically, but how do you want to do this? Do you want to do foreplay or anything?' she asked him.

'I don't know much about foreplay,' Freddie replied.

'It's just that it might be more comfortable, for me at least, if we just warm things up a little? I mean, we haven't even kissed yet.'

Kate hated how complicated her brain was making this. She had been hoping that somehow biology would take over, that they'd get to her room and start ripping each other's clothes off, but each thing she said just sounded so extremely forward, all she was doing was squirming and second-guessing herself.

'What are you thinking about?' Kate asked.

'Do we have to kiss?' he asked eventually.

'I think so,' Kate said. 'I think it would be weird if we didn't.'

A beat of silence. Freddie stared at his socks.

'I know about the OCD. Is this part of it?' Kate asked carefully. 'I get it if it is. I mean, I don't, but I also do. Does that make sense?'

'Mouths are a thing,' Freddie admitted. 'There are just a lot of germs there.'

'But you've kissed girls before?'

'I have, but I was either really drunk, or it was before things got bad.'

'Well then, maybe it's time to . . .' She struggled for the word, and then to say it in the right way. 'Time to desensitise you to it? Because I think kissing might be important for me. And well, isn't this whole project about overcoming the stuff that's been getting in the way for both of us? Isn't kissing another person part of that? When you get a proper girlfriend then you're going to have to kiss her, so why not practise with me?'

He was still staring at his socks.

'I can brush my teeth first, if you think that would help?' Kate offered.

I suppose this could be weirder, Kate thought as she scrubbed at her teeth.

She watched them together, side by side in her bathroom mirror. Freddie was brushing his teeth as well, sheepishly, like he felt guilty about it, but Kate was brushing hers with gusto. She wanted to make sure that Freddie knew she was taking it seriously.

Their eyes met in the mirror, and although Freddie still looked shy and guilty, Kate smiled. There was something about doing this together, while both of them were shirtless and it being such a mundane thing, at least for her, that gave her a shiver of satisfaction. She wondered if this was what it was like to have a boyfriend. All these silly little things that you didn't think about ordinarily suddenly became so immensely pleasurable when you did it with another person. Especially when it was a person you were intimate with. She could definitely get used to this.

They spat out the remnants of the toothpaste at the same time, and Freddie seemed to take a moment watching it all intermingle as it swirled down the drain.

'Better?' she asked him carefully.

'Do you use mouthwash?' he replied, face serious.

'Sometimes.'

'I have some.'

Freddie darted back into the bedroom and into his bag, coming back quickly with a purple bottle. He poured a shot into the cap and chugged it back, swishing it in his mouth and gargling before spitting it out into the sink. He then handed the cap over to Kate.

'Are you OK with me using the same cap?' she questioned.

'You've just brushed your teeth, so yeah, I guess,' Freddie replied. Kate wondered if he was lying, and just trying to force himself past his reluctance.

She poured herself a shot nonetheless, and repeated what he had just done, keeping the mouthwash in her mouth for as long as she could handle. By the time she spat it out, her gums stung.

Unexpectedly, as soon as the cap was screwed back on the bottle, he reached down and kissed her. Kate wasn't prepared for it, so she just stood there for a moment, shoulders tense and eyes wide, before she realised what was happening and willed herself to relax.

It was never going to be the best kiss in the universe. Freddie obviously had no idea what he was doing, but it wasn't as if Kate was enough of a seasoned pro to guide him either, so they both just stood there, lips pressed together, unmoving and awkward. By the time he pulled away, Kate was wondering if she could make do without the kissing after all.

But now it was her turn. He had been brave and, after his kiss, she figured she had to do something equally brave.

So the bra came off.

She kept her eyes on the floor for a moment, but when she finally tipped her head back up to look at him, she saw that he was staring. Goggle-eyed, unabashed, staring. Kate felt a warm rush of pride and pleasure surge through her. It was nice to be looked at like this. Another thing she added to her mental list of things she could easily get used to.

When she sensed that he wanted to move his hand up towards her, she gestured for him to go ahead. His touch was tentative, maybe shaking ever so slightly. She tried not to let herself tense up. Maybe the cold, stark lighting of her bathroom wasn't ideal, and her gums still stung uncomfortably, but she let herself breathe, despite the anticipation of his touch making her heart race. She didn't want to seem in any way frigid and uncomfortable, even though she was.

He wasn't cold. His hand there, right over her left nipple, gently holding her, cupping with an unexpected tenderness, was surprisingly nice. She felt the warmth of him and reacted in a pleasing way. All over.

'Is this OK?' he asked, stopping himself from going any further.

'It's fine,' Kate replied, her voice coming out high and fraught.

'Are you sure?'

'Yep!' She wasn't lying, not exactly, it was just that she wasn't used to it.

'You can touch me too, if you like?' Freddie offered, trying to help.

She brought a hand up to his chest, to that patch of fine, hair she had admired earlier, and placed it right there, near his heart. His breath caught.

'Are you OK?' it was her turn to ask.

'Your hand is cold,' he said.

'Really? Oh God, sorry. Your hand is quite warm and I didn't think that mine wouldn't be. I'm sorry, perhaps I can—'

He stopped her from talking by kissing her again, and this time it was different. This time it wasn't like two robots pressing their mouths together in an attempt to do what they thought kissing was. This time it was softer and warmer, and this time they both had a hand on each other's body and could feel the other's heart beating.

Kate parted her lips, just slightly, and without thought. It was just happening, and she couldn't help it. She pressed into him, stroked her hand down his chest, the other one reaching up to his face. He pressed into her too, the one hand still holding her left breast.

Kate's list of things that she could get used to was getting longer. Pressed up close like this, a hand holding her, tentatively massaging her, and his mouth warm and questioning. They just seemed to be fitting together. She almost couldn't believe it.

'Shall we go back to the bed?' Freddie asked. It was a whisper really, his voice low against her face, the vibrations of him running through her neck and down her spine. Kate nodded in reply, her forehead pressing against his cheek – she liked that he was taller than her – and then his hand left her body, and went to find her hand so that he could lead her back to the bedroom.

She was surprised at how easily these feelings were happening, how ready her body was to respond. She was already hot and bothered, her blood flooded with all those pleasure hormones. When they settled themselves back on the bed, on their sides and facing each other this time, Kate marvelled at how fun this was, how much she wanted Freddie to touch her again, wondering if he'd be open to kissing with tongues this time.

'Maybe we should take off the rest of our clothes?' she asked. He nodded in reply.

Kate turned away to sit on the edge of the bed and shuffled out of her jeans. She could feel him sneaking glances at her and then, when she was done, wearing just her knickers now, she turned to him, hoping he was as excited as she was.

He was definitely excited.

'I . . . err . . .' he stammered.

'You OK?'

'I'm just embarrassed,' he admitted.

'Of what?'

'Of . . .'

Kate knew what he wanted to say, couldn't mistake the denim tent between his legs, and felt just as unsure as him on how to talk about it. If they even needed to talk about it at all.

'I mean, that's a good thing, isn't it? Isn't that what we want to happen?'

'I guess,' he mumbled.

'If it helps, I'm feeling the same? I know you can't see it, but I promise you it's the same for me right now too.'

'It is?'

'Yup. Definitely. And I'm scared too.'

They nodded at each other, and then Freddie undid his jeans and let them slide off towards the floor along with his underwear. Kate did the same with her knickers. They were naked now. Both of them. Naked on her bed.

'I can turn off the lights?' Kate offered, worried.

'No, I think I want to see you,' Freddie replied. Then he added carefully: 'You can back out of this too, you know, at any time.'

'No, no. This is fine. This is all totally, unquestionably, fine.'

'I still think you look really nice. You don't have to worry.'

'You don't have to worry either.'

It was true, she felt it. And the more she realised how much she liked his body, the more she felt comfortable in hers, with him looking at hers.

Then Freddie leaned over and kissed her again, this time deeper and more urgent.

'Oh my God,' he suddenly whispered, coming up for air for a moment. He pressed his forehead against hers and kept his eyes closed, breathing unsteadily.

'Freddie, it's OK,' Kate replied, her lips feeling swollen, her voice breathy. 'Do you want a condom?'

He nodded back at her, keeping his eyes tightly shut.

Kate went into the drawer of her bedside table and brought out the tiny square packages.

Pick a condom, any condom, she wanted to joke, his erection pointing obscenely towards her while she fanned them out like tiny playing cards.

Freddie didn't say anything, just took the middle one and stared at the packet for a second before tearing it open.

'I can help you?' Kate tried again. She had been doing research earlier that afternoon and had watched a video of a condom being placed over a cucumber, just to make sure that when the time came, she could do it right.

'It's OK,' Freddie muttered.

His penis was suddenly very near and the thought of it entering her suddenly seemed like a horrifyingly close prospect. Kate wondered what it felt like for him, whether the feeling of being erect was a tangible thing, then she worried about whether she was aroused enough too. She hadn't been lying to him before, and she couldn't forget the pleasing warmth she felt, those shivers that spun though her like electric darts. But they were fleeting, and they weren't nearly so vibrant now. Looking down at him, as he clumsily worked to sheath his erection, those electric darts were starting to feel like the early signs of a panic attack.

'Do you want to talk?' Kate asked Freddie. She wanted to talk. She wanted to say everything she was feeling, to let it roll out of her and find out whether he was feeling the same.

'What about?' Freddie asked. He was wearing the condom now, and the sight made Kate think of a balloon, the kind used to make balloon animals, before it was contorted into shape.

'I don't know. Nothing I guess. Have you thought about how you want to do this?'

'I could get on top?'

'OK.'

There had been flashes of romance, Kate was certain of it. When he kissed her deeply, when he had his hands on her, when she had touched him and felt the wild zap of connection.

But this isn't romance, she told herself sharply.

Freddie climbed on top of her, his hardness pressing on her belly. He seemed frightened to touch her, so deeply embarrassed that he didn't even dare look at her, and Kate stiffened in response. The weirder and more uncomfortable he seemed, the more distance she felt between them.

This isn't right.

This isn't right.

This isn't right.

She wanted to shush the inner voice, because this was meant to be simply about the sex and getting it over with. This was what she wanted, what she had wanted for so long, and what they had planned. And yet.

'Is this all right?' Freddie asked. Kate wasn't doing a good job of masking her fear any more. She felt sick and cold.

'Of course it is,' she said, but her mouth was dry as she said it and the words hard to form.

'We can stop?' Freddie offered. 'I wouldn't mind.'

'We've come this far,' Kate replied. And then added, as if she were a teacher recognising that a struggling student needed validation: 'We're doing really well.'

Kate had her hands clasped around Freddie's back – it was a wide stretch of back, Kate couldn't quite believe how much of it there was – when he put his hand down between her legs to find a way in.

'*No!*'

She thought she said it in her head. Kate only realised that it was out loud once Freddie froze.

17

'No?' Freddie asked.

He was hyper-aware of how close his body was to hers, her hands on his back, one of his between them, the other working to prop himself up so that his entire weight didn't fall on her. He had never been this close to another human being. Could hear his heart pulsing in his ears, in his fingertips, everywhere.

'No,' she said again.

'We can kiss some more?' Freddie offered, but he knew that he didn't sound enthusiastic. He rolled off her as gingerly as he could and lay back on the bed next to her. 'We can try more foreplay-type things? If you like?'

'No,' Kate repeated, her voice softer this time, like she was trying not to cry. 'I'm so sorry.'

'Don't be sorry.'

'I thought I could do this. I thought I was being the strong one,' she rubbed her hands over her face so that he couldn't see her. 'I was freaking out. I was trying so hard to be cool, to be the one who would make this happen.'

'I'm relieved,' Freddie revealed, only knowing that it was true once he had said it. 'It's like we've been playing this gigantic game of chicken and I guess that if you hadn't backed out, then I was going to end up having to.'

He felt deflated; he was deflating. But he was genuinely relieved too, felt like he could breathe properly for the first time that whole evening. He took in a lungful of air and let it out slowly.

Kate leaned over to reach down to the foot of the bed to grab the duvet, which she then spread out, hiding them both. For Freddie, this had the unexpected impact of making him suddenly very aware of their nakedness. A boyish thought in that moment, one he knew was stupid and immature and yet gave him an electric thrill all the way through his body, even whilst he was reaching under the blanket to remove the condom: 'I've seen her boobs.'

He sighed when it was done, and then looked around awkwardly as he wondered what to do with it before Kate handed him a tissue to wrap it up in.

'I'm really sorry,' she said again. 'I thought I could go through with it.'

'I thought I could too.'

'I thought you were fine. *It* was right there.' Her face reddened as she said it. Freddie realised that people don't just blush on their faces, but right down their chest too.

'I really wasn't. I was worked up, but not comfortable. Arousal is . . . weird.'

'But even so. Men can't fake *that*, can they?' Kate awkwardly gestured to his crotch.

'No, but that doesn't mean I was going to actually do it. I don't think,' he paused, fighting for the right words. He had been excited, he had been ready. But he had been frightened too. 'I was relieved when you said no.'

'It wasn't right, was it?'

'No.'

'I really thought we could hook up and get it over with. Don't people do that all the time? People just have sex everywhere, don't they? Why couldn't we?'

Freddie let out another long, deep breath and looked up at the ceiling. 'If we had done it, if you had let me do it, do you think it would have been too much?'

'Too much?'

'It's just a lot to happen all at once, maybe.'

'Maybe.'

He sat up and swung his legs over the side of the bed, facing away from her, and wondered if she would think it was weird, or rude, if he went to brush his teeth again.

'Stay.'

Freddie turned and looked over his shoulder at her, one eyebrow crooked and confused. He didn't know if he'd heard her right.

'Stay the night,' Kate clarified. 'You don't have to go. It's late, and—'

'And what?'

'And I want you to stay. I don't know, maybe this can be a first step? We may not have slept together, but we can still *sleep* together?'

Freddie wasn't sure. He didn't know what was appropriate, couldn't work out how comfortable he felt. His brain was still a muddle of conflicting instincts, plus he had no script for this scenario, no template to work through. But more than anything, he didn't want to do anything that he or Kate might regret at some point. He desperately didn't want to hurt her.

Carefully, he nodded. He would stay. They would sleep. He would have liked to go home and fold himself into a ball of despair and shame, but it was late, and he was tired. There was also the vague idea in his head that he didn't want to leave Kate, that he wanted to stay with her for reasons that he had no idea how to properly articulate, but he brushed those aside. It was late, he was tired, therefore he'd stay. That was all there was to it. He was sure.

Freddie could feel that she had fallen asleep next to him. He didn't really understand how anyone could sleep after what they had just been though. He wondered if he would ever be able to relax ever again, if every time he closed his eyes he would see her face, contorted with tension, making him feel like a torturer. He didn't want anyone ever to feel the way she had looked.

I like Kate.

There it was. The thought suddenly fused with clarity. Not the same kind of like he had for Baz, for his niece Lacey, for that one shift at work that seemed to go more quickly than the others. This was a different kind of like. A like that was meaningful, charged with energy. A like that made him exhilarated and sad all at once. Because she didn't like him back. Couldn't like him back. Hadn't her actions in the moment made it even more clear? When they were as close as two people could be, she'd pushed him away. She hadn't said it, but she seemed repulsed.

Freddie shuffled, testing out how the duvet lay, how much the bed creaked, to see if he could feasibly get up and escape without disturbing her. She'd wake up in the morning and he'd not be there. Then they could both go back to their lives and relegate this whole thing to some deluded frenzy, a failed experiment.

He'd be a virgin for ever. Perhaps that was something he could be OK with. Perhaps he'd been foolish for wanting anything more.

'Are you all right?'

Kate was awake. She'd been so still and so quiet that Freddie didn't think it was possible.

'Can't sleep,' Freddie admitted. He should never have agreed to stay. He should have escaped as soon as he'd been able.

'Neither can I,' Kate sighed.

The silence between them was excruciating.

'This was all so stupid, wasn't it?' she said eventually.

'Maybe? I don't know,' Freddie replied. It hadn't seemed stupid before.

'I just thought it would be such an easy thing. We get on, we're both in the same situation . . .' Her voice trailed off, and Freddie wondered again if she was going to cry.

Instead she just sighed again and turned over to face him. He couldn't see her properly, just the outlines of her face, contours within the shadows, and the tiny, jewel-like gleam in her eyes from what little streetlight was peeking through the curtains. Freddie had a tremendous, inexplicable urge to trace the shape of her jaw with his fingers, to check that she was real. He forced the instinct away and clutched his fingertips into his pillow.

'I feel like I led you on,' Kate admitted, her voice barely a whisper.

'You didn't,' Freddie reassured her. He felt sad that he hadn't done more to make her feel more comfortable. Sad that she didn't like him enough. He didn't tell her this.

'Can I ask you something?' she tested.

'Sure . . .?'

'Do you have blue balls?'

He snorted in surprise. 'What?'

'Isn't that a thing? Blue balls?'

'No, I um . . . I mean I guess it was a bit awkward. But, no. I'm not sure.'

'I have no idea how men's bodies work. I had it in my head that once the process started, that you couldn't stop or something.'

'No, I guess I'm fine. I don't know.'

More silence. And then, questions started sprouting in his head. Things he had never thought to ask before, because he had never had a real human girl in front of him to ask.

'Do women get blue balls?'

'Well, we don't have balls, so . . .'

'No, not literally. But, like, if you were ready to go, and then I had stopped things, would it have been . . .' He struggled for the right words. 'Difficult? Would it have been *difficult* for you?'

'I don't think so. I guess it can be frustrating. I might have been annoyed, I guess.'

Her voice sounded sleepy. He had more questions, more things that he wanted to know, but maybe now wasn't the time.

'We're going to stay friends, right?' Freddie asked.

'Of course,' Kate said through a yawn, but Freddie didn't believe her.

The tension broken, at least on her side, she fell asleep. He could tell, even under all this darkness, because he could sense her soften, her breathing deepen in a way it hadn't done before.

Freddie suddenly felt very alone and very scared. It had been a long time since this had happened, since he'd liked someone this much, and it hadn't exactly worked out well then. He didn't want another Camellia situation, flinging all his feelings at someone when he had no guarantee that she was going to feel the same things back.

He listened as her breathing became deeper still, and felt his own eyelids become heavy as a result. As Freddie finally drifted asleep, the thought occurred to him: if this was all they were going to be, then it was better than nothing at all.

When he woke up again, the sliver of light that fell through the windows was pale lilac, and made Kate's room glow. Freddie hung there, in that woozy place between sleeping and waking, wondering if the girl next to him was a dream.

He concluded that he must still be dreaming when she shuffled herself closer into something almost like a snuggle. It felt good, the warmth of her, the feeling that he was grounded by her presence, made more solid just from being there. Freddie stretched out an arm and wrapped it around her in a way that could be construed as accidental if she woke up and questioned it. But instead of surprising her, Kate just rolled into it, tucked herself in closer, made a quiet noise almost like a purr.

That was when Freddie realised he was hard.

He felt intensely embarrassed and ashamed, and started analysing whether it was safer to stay and risk her noticing or whether it was riskier to untangle himself from her and escape, which could wake her up.

She must have been awake to notice, because Kate moved suddenly, slipping out of the bed and out of the room so quickly he was instantly scared. Where had she gone? When she came back five minutes later and ducked under the covers, he could feel the cold air lingering on her skin.

'Hey,' he heard Kate whisper, her mouth so close to his face that she was practically kissing it. Her breath was minty and he felt a rush of gratitude, of affection. She'd gone to brush her teeth.

'Hey,' he whispered in reply.

She kissed him. Not directly on the mouth, but just to the side, and feather-light. He moved again, just a bit, allowing Kate to get closer still. Now her face was right up against the sharp angle of his jaw, and she kissed him there too, as gentle as the sunrise.

Maybe it was the dreamlike haze of the early morning, or the woozy drunkenness of his just-woken brain coupled with the warmth of the cosy duvet, but Freddie found kissing much easier now. There were things he knew he would normally have worried about, but instead of wild sirens his anxiety felt more like far-off bells, distant background noise. He wanted to brush his own teeth, but he also felt like he didn't really need to. With Kate right there next to him, the freshness of her mouth felt clean enough.

They were kissing in slow rhythms, lazy and sensual. He let his hands move, tying the pleasing memory of her breasts from the night before with the real-life feel of them now, getting as much of a thrill from sensing them under his fingertips as he was from the sound of her responding to him. A feedback loop of pleasure; the more he touched and explored, always carefully, at least at first, the more she explored right back. At some point, Kate reached for him under the duvet, tender like a tiptoe. When she got there, finally, he couldn't help the response.

'I think I want to . . .' she suggested, her eyes closed, her face nuzzled against him.

'Yeah?' Freddie asked, wondering, hoping he had understood her properly.

'Yeah. Do you want to?'

'Yes, I do,' he said.

Kate shifted away and went to her bedside table, and he stayed perfectly still, scared of breaking whatever spell this was. There were no words as Freddie shifted up in the bed and turned to get ready for her. No awkward chitchat, and no anxious fumbling. Just the silence of the morning and the surprising peacefulness of it all.

When it happened, it was soft and slow. He felt her tense beneath him, a tiny moment of something that might have been discomfort, but when she didn't say anything, he continued, tentative and aware. She made noises; not the wild moans of porn stars, but something more like the sound of someone who had found the most delicious ice cream in the world. It felt good for him too, like roaring and punching but also like collapsing into a comfy chair at the end of a long day. Power and relief all at once. He was scared by how good it felt.

They were silent for a while afterwards. There didn't seem to be any need for words. Freddie thought that they might even be able to fall back asleep; but not long after, the mattress tilted as Kate got up and dashed across the hall to the bathroom. The coldness of the air as the duvet lifted and revealed him was enough to snap Freddie out of the reverie and back into real life. Through the single-glazed windows he heard birds chirping, the rush of car engines and planes flying overhead.

His ease collapsed around him once he was alone, allowing the worry and panic to come crowding in.

'So . . .' Kate said hopefully when she got back from the bathroom, climbing back into the bed with him.

'Yeah,' he replied. He was thinking. Thinking about what he should be saying, what he should be doing.

'We did it!'

'We did.'

Silence again. He could tell that Kate wanted to talk, but just didn't know what he could say back to her. There were so many wrong things, and the right things felt impossible to conjure.

'Was it OK?' she asked. All he could do was nod in return, as he bit at his lips. 'Do you want some tea? I can make breakfast?'

'Sure.'

'I'll be in the kitchen if you need anything.'

She wrapped herself up in her dressing gown and crept away, but even as he thought that he should be getting up to help, he found that he couldn't move.

Freddie blinked hard as he replayed what had happened. How did he know how to do that? Nobody had taught him, as such. But when he was there, in the moment and on top of her, that pressing need for friction, and the desire to just keep going and push through, had been intense and automatic. He had tried to be slow and gentle, but now he was scared that he had been too wild, that he might have hurt her, that she was too polite to say anything about it. He supposed that he could just ask, that they could talk about it, but he didn't think he could possibly handle that right now.

His plan now was to eat a little something and then get himself out of Kate's flat as quickly as possible. His stomach rumbled.

Kate was glowing. Freddie took her in as he stood in the kitchen doorway. In that tiny moment before she noticed him and he felt forced to retreat into his mental hole of worry, he watched her and marvelled at how happy she seemed. He had never seen a woman glow before, but there she was, stirring eggs in a pan over the hob, and she was shining.

Had he done that? Had he made her feel that way?

'I guessed you couldn't really go wrong with scrambled eggs,' Kate offered when she saw him. The shine dialled itself down, she was retreating.

'Yeah, that's fine,' Freddie said, coughing through an unexpectedly dry throat.

'How do you take your tea?' Kate asked, switching the kettle on. At the very moment she did so, two slices of toast pinged out of the toaster.

'Brewed a while, not too much milk, one sugar,' Freddie mumbled, before adding, 'but let me get the tea. I'll do the tea. Where do you keep the mugs?'

They danced around each other in the kitchen. Freddie was reminded of a science project he once had. He had spent an entire weekend making one of those games where you passed a wire circle over another wire and tried not to have them touch for fear of connecting the circuit and making the buzzer go off. Now, in her tiny, cupboard-sized kitchen, they were both charged wires, and Freddie was using all his energy and attention to make sure they didn't touch and spark.

The breakfast was good and Freddie wondered if he had ever been this hungry in his whole life. Without him asking her to, Kate got up to put some more bread in the toaster and refilled the kettle.

'This is really nice,' he said, and he meant it.

'I like making food for more than one person,' Kate said. She had come back to the table and was using her fork to play with the last remnants of egg on her plate.

'You're a good cook,' Freddie offered, not knowing what else to say.

'It's just scrambled eggs,' Kate scoffed.

After the next round of toast, Freddie decided that it really was time for him to be leaving. He had always thought it would be perfectly easy to stay friends after their little experiment had ended, that life would go back to being exactly how it was before. It was meant to be easy. What Freddie hadn't taken into account was the sheer complexity of emotions involved, and the fact that he would enjoy it so much. Because he had, hadn't he? He thought he had enjoyed it. At least, he figured that he would want to do it again at some point, if he ever got the chance.

'We don't have to talk about it, if you don't want to,' Kate said finally, noticing that he was hesitating over his empty plate and finished cup of tea.

What was Freddie meant to say to that? He had no idea.

'I think . . .' He looked up at her guiltily as she struggled to find the right words. 'I think that it was good and I just wanted to tell you that.'

'It was good,' Freddie conceded, the shame reaching his face in a fierce red blush. He thought about that moment of release, the pure ecstasy of it, with all the associated noises and facial expressions, and wondered how Kate could stand to look at him.

'I just feel like maybe I sprang it on you, and the way I sprang it on you wasn't fair, especially after how things were last night. I'm sorry for that, I wasn't expecting it either.'

'No, it's fine. It worked out fine,' Freddie said. He realised that he probably didn't sound like he meant it, but he did.

'Well, I'm pleased it happened. I'm pleased it happened in that way too.'

'So am I.'

'OK. That's good then.'

'Yeah.'

Freddie helped Kate clear up, still sensing and avoiding that static electric thing that was happening between them, and then went to brush his teeth and wash his face, before collecting his things and getting ready to go home. He felt Kate watching him the whole time. Thinking about him.

'Busy Saturday planned?' Kate asked as he stood in her entryway, backpack over one shoulder.

'Not really. Was going to play some games. Maybe read some comics. You?'

'Packing, mostly,' Kate sighed, looking back over her domain. Freddie noticed the flattened cardboard boxes ready to be assembled, the chunky roll of black bin liners on the coffee table in front of the sofa.

'OK, well,' he paused. Now was the time. He could kiss her again – surely she wouldn't mind if he kissed her again? 'I'll see you around?'

The chance was gone.

'Sure,' said Kate.

He couldn't make out her expression, it was hard to read.

And then Freddie was outside her flat, and the door was closed behind him.

18

Freddie hadn't called her, hadn't texted her, hadn't anything-ed her. It was as if, once he had said goodbye after breakfast on Saturday morning, he had vanished off the face of the earth. Kate remembered his expression, something like terror, something like reticence, his inability to look her in the eye. She wondered if he regretted what they had done. She wondered, even though he had said that he had wanted it, if this whole endeavour was something Kate had forced upon him, whether Freddie was someone too shy to be able to say no. She felt like a terrible person.

But she also couldn't ignore how she had felt that morning. How he had felt. There had been no screaming orgasm, but there had been something, a feeling of blooming deep inside her, a feeling like real pleasure was there and reachable, but still buried. She just had to dig a little further, she just had to be a little more patient. Kate thought about Freddie's body, the weight and the warmth of it, and was surprised at the feelings it conjured in her now, wondered if they were directly related to him, or more generalised. Was it having sex with Freddie that she had enjoyed, or the feeling of having sex itself? Would it be like that with others? Could it be better?

'You OK?' Renee asked as they sat in the staff room waiting for the morning briefing.

'Yes. No. I don't know,' Kate sighed, adjusting the shirt of her uniform. She felt self-conscious.

'So, how's Freddie?'

Kate stopped suddenly and glanced at her friend, worried. Was '*I just had sex for the first time*' written in felt-tip pen right across her forehead?

'Has something happened?' Renee asked again.

Kate didn't get a chance to reply because suddenly Beth was there, shuffling her papers and delivering the daily briefing. After she had finished and officially dispersed everybody to their posts, she called out: 'Oh Kate, before you go upstairs?'

'I'll talk to you later,' Renee mouthed meaningfully as she left with everybody else.

'So, I've been talking with the Learning and Development team about that role you were interested in.' Kate prepared herself for bad news, but Beth was smiling, her tone cheerful. 'It turns out that the team there are in a bit of a pickle, and need some interim help before the new role can be properly filled. I put you forward – I hope you don't mind?'

'No, I don't mind at all,' Kate replied, trying to contain her eagerness.

'They're willing to consider it an elongated interview. A chance to see if it's a good fit for both of you. What do you think?'

'I think that's fine; better than fine, in fact. I'd be happy to do it.'

'Great. In which case, you start first thing tomorrow morning. Check with them what code you need to put in when you do your timecard. Don't forget, otherwise you won't get paid properly.'

'I'd get paid more?'

'Not much more, I'm afraid, but a bit. You know how tight things are around here. But it's something.'

'Thank you so much, Beth. I really appreciate it.'

'Don't worry – you've been putting in the work here. I'll be sad to see you go, but you'll just be upstairs.'

'It's just temporary, I'll be back.'

Beth smiled, and then was on her way.

* * *

'What did Beth want to talk to you about earlier?' Renee asked when lunch rolled around.

'They're trying me out in the Learning and Development office, for that job I wanted to go for,' Kate replied happily.

'No *way*. That's so cool. I knew good things were around the corner for you!'

'I start tomorrow, can you believe it?'

'So soon?'

'I guess they're desperate. It's temporary, but I think if I impress them then they'll let me stay on.'

'Gosh, look at you,' Renee stared at Kate curiously. 'There's something happening . . . a vibe. Is it the job, or is it that Freddie guy? Or both?'

'We're just friends, me and Freddie,' Kate said quickly.

'I don't believe you.'

Kate took a moment to consider if now was the right time, if this was something that she wanted to reveal. She hadn't even told Lindsey the full details. They'd messaged afterwards, but Kate had felt coy, wanting to keep it to herself for a while before letting her friends in. She'd wanted to protect the moment in a tight warm hug inside herself for as long as possible. But it was easier with Lindsey. A few blushing emojis followed by the aubergine emoji was enough to keep her at bay. With Renee right in front of her, it was harder to be discreet.

'He came over on Friday night.'

'And?'

'And we . . .'

'You didn't?'

'I did.'

'Good for you! I knew you liked him!'

'I'm not sure I . . .' Kate stuttered before Renee interrupted her, eager for gossip.

'So, was it good?'

'Um . . . I guess?'

'Which means it wasn't good.'

'No, it was good.'

'If it was good, you'd know. You hesitated. If it was good, there'd be no hesitation.'

Kate didn't know how to tell Renee that she didn't have much to compare it to. She had liked it. She wanted to do it again. But there were threads of angst tied up in it too, and confusion about how Freddie had reacted afterwards. It made her uncertain to claim the experience as a total success.

'No, it's not that: it was good and I think it could be even better next time. But the problem is, I think it might have been a one-time thing,' Kate admitted to Renee, trying to sound confident, and not too sad about it.

'Really?'

'Yeah. We're really different, and he's got a lot going on—'

'So that means you need to get back on the horse. Pronto.'

'I do?'

'Yes, you do. Freddie is the past. More boys are the future. This is your time, Kate! Everything is looking up for you and you need to make the most of it. What about finally embracing online dating?'

'Tinder is awful though.'

'Doesn't have to be Tinder. There are loads of other ones out there. Ones where you get to read more about the person. Personality type stuff.'

'I'm not sure, it feels a bit soon.'

'Kate. You can do this. If you want to get yourself over a one-time guy, the only way to do it is with another one. Just have fun.'

Renee reminded Kate of a sweet puppy when she was sincere. Her eyes were glittering in the staff-room light, large and hopeful. It made it very hard to say no to her.

'When I get home later, I'll try some apps and see what happens.'

Once Kate got home, she got to work. She downloaded the app Renee had suggested, wrote a basic profile and started flicking through the pictures of eligible men. Somehow, some of Renee's electric hope had fired its way into her and she was happy and excited. She felt good. Her body felt good. She remembered again the way Freddie's hands had felt, how she had discovered nerve endings she had no idea previously existed, and knew that she wanted to feel like that again. If all she had with Freddie was their silly little virginity pact, if he didn't feel anything more, then what was stopping her from finding someone else and trying again?

She was a little stunned when she matched with Ethan. He was good-looking, in a quirky, interesting way, with a patch of white in the stubble of his otherwise dark beard. The written part of his profile was appealing too: he'd just come back from a three-month trip to East Asia, undertaken after he'd decided to jack in his desk job in the City, and was now a freelance creative, whatever that meant. He said that he hated being tied into gym membership contracts and preferred to go on long runs instead. He cycled around the city, didn't have the head for novels, but liked popular science audio books by 'leading thinkers'.

Kate was nervous about her photos though, not because she thought they were bad; the opposite actually. She liked the way she looked in them, but wondered if they told any objective truths. There was a way to position the face, a way to hold the camera, and a direction against the light, which all conspired to give her face sharpness, and give her cheekbones some semblance of definition. She hoped that she was being fair to herself, that she was being fair to whoever ended up picking her.

Hey, Ethan had messaged.

Hey back at ya, Kate had replied, smiling.

What are you up to? he had asked. She wondered if it was a sexual question, but then reasoned that it was still only seven in the evening.

Pretty tired, long week at work.

What do you do?

I work in an art gallery.

That's really cool. I used to paint a lot, Ethan typed.

I did too but haven't for a long time. Keep meaning to take it back up.

Ethan was cute, at least in his messages. He kept the chat restrained to conventional conversation, no asking what she was wearing, or requests for photos. He professed to being a feminist, which impressed Kate, and told her that he always thought of himself as a sapiosexual. She had to look that one up and was relieved by what she found.

He seemed genuine and easy-going, and the arrangement to meet came quickly.

Kate was waiting for him by Bill's just behind Long Acre, the night bright with the Covent Garden bustle, the air cool after a heavy rain shower that had passed quickly earlier in the afternoon.

She was a little surprised when he didn't look exactly like his photos, but not enough to be turned off the idea of spending the evening with him. Ethan had listed his age as twenty-nine and his height as six foot two. Neither seemed to be accurate. If Kate had to guess, she would have put his age nearer thirty-five. Also, she was five foot nine and he was only a bit taller than her. But she pushed her concerns away and considered that as her photos were styled to be as flattering as possible, he might be a little surprised seeing her in the flesh too.

At least it was definitely him. The beard had grown out since he took the profile photos, and was a little unkempt, but there was that distinct white patch regardless. He smiled when their eyes met.

'Hi, Kate!' He went right in for a hug, which she found reassuring, and flattering. 'Did you get here OK?'

'Yes, I only work around the corner.'

'At the gallery?'

'Yes.' She liked that he had remembered. 'How about you? A good day?'

'Ah, you know. I'm between contracts at the moment, so just trying to keep myself busy with other things.'

Kate wondered if that was code for him being unemployed, but chose not to dwell on it.

They went into the restaurant and Kate felt herself stiffen when Ethan held out the chair for her when they got to their table. It seemed a pretty old-fashioned gesture for someone who had proudly announced that he was a feminist. She took him in, noticing that his T-shirt was a little stretched out and faded, his jeans battered and slouchy. Another thing she brushed aside. First dates from online apps were casual and informal, weren't they? Wearing a nice wrap dress and her black boots, maybe she was the one who had got the date-wear wrong?

'Starters?' Kate asked, glancing over the menu.

'How about straight to mains?' Ethan countered.

'OK, I'm more of a dessert person anyway.'

'Oh, I'm not really that into sweet things,' he added. Maybe he was broke; Kate could empathise with that. Except that when she checked the menu, she decided that she really wanted a starter. She resolved to offer to share, and to insist on paying her side of the bill. Once again she thought about his profile, how he had declared himself a feminist, and thought that it wouldn't be a big deal.

Ethan watched her eat her fried halloumi sticks in silence, his hands in his lap.

'So, tell me about your travelling? Where exactly did you go?' Kate asked between mouthfuls.

'Oh, you know, the normal places.'

'Like where?'

'I did Thailand and Singapore, then South Korea, finally ending up in Japan.'

'Wow. I wish I could just escape like that. What was your favourite place to visit?'

'I honestly don't think you've lived until you've slept on a beach in Thailand, under the full moon. It just puts everything else into perspective, you know? Like nothing really matters in this life, like all the things we think are important are actually not that important at all.'

'I feel that. Or, at least, I wish I could feel that. But, you know, rent. And money in general. Are you sure you don't want one of these?' she said, gesturing at her plate.

Ethan declined, and Kate detected a slightly worried look on his face.

Conversation was stilted as they ate their mains. Kate had chosen a Caesar salad because she figured it would seem a little more delicate after the halloumi, plus there was less chance she would end up with anything down her front, while Ethan went straight in with his hands on his burger, chomping down and getting covered in sauce in the process. It wasn't pretty.

'Are you really going to have dessert?' Ethan asked when she asked the waiter for the menu.

This was the first nice meal she'd had out in ages, and she had wanted dessert. Then she wondered: was he commenting on her weight? Or was he just in a hurry to leave?

She put the menu down and asked the waiter for a decaf coffee instead. She felt deflated and uncertain. But otherwise, he was being fairly pleasant, so she put her insecurities about him aside, yet again.

'Let me pay for what I had,' Kate said when the bill came. Ethan was being strangely protective over letting her see it, even though she could easily guess what was there.

'No, this is a date. I've got this.'

'I insist. I had a starter, and a glass of wine. You didn't even drink.'

'Well, I insist too.' With his head bent down as he got his wallet from his pocket, the subdued lighting cast angry shadows over his face. He wasn't being playful. Kate wondered if he was angry with her but let him get on with it.

Afterwards they walked. He was being nice again. They joked, she laughed. They talked about South Korea and Japan, and Kate told him about the big corporate job she used to have. She didn't mention she'd been made redundant from it, but she wanted to tell him about her life there because she thought that breaking free of it was something they had in common.

She knew where they were headed, and felt a tangle of hope and dread as she rounded the corner and saw it: the rainbow alley she'd found with Freddie. This time it was stuffed with people posing for pictures, and Kate didn't suggest that they stop to experience it. She didn't think that Ethan had noticed it at all, or if he had, he clearly wasn't interested.

As they walked, Kate tried to imagine having sex with Ethan, and what it might be like. There would have been a time, not so long ago, where she would have been freaking out by this point, wondering how she was going to broach the subject of her virginity. She imagined all sorts of possibilities: men getting angry with her, men laughing at her, men simply walking out of the door without any further attempt at communication. She liked that she didn't have to have that horrible conversation any more and reckoned that she could probably get away with passing off her still considerable inexperience as nerves.

Ethan was nice enough. She wasn't experiencing any fire-cracker emotions but Kate was beginning to wonder if they even existed. Maybe she just wasn't a fire-cracker emotions kind of person. She didn't mind Ethan's body, and if he didn't mind hers, then why shouldn't they sleep together? This could be fine. Kate was determined this would be fine. She looked up at Ethan and smiled at him. He smiled back.

'Sorry it's all in boxes,' Kate said when she brought Ethan back to her place. She had wanted to see where he lived, but he said that it wasn't a good idea.

'I'm in the process of moving,' she added.

A lot had made its way over to her parents since Freddie had been there just a week before. There were only bare essentials in the kitchen, and all her knick-knacks assembled over the past few years had been packed up and shoved out of the way. She offered Ethan a drink in the only glass she had left and made herself a drink in the one remaining mug. It wasn't even a fresh bottle of wine, but one that was already half-empty from a few nights before.

When they sat on the sofa she asked about the white patch in his beard.

'Everyone asks about it,' he moaned. 'And it's not even that interesting. It's just a patch, it doesn't mean anything. I've had it forever, but I guess no one could really see it until I grew my beard. To be honest, I'm a little bit tired of talking about it. I don't ask you about the colour of your hair.'

Kate sat still, holding tight to her mug of wine. She had this sensation of forcing herself smaller, of folding herself up into a tiny box so that she didn't take up so much space.

'Sorry,' Ethan said finally, after noticing the silence that followed it. 'I snapped, I'm sorry.'

'It's fine. It was a stupid question.'

'I just hate small talk, you know? After everything I've experienced, after you feel that kind of bliss, it's just hard to go back to things that are so trivial and meaningless.'

'I don't think that making conversation is meaningless. I was just trying to get to know you.'

Kate absently wondered how she was going to get Ethan out of her house, if she needed to. But then he started being sweet again.

'I think I'm nervous around you,' he admitted, looking down into his glass of wine. 'You make me nervous; I think you're pretty amazing.'

'You do?' Kate did not feel amazing.

'Well, look at you. You're beautiful, and you're confident, and you know what you're talking about. I like that about you. I like it a lot.'

Kate blushed and felt her heart move inside her; not a pang of desire exactly, more of a lurch, but maybe it was possible she was confusing things. Nobody had ever called her beautiful before. Nobody in her whole life, bar maybe her parents when she was a lot younger, had ever told her that they thought she was beautiful.

'I think you're someone I could see a future with.'

Kate couldn't think of any meaningful words to say back, but it turned out that she didn't need to, because suddenly he was kissing her, hungrily. He was almost climbing over her, pushing her back on the sofa, his hands already on her breasts. Kate barely had the chance to put her mug of wine down before she gave in, letting him push into her, completely dominating her space. His physicality was just as overwhelming as his words, leaving her no room to breathe or think. He was just suddenly there, all over her.

'Wait, wait,' Kate said, pushing back, trying to gain her breath, trying not to dwell too long on the strange, new taste of his mouth.

Ethan sat back in his place on the sofa, looking like he was struggling to regain his composure.

'I'm sorry,' he said. 'It's just, I think you do something to me. It's like I can't help but be an animal around you. I've been holding back all evening, you're just so beautiful.'

Now Kate knew that he was lying, but she also wasn't sure if she cared. It was just sex. Sex that she wanted.

I can turn the tables on this, Kate thought. *I can control it.*

Ethan was just as much an opportunity for her as she was for him. There was sex, laid out on the table right in front of her. He clearly wanted it, wanted her, and she was allowed to want sex for sex's sake too, wasn't she? Yes, it was a shame that it came wrapped up in a scumbag package (by this point Kate was wondering how much else he had told her was a lie; whether he had ever been to East Asia, or if he had been on a long-distance run in his entire life), but who was she to be choosy?

Kate told herself that this was what she wanted. That this was what she had to do to get the feelings that she wanted to feel.

'Let's go to the bedroom,' she decided, and his eyes grew wide with surprise and satisfaction.

There was no hesitation here either, just instant and insistent fumbling. The fact that Kate didn't know what to do or where to put her hands didn't matter as Ethan's mouth was constantly attached to hers, his hands heavy on her, pawing and prodding. The moment her dress was unwrapped, his hands moved to the top of her tights. The moment they were rolled down, he was unhooking her bra. Then, after he flung his top off and to the other side of her room, he announced: 'I'm turning the lights off.'

Again, there was no chance to object. Ethan practically jumped off the bed to flick the switch, before he was suddenly back to kissing her. There was something automatic about his technique, like a machine hard at work, but she didn't know how to tell him. In fact, there seemed to be no way to tell him anything, because the kissing could have almost been designed solely to shut her up and stop her complaining.

'Slow down, slow down,' Kate said, eventually managing to pull herself away.

'What?' Ethan asked. In the darkness, he seemed to have lost his ability to tell her she was beautiful. His tone was gruff and impatient.

'I just don't think we have to move this fast,' Kate said.

'You're not one of these "three date" girls, are you? I thought this was a done deal.'

'No, I'm talking about this precise moment. It's a bit much. What's the hurry? Why the rush?'

'Look, you took me to the bedroom, so is this going to happen or not? I have an interview in the morning and I'd like to get off sometime soon, before it gets too late.'

'Wow, that's romantic.'

He growled. Or was it a groan? Either way, a sound came out of him that revealed his annoyance.

'I thought I was the one doing you a favour here.'

'Wait, *what?*'

He sighed and the bed shifted as he fell backwards, as if he had given up. Kate sat still, utterly paralysed with contempt. She had him pegged on the scumbag scale for sure, but not to this extent. Who the hell was this guy?

'So this is clearly not going to happen now, so I give up. Home truth time. I don't like you, you're not exactly my type, but I thought this would be easy.'

'Easy? Your type? So what was the plan here?'

'Don't be an idiot. You know what's going on.'

'Clearly I am an idiot. Enlighten me.' Kate got up and went to get her dressing gown before she turned on the light switch. She looked back at the bed, at the man who was there, lying all the way back, his hand rubbing his forehead in frustration, his proud erection clearly still in evidence. Kate wondered if she was going to vomit with repulsion.

'You're going to make me say it?'

'Say it.'

'I just needed to get laid. I've got a big day tomorrow and

I need to relieve the tension. I know girls like you need a bit of wining and dining first, so I did that. I even paid for it.'

She stared at him, feeling her rage build, and determined not to let him see the tears that were forming. 'So what, you think I owe you?'

'Whatever.'

He paused. Kate wondered if perhaps he had enough humanity to stop talking because he could see that she was upset, but apparently not.

'Are you at least going to let me jerk off before I leave? I'm not going home like this,' he gestured to his penis.

'Get out,' Kate snarled. He stared at her, disbelieving, so she repeated it, louder: 'Get out *now*.'

Without time to get himself together properly, Ethan was forced to put his jeans on first and stuff his underwear into his pockets. Kate stayed intimidatingly close as he grabbed his socks, shoes and coat, before slamming her front door behind him, so that he'd have to finish sorting himself out in the hallway.

'Damn it,' she murmured to herself, after she had heard him leave the building.

Still, she would not let herself cry. She would have broken utterly if she had let a single tear fall. She briefly thought about ringing Renee, but couldn't bear the thought of her friend's ferocity. She'd surely want to hunt the man down and shred his flesh with her fingernails, before telling Kate to pick herself up and try again. But that wasn't what she wanted. Calling Lindsey was out of the question too; it was very early in the morning in Hong Kong, and she didn't want to cause any upset when it was impossible for Lindsey to do anything from the other side of the world.

She didn't want Renee, and she didn't want Lindsey.

What she wanted was someone who would listen to her and be kind to her.

What she wanted was Freddie.

19

He'd drafted a bunch of messages to send to her, but none of them had been quite right. Some sounded too chill, some not nearly chill enough. He didn't know if he should say a simple thank you, or if she had expected anything more. He thought briefly about sending her flowers, but wondered if that was corny and old-fashioned, and also whether it was appropriate for 'just friends'. Flowers felt like something more. So he waited, hoping that the right idea would pop into his head suddenly, but the inspiration never hit, and the moment passed. The moment was still passing. The moment had gone on longer than a week.

This wasn't a romance and could never be one. So why couldn't he stop thinking about her? Why did the very idea of sending her a simple message fill his head with so much turmoil? Eventually he started thinking that forgetting everything, and just disappearing from each other's lives, would be the easiest thing. The only way to avoid any awkwardness. The only way to stop him getting hurt.

'So, you're not dead then?' Damien peered around the doorway, eyes squinting in mock concern, tone droll. 'Thought I should probably check.'

Freddie was lying on his bed staring at the ceiling, the comic he was reading dangling from one hand towards the floor.

'Aren't you meant to be asleep?' he asked. 'It's daytime.'

'Things to do today, people to see. Which is more than can be said for you, apparently?'

Freddie groaned and rolled over on to his front, hoping his flatmate would take the hint and leave him alone.

'Freddie, are you depressed?' Damien asked in a matter-of-fact but not unkind voice.

'What? No.'

'Because you seem pretty depressed right now.'

'I'm not depressed.'

'I just think it's good for me to know these things in case I have to get in touch with your emergency contacts or anything.'

'We haven't swapped emergency contacts, Damien.'

'No, but should we? In case your depression gets worse?'

It was hard to tell whether Damien was joking or not. It was possible that this was his way of expressing concern, Freddie pondered, but it was doing little to help.

'Is this about that girl?' Damien asked. 'Did you try the frog?'

'I just want peace and quiet, please.'

'Did she dump you?'

'No, she didn't dump me.'

Damien stood in the doorway, impassive, like a heavy, expressionless statue.

'What is it, Damien? Why are you just standing there?'

'I think it's time to pop the kombucha,' he announced finally.

'The what?'

'Come with me.'

Curiosity getting the better of him, Freddie met Damien in the kitchen, where he was hovering over his personal cupboard. Most of the space in the small kitchen was shared, but where they could, both Freddie and his flatmate had found private places to keep the food and treats they didn't want the other to know about. Freddie's contained a box of too-sugary cereal he saved for weekends and some other guilty pleasure snacks, as well as his favourite frying pan and a couple of mugs he felt protective over. Damien's cupboard, on the other hand, contained three mysterious flip-top bottles filled with what could only be described as luminous golden liquids.

Damien studied the bottles carefully, lifting them up to see them catch the light, gently swirling the contents, and on one of them, flipping the lid to take in the aroma. The expression on his face was the closest Freddie had ever seen him get to a genuine, happy smile. Just the tiniest of movements from the muscles around his lips.

'This one is ready,' Damien declared soberly.

'What is this stuff? Is it safe?' Freddie asked.

He had visions of his flatmate concocting illegal moonshine (was this illegal?) and running some sort of alcoholic drug-den from their home. And yet there was something magical about the potions too. The way they glowed in the light, and their intoxicating molten-gold colour.

Damien put the other two bottles back in his private cupboard and brought the chosen one over to the counter.

'This has been brewing for nearly two weeks now, and was crafted from the finest black tea leaves I could find,' Damien explained. 'I then flavoured it with blackberries and elderflower. Would you like me to leave them in, or strain them out?'

'Damien, what is it?'

'Kombucha,' Damien replied.

'Ah, yes,' Freddie tried to think about how to say it without coming across as too naïve. He had heard of kombucha, he just had no idea what it actually was. 'Explain what it is to me?'

'Fermented tea,' Damien said. When he saw Freddie's questioning face, he continued. 'Veronica, my friend who you have had the pleasure to meet, bestowed on me what is known as a scoby. A bacterial culture that allows the tea to ferment.'

'Bacteria?' Freddie questioned.

'I understand your concern. It's not going to do you any harm. No more than yoghurt would, I suppose.'

'Right.' Freddie understood the logic of it. He knew that not all bacteria was bad, that a fair bit of it was actually good and useful, but even so, he still wasn't sure.

Damien stood poised over two glass tumblers, the kombucha bottle hovering over the first one. 'Strained, or no?' he checked again.

'No,' Freddie replied softly. His flatmate proceeded to decant the drinks with the reverence of a priest pouring the wine for Mass.

Finally, Damien handed Freddie the glass, which he then brought under his nose for a cautious sniff.

'Is it alcoholic?' he asked, still worried about the possibility of illegal moonshine.

'Barely,' Damien replied.

'It's not hallucinogenic or anything like that? And the bacteria is definitely good bacteria?'

'It'll do you good, I think.'

Damien went first, taking in a hearty sip before expressing his satisfaction with a loud sigh.

'You really didn't have to go to all this trouble,' Freddie said, still vaguely worried, although it did smell good.

'Dark times call for extreme measures. And you have just been dumped, after all.'

'I haven't been dumped,' Freddie said quietly. He almost wished he had, as that would at least mean that whatever he had with Kate had a label that he understood.

'If by sharing this with you, my most prized concoction, I can make you feel just a little bit stronger, just a touch more powerful, then I will feel like I have done a good thing. Women are an unfathomable species. They fill our hearts and then they break them,' Damien intoned like a sermon. 'Now, please drink.'

'This all feels a little ritualistic.'

'We are celebrating freeing your heart from the shackles of mighty Venus. We are celebrating your victory over the forces of feminine wiles.' Freddie wondered what exactly the deal with Veronica was.

'Right.' Freddie took a sip of the precious kombucha, swallowed it back too quickly, and instantly regretted it.

'Good, isn't it?' Damien asked.

'No!' Freddie cried, before catching the hurt in his flatmate's eyes. 'I mean, it's unexpected.'

'An acquired taste, perhaps,' Damien reflected.

Freddie had caught the blackcurrant and elderflower, but what he'd also caught was something distinctly vinegary, a potent tang that he wasn't prepared for. He remembered what it had been like when he tried alcohol for the first time. Freddie had been twelve, his brother fifteen and surrounded by friends who looked even older still. David had goaded his little brother into drinking from a bottle of vodka, reassuring him that it was no big deal, and that he would like it. Freddie hadn't been prepared back then either, had felt the rush of heat at the back of his throat and thought he was going to lose all his breath. It took a while before he learned to appreciate the kick, and then to want it.

Not wanting to disappoint his flatmate when he had made such a rare and poignant gesture, Freddie took another nervous sip and waited for the sensation to become pleasurable. It was easier to hide his revulsion this time, but the taste was just as potent and strange.

Freddie winced as the fruity-vinegar tang travelled through him, then put the tumbler back down on the counter. There would have been a time, not even that long ago, when the thought of his mouth being potentially contaminated with weird new bacteria would have been enough to send him into a spiral of self-hate and despair. He would have been desperately looking up diseases, checking his temperature every half hour, brushing his teeth until his gums bled and his tongue was stripped and raw. The thoughts would have been insistent, loud and inescapable. And they *were* there, Freddie realised, creeping around his head and flaring like faraway fireworks, but he could ignore them.

'You won't mind if I don't finish it?' he asked.

'No,' Damien replied, but Freddie noted the subtle inflection of disappointment.

'Really? Because I'm grateful and everything, I really appreciate the gesture, I just . . . I don't know if it's for me.'

'I won't be upset, Freddie.'

'You sure?'

'All the more for me,' Damien sighed quietly, turning away to finish his home-brewed kombucha in peace.

Reluctant to stay in the flat when he knew Damien was going to be around, Freddie decided that it would be just as easy to mope outdoors as it would inside. Besides which, he had a week until his parents' big anniversary party, and he needed to get them a present.

Freddie hated present-buying. The last one he bought, Lacey's cuddly dinosaur, hadn't exactly gone well. There were just too many options, and no accurate way to predict whether someone was going to like it or not. Plus, there were other unknowable factors, like duplicating something the gift-receiver already had, or getting them something that would conjure up bad memories. He always wanted his gift to be meaningful, special, a token of himself that he could hand to the other person, but the pressure of that only brought added anxiety.

He found himself on Oxford Street on a Saturday afternoon. It was not a pleasant experience. His walking pace seemed to be completely at odds with the pace of everyone else around him; sometimes too slow, sometimes too fast, and sometimes groups of people walked in a way that blocked up chunks of the pavement, meaning he'd have to clumsily zigzag around them. There was none of the order of commuters early on a weekday morning, all on a mission to get to where they needed to be at a reasonable, brisk pace. This was chaos.

Finally, Freddie managed to divert himself into a department store, gleaming and clean, and set himself the task of discovering the perfect gift. He stared at the store directory for so long that an assistant in a badly fitting blazer asked if he needed help.

'Gifts?' he'd asked back, awkwardly.

The assistant, not dropping their perfect customer service smile, replied, 'Everything here could feasibly be a gift.'

I know, Freddie thought.

He shrugged at the assistant before extricating himself, letting a nearby escalator take him to another floor, hoping that the perfect gift would jump out at him. Just like he had hoped the perfect message to send to Kate would creep into his brain unannounced too. Freddie wondered if he expected too much from his brain, if his brain wasn't on his side after all.

He wandered through menswear, and found himself in a section devoted to lingerie, which just made him think of Kate. Hurrying out, one floor up and in the children's department, he wondered if he was too old to buy himself a Lego kit, before he came to the lighting department. Freddie was immediately drawn to one fixture in particular, a set of panels affixed to a wall that was programmed to run through a sequence of colours, like a rainbow. As he stood before it, he felt himself washed with reds, then oranges and yellow, and as he closed his eyes the darkness became infused with greens, and then blues and violets. He remembered the alleyway. How happy Kate had looked smiling in the colours.

Before he had a chance to think it through, Freddie whipped out his phone and took a video, just a few seconds of footage as the light panels ran through their sequence. Then he sent it to her.

He hated himself once he had done it. Hated that he hadn't even bothered attaching words. Worried that it was too abstract and she wouldn't get it. What if she didn't remember? As he shoved it in his pocket, he felt it vibrate in response. Kate had messaged back. He was too nervous to bring it out again, scared that she might hate him, that she had replied with abuse or, somehow worse, baffled question marks. He kept walking through the lighting department, pretending that he was interested in filaments and desk lights and shrugging off attendants who came to help him.

On the escalator heading up to the next floor, he finally dared himself to see what she had written.

Where are you? Followed by a smiley face and a rainbow emoji. Freddie's heart fluttered with relief.

He replied with the name of the department store.

I'm not far from there right now. Want to meet?

Freddie didn't know what he wanted, didn't know what Kate really wanted either, so he replied: *Sure.*

They met in the café at the top of the department store, which had windows that looked out over the roofs of Oxford Street and Mayfair beyond. Freddie couldn't remember being this nervous meeting someone. He was more nervous than when he went on his date with Mia. Here, right now, he felt like he had no control, had no idea what Kate might be thinking or feeling. Was she angry at him for not contacting her? Had she been lying when she said she had enjoyed their night together? He had no protocols for this situation. No script.

'Hey,' she said as she sat down. She looked pretty. The weather was starting to get warmer, and she was wearing a dress under her coat.

'Hey,' he mumbled in reply.

Neither spoke for a long moment. Freddie played with his coffee cup, moving it around in its saucer, seeing how much he could do without making it cause a sound. Kate was feeding sugar into hers and stirring vigorously. First one sachet, then one more, and then another. He got the sense that she was just as nervous as him, but had no idea how to solve it.

'Sorry I didn't get in touch after,' she said finally.

'No, I'm sorry I didn't get in touch with *you*,' he replied, startled. 'I should have reached out, thanked you, or said something.'

'Yeah, maybe. But I could have done too.'

'I was nervous,' Freddie admitted. 'I didn't know what to say.'

'I didn't either.'

'You're not regretting it?'

'No!' Kate blurted, almost too loud. 'No, God, no. I'm really not regretting it. Please don't think I am. I told you after, I liked it. It was good.'

'I thought it was good too.'

'Did you really? Because afterwards, you seemed . . . I don't know, distant? I worried that I had put too much pressure on you.'

'You didn't. It was fine. It was the right amount of pressure.'

'That's good.'

Silence again. Kate poured another sachet of sugar into her coffee.

'So why are you here?' she asked eventually.

'I have to buy a present for my parents. It's their anniversary this week. There's a big party next weekend.'

'Have you found something yet?'

'Nope. I have no idea what I'm doing.'

'I could help you, I guess. I used to work somewhere like this, once upon a time.'

'You did?'

'It wasn't as fancy as this one, but you end up knowing your way around a department store.'

Freddie let himself be led back down the escalators, down to where they kept home furnishings and scented candles. Kate picked a few out and held them up to her nose, which he liked to watch wrinkling up from either a frown or a smile, depending on the smell. He liked the way she wasn't afraid to touch things, picking pieces up and holding them close to inspect them, whilst Freddie had always felt that shops were a little like museums, and that you should keep a respectful distance from objects unless you meant to buy them.

'What do you think of these?' she asked, holding up some large fringed curtain tassels to the side of her head as if they were earrings. 'Too much?'

He smiled back at her, before nodding his head vigorously. She put the tassels back on the table and made a dramatic face like her heart was broken. He found her adorable.

Freddie liked how it felt being with Kate, how it felt knowing that she wasn't thinking about anything but being with him in that moment. Once more he had the feeling that if this was all there was left between them, if there was never anything more, that would be fine because it was comfortable, and safe.

Every time an invasive thought crept in, every time his imagination started to wonder what it might be like to spend all his time with Kate, to have her share the feelings he felt and return them to him, he cut them off. He'd been there before. He'd had hope, had bought it a Yorkie bar. He didn't want to get let down again.

'What about a photo frame?' Kate asked.

'My parents have lots of those,' Freddie replied.

'Well then, that's a good thing, isn't it? If they're the kind of people who like photo frames, then one from you would be meaningful. They could put their favourite picture of you in it.'

'They'd probably use it to put a picture of Lacey in. Lacey's my niece.'

'Well, that's fine too. Maybe you've got a picture of you and Lacey together? Or the whole family? You could put it in the frame for them.'

'You don't think it's too simple?'

'No, I think it's a good bet. But maybe you should get flowers too, or champagne or something.'

'You don't think flowers are corny?' he tested.

'I like flowers,' Kate replied.

Freddie stored the information away, and then berated himself for doing it. There would be no need for flowers in the future.

'So go on,' Kate said, indicating the array of photo frames in front of them. 'Now you have to pick one. One that you think your parents are really going to like.'

He cast his eyes over what appeared to be a vast field of options, conscious that Kate might be judging him for his choice too. He wanted to show her that he had taste, that he could make good decisions. Finally, his eyes fell on one that was formed from simple, silver geometric shapes, which reminded him in some way of the Chrysler building.

'My parents went on holiday to New York last year. This reminds me of that,' Freddie explained. Kate was smiling.

Then he remembered that his brother and Stella knew about Kate, that they expected her to be there too. He hadn't been planning on telling her about it, had hoped that if he just turned up alone, then nobody would bother to say anything to him anyway, but now, as he watched Kate investigate an incense burner, he wondered if maybe it would be fun, just another chance for them to hang out.

'You know. I never did tell you what happened at my brother's place that time, at the dinner party,' he started.

'When they tried to set you up with that guy?'

'Yeah. I only got out of it because they discovered that I was texting you.'

'I remember.'

Freddie steeled himself. Tensed his tummy muscles and faced a slightly different direction, hoped that he seemed casual enough, like nothing he was saying really mattered.

'They thought you were my girlfriend.'

'No *way*. Why didn't you tell me that?'

'I thought it would be weird. We didn't know each other as well as we do now.'

'That's hilarious!'

'Is it?' he asked. Kate didn't say anything. She seemed embarrassed. Freddie was starting to regret bringing this up, but he'd come so far now and would only hate himself more later on if he hadn't tried. 'They invited you to the party. They wanted to meet you.'

'Really?'

'I said that you'd be busy. But if you were free, if you wanted to come, then it might be fun?'

'I'll have to think about it,' Kate said. As they walked over to the tills, his steps felt slow and heavy.

'Sure.'

'But thank you, though. I mean, it sounds nice. And it would be great to see your parents receive their present.'

'It would be weird though, wouldn't it?'

'Maybe? I don't know. But if it would get them off your back? Make them stop setting you up with eligible men?'

'I wouldn't want you to come for that.'

'I could get on board with the pretend girlfriend thing . . .'

'It's silly.'

'Yeah, it's really silly.'

They reached the tills and Freddie presented the frame to the assistant, who offered to gift-wrap it for him. Freddie declined, thinking that he might try Kate's photo idea. He'd need to find a good one and get it printed somewhere first. Kate stood next to him, closer than she needed to be, he thought, and then suddenly, without warning, she placed a comforting hand on his arm. Despite the layers of clothes between them, his top and then his thick coat, somehow her hand felt warm, a warmth that radiated and heated up his face, making the back of his neck prickle. He pulled away, frightened that she would noticc.

'I did something the other night,' Kate said carefully when they were back on Oxford Street.

'Yeah?'

'I decided to give the whole online dating thing another go.'

'You did?' Freddie said carefully.

'I met this guy, someone online. It was a nice date, I thought, so I invited him back to mine.'

Freddie's chest restricted with an angry tension he was determined to not let show on his face.

'But it was horrible,' Kate continued 'He was awful, it was all awful.'

'What happened?'

'I'm fine, nothing happened really, and he didn't do anything. It just turned out he was an awful human. So I chucked him out.'

Freddie was further surprised by the jolt of energy he felt then, a restless need to do something, to punch something. He wasn't sure what, but something.

'Are you sure that you're OK?' he asked again, concerned.

'I'm fine. Thanks for asking, though. It was all so stupid.'

She looped her arm through his as they walked down Oxford Street towards the Tube station. He never realised an affectionate gesture like that had the capacity to make anyone feel so sad.

'I'm pleased you're not one of those guys,' she looked up at him, her eyes round and pretty. 'I know that whoever you end up with will be great, and you'll treat her really well.'

'Thanks,' he replied, shy of her.

They stopped by the entrance to the Tube station. Kate had taken herself away from him and was preparing to head home. The space on his arm felt cold and empty without her holding on to it, which only made him sadder.

Before she descended underground, she looked back at him as if struck by inspiration and said, 'Let's do it – I'll come to the party.'

20

'Well don't you look nice!' her mum said, pulling her glasses down on her nose so that she could get a better look.

'It's nothing,' Kate replied.

'Look, Jack. Look at your daughter! Tell her she looks nice. Because doesn't she?'

Jack Mundy peered over the top of his newspaper and jutted his bottom lip out as he nodded approvingly.

'Very nice,' he agreed.

So far, living with her parents again felt almost like a holiday, her parents treating her like a treasured house guest. Kate's laundry was folded and placed neatly on the end of her bed, her favourite foods were stocked in the fridge, and they always asked what she wanted to watch on TV in the evenings. It wasn't an ideal situation, but she knew she was lucky.

Still, the gauntlet of having to parade in front of her parents in her Sunday finery was something Kate could have done without. It was a dress she hadn't worn in a while, dusky pink and tea-length, with a sweetheart neckline that flattered her curves. She felt cute, even pretty, in it. Kate left her hair loose and had made up her face to emphasise her eyes.

'I really do think you look lovely,' her mum repeated. Kate felt it. 'Where are you going again?'

'Nowhere important.' She hadn't told her parents about Freddie yet, and certainly didn't want to divulge that she was accompanying him to a family celebration. They weren't ready for that. Kate didn't feel ready for that. 'Just meeting up with some friends.'

'That's very fancy for meeting up with friends,' her dad remarked, not looking up from his newspaper.

Kate was nervous. She had wanted to go, wanted to be there for Freddie, but now that she was standing in her parents' kitchen, checking for dog hairs and shifting the neckline of the dress so that it didn't sit too low, she wondered what she was doing. It felt inappropriate somehow, too soon. She was meeting his parents, for goodness' sake.

We're just friends, Kate told herself, even though she realised now that it wasn't true. At least, not for her any more.

She'd jumped when he'd sent her that video of the light rainbow. She didn't know why, but then also she did. She did and she hated that she did. She had yearned for him as they wandered through the department store, tried to find ways to make him look at her, to find reasons to touch him. Outside, she'd threaded her arm through his and pretended that it was a natural, easy gesture. She'd wanted to come across as light, carefree, and therefore more attractive. Instead she had felt stupid and confused. It wasn't as if he was giving her any signals back. Sure, he'd seen a light fitting and thought of her, but where were the words? Where was the meaning?

Then she had tried telling him about Ethan. She wanted to see how he would react, if there were any clues that would tell her that she wasn't acting like a stupid, smitten teenager, that there was really something there. Something like jealousy. But no, nothing.

She wondered why he had asked her to the party. She wondered why she had said yes. She told herself that she would do this for any of her friends if they asked her. That this was a silly bit of fun. Just helping him out, getting Freddie out of a pickle with his relatives, pretending to be his girlfriend so that they'd give him some room to find a real one.

Which meant that she wasn't real. That these feelings weren't real either.

'Well, you make sure you have fun,' her mum said, giving Kate a brief flashback to when she was fifteen and leaving to meet her friends in the park.

I can back out, there's still time, she told herself as she locked the front door behind her and made her way to the station.

The golf club building was a boring concrete affair, built in the seventies to serve the growing, upper-middle-class neighbourhood nearby. Now, despite various renovations, it was tragically old-fashioned, but Kate thought it had charm. The suburb didn't feel too dissimilar from where she had grown up; both were slices of a familiar Middle England despite being on opposite sides of London.

Freddie had been waiting for her outside the train station, a dark grey suit over a navy sweater. He tugged nervously at his collar, too tight even though it was open. He then briefed her on the bus ride to his parents' house.

'David is my brother, his wife is Stella, and their baby, my niece, is Lacey. My mum is called Christine and my dad is called Hugh. This is their thirty-fifth anniversary. There are hundreds of cousins. I mean it, hundreds. Some of them look so similar I can't remember who is who, even though I grew up with them, so don't worry about that.'

'It'll be OK,' Kate said, 'it'll be fun.'

'I don't know. I've never had fun at these kinds of thing. They always make me nervous.'

'Why?'

'You'll understand when you meet David. He's the life and soul of everything. He's just . . . he's just perfect. And I'm not him.'

They were in the restaurant space now, and Freddie pointed out his mother, who stood in the centre of a group of ladies all holding Champagne glasses. She was wearing a tight black dress that wrapped her up like a bandage under a lime green shawl. Not too far away, standing near the bar, Freddie pointed out his father, holding a court of his own in a navy blazer with gleaming gold buttons over expertly pressed beige trousers.

'I don't expect you to actually pretend to be my girlfriend,' Freddie had said on the bus ride. 'I don't want to make things weird, or for you to feel uncomfortable.'

'I wouldn't feel uncomfortable,' Kate said, looking for a reaction, but only seeing his nerves. 'And besides, we don't have to give any details about anything. We can be one of those private couples. Coy and mysterious.'

Now Freddie pointed out David and Stella, holding court next to the table where the presents were being collected, all enthusiastic waves and gleaming smiles. Kate liked the way Stella looked. She was wearing a floaty mint-green dress and holding a baby swathed in pink frills, but despite being a new mum, appeared totally immaculate. David was too, Kate noticed. Like a more refined version of Freddie, broader and bulkier and with glossy hair that swooshed and conformed perfectly.

Kate could feel Freddie breathing heavily by her side and gave his arm a brief, reassuring squeeze before they ventured over.

'Freddie!' Stella cried out excitedly when she saw them enter. 'And this must be Kate? We've heard so much about you. It's so nice to meet Freddie's girlfriend!'

Kate noticed that Stella's voice was just a little too high, just a little too loud.

She felt Freddie tense up next to her and, without thinking, reached out to hold his hand so that he remembered she was there for him.

'It's lovely to meet you too!' Kate found herself replying breezily. 'I've heard so much about you all, and can I meet little Lacey?'

Stella held the baby up and let Kate coo over her. She really was a very cute baby.

Kate smiled as Stella talked about Lacey's dress and how difficult it had been to choose the right one. She was good at this. A couple of years of greeting and guiding visitors at the gallery had given her the ability to chat comfortably to people of all ages. But at the gallery all people ever really saw was the uniform. Here they were seeing her, wondering about her, and Kate could feel it.

Freddie left her side to place the wrapped photo frame on the gift table, and then veered off to the bar to say hello to his father. He returned shortly after with two flutes of Champagne, looking guily and burdened.

'What's wrong?' she asked him, taking a drink.

'Nothing,' he replied.

After another round of introductions to people whose faces all started to blur into one another, Kate was relieved when Freddie guided her over to the buffet. They filled their plates, then found an empty table near the back of the room where Kate hoped nobody would bother them for a bit.

'You have such a nice family,' she said, smiling.

'I have a big family,' Freddie said. 'I don't even know who half these people are.'

'But it looks like they all care about you.'

'I feel like they're staring at me all the time.'

'I don't think they're all staring, even though it feels that way. People are curious. And they care about you. Maybe you don't have to be so scared of them.'

She extended a hand across the table and carefully entwined her fingers with his and let their hands stay there, right on the tablecloth, for everyone to see.

'Well, we are boyfriend and girlfriend,' Kate said as Freddie looked down at their hands. 'Might as well be believable.'

'I didn't have a chance to come and say hello before.' David strode over and sat himself next to them at the table, his shoulders broad and his legs planted wide.

Kate still couldn't get over the similarities between them, and the differences too. That same nose, a little large and aquiline, possessed David's face in a completely different way; his chin too was the same shape but bolder, sharper. Like someone had taken the form of Freddie, and puffed it all the way up as far as it could go.

'So, Kate, tell me about yourself.' David didn't ask it, he demanded it, running a hand back through his hair.

'Well, I work at an art gallery. The Central Art Gallery. The one near Trafalgar Square?'

'Never been there,' he replied proudly.

'Oh, well you should visit. It's pretty nice.'

'Tell me something, Kate, why should I go and see a piece of art in a gallery when I can see the entire thing on my phone? I've got the whole Louvre right here!'

She couldn't tell if he was teasing her.

'I mean, you can, sure. But I think that seeing a real work up close, seeing the brush strokes, how the colours react under the lights as you move. I don't know, it makes you feel connected to it somehow. Like, you're seeing exactly what the artist intended. It feels important.'

David was watching her, assessing her. Something rose up in Kate, making her feel like she had something to prove. He turned to Freddie. 'Perhaps you could learn something from this one.'

Kate watched as Freddie stared at his knuckles. She got the sense that he was shrivelling right in front of her.

'You know, we've been trying to convince Fred to come and work for me for ages now? There's a space for him at my place, but he's always said no. Maybe you're the one to help convince him.'

'Who's we?' Freddie asked.

'You know, Mum and Dad, Stella and me. We just want the best for you.'

Kate looked at Freddie again, her concern growing. Why wasn't he saying anything?

'But if he's happy,' she wasn't intending on saying anything more, but now David was looking at her, 'I mean, if you're happy and enjoy the work, and you're paid enough to live, isn't that OK? Shouldn't that be enough?'

'We all love Fred and want the best for him,' David reiterated.

'But what about what Freddie wants?' Kate felt as though she had gone too far. David was looking at her curiously now, cool disdain tempered by a polite smile.

'Oh, I think I know my brother fairly well.' He turned to face Freddie directly. 'Come on, tell her.'

Freddie didn't say anything.

'For goodness' sake.' David rose from his chair. He looked as though he wanted to say something more to them both, but then thought better of it. 'I must go and say hello to Cousin Giles. I'll leave you two to enjoy the party.'

'I'm sorry about him,' Freddie mumbled once he was out of earshot.

'He was all right. Are you though?' Kate asked, leaning over the table so that she could be closer. She was holding his hand again. She hadn't noticed when she'd decided to reach for it or whether it had been him who had reached for her.

'Well, now you've met David.'

'He wasn't so bad.'

'I think he liked you, to be honest.'

'That was him liking me? It felt like a job interview. And I didn't get the job.'

They sat for a moment together. Kate slowly chewed on a sausage roll.

'Thanks for sticking up for me,' Freddie said eventually.

'I didn't do anything.'

'No, it was me who didn't do anything. I really should have done. But I don't know what to say to him sometimes. He's always been better than me. In school, in sports, in life in general. I've always felt like I never met his standards, like he was always a bit annoyed by having me for a little brother. He can't understand that I might think differently from him, that I might want different things.'

'I do genuinely think he wants you to be happy, in his own way.'

'But his idea of happy, it's not the same as mine.'

Kate nodded in silent agreement, watching David on the other side of the room, the ease with which he chatted to family members and other guests, the way he threw his arms out when telling stories, how his head tipped all the way back when he laughed. What Freddie perceived as perfection, Kate realised, was probably just a costume David had practice wearing. He wasn't perfect – he just knew how to appear that way.

'Hey, want to have some fun?' she then asked, turning back to Freddie after what was starting to become an uncomfortable silence.

'Fun? Here?'

'Look, I don't know what your family really make of me, but while I'm here and pretending to be your girlfriend, why don't we dance? You up for it?'

'I can't dance,' Freddie said, and the worry in his eyes made Kate want to laugh.

'Everyone can dance,' Kate retorted, standing up but still holding his hand, pulling him along with her. He let her lead him into the centre of the room, where the music was loudest and most guests were gathered.

She knew people were watching them, but she didn't care. There was a strange confidence that came with knowing that she might never see these people again, that this might just be a one-time thing.

Just friends, Kate reminded herself once more, this time with an added sense of sadness.

'There we go,' Kate encouraged.

It was not so much dancing as shuffling to the rhythm of the music, she knew, but it was fun anyway. Kate hadn't heard S Club 7 in years. She noticed Freddie looking around at his relatives, nodding small acknowledgements, offering waves and quiet smiles. She knew this was harder for him, that he was worrying too much about other people and what they were thinking.

'Want to do something even more fun?' Kate asked, but before he had a chance to reply, she leaned into him and planted a soft, chaste kiss on his mouth, before pulling away and smiling.

'What was that for?' Freddie asked in a low whisper. His face and body were still close to hers, so close that she didn't dare look to check his expression. She had wanted to do it, for herself and for him, but now that it was done, she was scared that he'd be angry.

Because I like you, Kate thought. But instead she said: 'Does it have to be for something?'

She'd made a mistake. He didn't feel the same as her. She'd given him all the clues she knew how to give, and it wasn't enough. The song ended and they went to sit back down.

The speeches were fun. There were jokes that Kate didn't get, and then jokes that she did. Freddie's father gave a speech about how wonderful it was living with Freddie's mother, and then Freddie's mother gave a speech about how terrible it was living with Freddie's father. It was merry and sweet.

'Here comes Mum,' Freddie warned once the speeches were over.

'Now, I just had to find time to stop by,' Christine Weir came and sat right by Kate's side, and immediately reached down to hold Kate's hand in her own. The sudden familiarity was startling, the intensity of her attention even more so. 'I had to make time for you both, because this is something special, isn't it?'

Kate didn't know if Freddie's mum was talking about the party, or the fact that Kate existed, but she smiled anyway.

'How are you finding things? Enjoying yourself?'

'Yes, I am. I'm really pleased I could come,' Kate replied.

'I'm so happy. I'm so happy you're here.' She turned to Freddie: 'Are you looking after her? Making sure that she knows who everyone is?'

'Yes, Mum.'

'And have you told Kate that I want her to come over to ours? Spend some real time with us?'

'I hadn't told her that, no.'

'I'm sure we can arrange something,' Kate interrupted nervously.

'You know, I've never seen Freddie dance?' she told Kate. 'I've never seen him out there, on a dance floor, enjoying himself?'

'I've danced before, Mum,' Freddie groaned.

'But I haven't seen it. I haven't seen you like that. You seemed . . . you seemed yourself. Does that make sense?' She turned back to Kate: 'I can tell from the way he stands when he's next to you. It's in his face. Does he tell you?'

'Not enough,' Kate replied lightly, hoping it was the right thing.

'Anyway. I've got to go and do my mingling. We're going to meet properly, though, spend some time together. I'd really like that,' Christine said, still holding Kate's hand tightly.

'I'd like that too,' Kate replied. She was telling the truth.

After she'd left, Kate looked at Freddie, who stared back at her with heavy eyes.

'This is all really intense,' he said apologetically.

'I don't mind,' Kate replied. But Freddie looked like he did. 'I guess we're going to have to stage some big break-up event if we don't want this to spin out of control.'

It was meant to be a joke, something stupid to break the tension, to stop Freddie from looking so worried. But he didn't say anything. Kate wondered if that's what he really wanted, if he regretted this whole endeavour and was thinking about staging a break-up too.

'Maybe it's time to go?' Kate suggested, and Freddie nodded back in agreement.

'I'll go and say goodbye to my brother,' he said.

'I'll get our coats,' Kate added.

She watched Freddie walk away, before getting up and heading over to the coat rack near the door.

'Oh Kate! Are you guys going?' Stella came over and reached around her for a hug.

'I'm afraid so,' Kate replied.

'I just wanted to grab you, if that's OK?'

'Sure . . .'

Stella led Kate away, just to the side, so that they could talk without being overheard.

'It's just . . . did Freddie tell you about the dinner party? The one at mine a few weeks ago?'

'He mentioned it,' Kate replied, careful.

'I wanted to say sorry. I had no idea he was seeing someone, and I honestly can't believe that I tried to fix him up. If I had known about you—'

'It's all right, really. We both found it funny.'

'I just wonder about Freddie sometimes. Why didn't he tell me? Any of us? That's not to say I'm not pleased that he met you, I am pleased. I'm thrilled! But I'd be lying if I said that I wasn't . . . *What on earth?*'

The conversation was cut short by a commotion that was happening on the other side of the room, by the bar. Stella hurried over immediately to do damage control, but Kate hung back, uncertain about how involved she wanted to be in any family drama.

But the gossip reached her quickly. It was another man walking away who said it, loud and apparently amused: 'Freddie just walloped David!'

21

Freddie felt the thrill of pain radiating through his knuckles and wanted to swear, but there were people around him. All those cousins, all those family friends and their children, his parents. They stood in silence, waiting for the next thing to happen, wondering what Freddie was going to do next.

They all think I'm crazy, Freddie thought. He felt it like a background hum, that sense that everyone thought he was odd, that they were all expecting him to flip out at some point, weren't they? He noticed how people averted their eyes, how they were scared to cross him, scared to say anything that might provoke more rage. It was a powerful thing, he realised, to have people fear you.

But the punch hadn't come out of nowhere. He hadn't planned it by any means, but at the same time, Freddie realised that he'd been building up to it for a long while. There was the constant feeling over the last couple of hours that David had been looking down on him, laughing at him. And even if that wasn't real, even if it was a misplaced impression, there was the way he had talked to Kate, the way he'd looked at her. He didn't know how to define it exactly, didn't know how to respond to it either, but it had made him feel so uneasy, and protective too.

And then what about all those other times throughout their life together? Like the time David had tried to trick Freddie into eating weird things, chalk and leaves and bits of paper he said were made of sugar, and then laughed about it with his friends. There had been that cold autumn evening when he'd locked Freddie in the garden shed and left him there for two hours, explained away afterwards as a plan to make him stronger. And then, when they were a little older, the time David had racked up a massive phone bill buying stupid expensive ringtones and convinced his younger brother to take the blame because David couldn't afford to be grounded, and besides, it wasn't as if Freddie had much of a social life to lose anyway. Those were just the things that he remembered. Freddie had taken it all, had never revealed how much it had hurt him, and then buried every moment deep.

He'd only gone over to say a quiet goodbye, a chance to be polite and to thank his brother for going to the trouble of organising the event. He hadn't expected much else in the way of conversation at all.

'So. Kate. Your Kate. Katie-Katie Kate,' David had trilled, hands in pockets, grin on his face. 'Quite something you have there, Fred.'

'Yeah, she's nice.'

'Finally got yourself the girl.'

'Yup.'

'She's got opinions too, hasn't she? Passionate.'

'I don't think she meant any harm in what she said,' Freddie had said, starting to worry. 'She doesn't know you, doesn't know us.'

'No no, it's fine. All forgotten . . .' David had paused, looking down at the wine in his glass. 'Still, you didn't say anything to her.'

'Like what?'

'Well, you kept yourself very quiet, didn't you. Didn't stand up for yourself. For me, for us.'

'Kate can say what she likes,' Freddie had replied, cautious.

'But she's meeting the family?'

Freddie had felt all his angst balling itself up inside him. He thought about how it had felt when Kate had led him to the dance floor, the terror and then the surprising ease. He thought about how he had frozen when she kissed him, how much he had wanted to kiss her back but was too scared of people looking, and of not knowing whether she was doing it just because she was playing a part. He had wanted it to be real so badly, but just couldn't be sure.

'Look, whatever happens, at least Kate made *an* impression,' David had continued.

'What do you mean, *whatever happens*?'

'Well, brother to brother, I can't see this lasting.' When David caught Freddie's shocked expression, he had added: 'Come on, I'm only looking out for you. There are plenty of fish in the sea. You don't have to settle for the first tiny minnow that comes your way.'

'Please don't talk about Kate like that.'

'Yes. You're right, you're right. She's less a minnow, more of a trout I suppose.'

Freddie didn't know how to fight with his words, didn't know how to say it, but he felt the ball of angst morph into rage. It was hot in his chest, and tense.

David had laughed right then, so hadn't seen the punch coming.

As punches went, Freddie figured afterwards, it couldn't have been too impressive. But what he lacked in power and skill, he made up for in sudden fury, and David's reaction was one of genuine surprise rather than pain. Once he had regained his composure, David put a hand up to his face to check for blood. There was none, but from the way he winced as he adjusted his jaw, Freddie wondered if he would end up with a bruise by the morning.

'You little shit,' David muttered. 'This is what I get for trying to help?'

Freddie felt the circle around him, the hum of wonder and disapproval. He looked for his parents, hoped they weren't around.

'Let's go,' Kate whispered, coming close, handing him his coat. Had she been there? Had she seen?

They walked out together, quickly, not stopping for anyone, not looking back to check on the commotion that had been caused.

'Are you OK?' Kate asked.

'No,' Freddie replied as they walked to the nearby bus stop. 'I don't know what happened.'

'What did he say?'

'It wasn't just what he said . . . he was just being David. But I'm sick of David being David. I'm sick of so much of it.'

'Did you fight lots as kids?'

'Never! That's the thing. He was always so much bigger than me, so much more powerful. Most of the time, I was scared of him. I did whatever he said. Whatever he wanted. Each and every time, I hoped that I had finally impressed him. That I'd finally done enough to meet his standards.'

They stood next to each other under the bus shelter.

I'm not just sick of him, Freddie thought. *I'm sick of myself too. Sick of not being able to say what I really want to say. Not just to David, but to everyone. To you.*

The bus arrived before he could tell her.

They sat together in silence on the way to the station, and then took the train into London in silence too. When they sat down in the carriage, Freddie still stunned, Kate let her head rest on his shoulder and held his hand – the one he had used to punch his brother – fast in her own. There was no discussion about where they were going, or what was happening. Without any words, Freddie led Kate back to his flat.

Damien was away for the weekend, visiting his family. Freddie was relieved. Kate had gone through so much with him that day, he didn't think she needed to meet him too.

He saw the flat with the eyes of someone who was seeing it for the first time. It was primarily Damien's flat, he had been there first, and Freddie had always gone along with his stark, minimalist style. White walls, beige carpets, stainless steel appliances. A row of tiny, inscrutable succulents in pots on the kitchen windowsill. The expensive coffee machine. Freddie wondered if Kate would think he was boring.

'This is nice,' she said softly.

'It's mostly Damien's. He's away.'

'Is your hand all right?' she asked after a beat. 'Maybe you should put some ice on it, just in case.'

Freddie went to the freezer to grab a bag of frozen peas and let out an extended sigh of relief when he applied it to his aching knuckles. Kate sat across from him at the kitchen table, silent and sad.

'I feel like I ruined the whole thing,' Freddie said.

'Your family will get over it,' Kate reassured him.

Freddie wanted to tell Kate that actually he was talking about her, that somehow he had ruined things with her, but once again, the words didn't come. He fumed quietly.

'What did he say that was so awful it got you to punch him?'

'Oh, nothing. Nothing important,' Freddie lied.

'Seemed like it had been building up for a long time,' Kate said, and Freddie nodded in agreement.

She was sitting closer to him than he first thought. She was stroking his arm, soothing him. Freddie never wanted her to leave. So, still stuck for words, he moved closer still and kissed her, returning the same soft, chaste kiss she had given him earlier. It seemed right somehow, to *do* what he was thinking, instead of having to say it.

This time there was no taking turns, one person testing the other, daring the other to go further. They were working together, gently at first, and then with a fierceness Freddie had no idea was in him. The bag of peas lay discarded on the table. His shirt was being unbuttoned, her dress lifted off and thrown to the floor – the sudden separation as he helped her do this was nearly unbearable – and then, without him even really understanding what was happening, they moved to the bedroom.

His body seemed to be doing all the talking that evening. He asked a question with his fingers and she would respond in turn. He heard what she needed just from the way she shifted and moved around him, and he replied. The ease and the instinct powered him to find new sensations with her, sweet and hot all at once, and when he heard her moan, louder than she had the first time they'd done this, he was moved to moan too.

Afterwards, he collapsed back on the bed, emotionally exhausted and sleepy.

When he woke not long after, Kate was getting ready to leave.

'Where are you going?' he asked, propping himself up.

'I live on the other side of London now. My parents will be wondering where I am,' she replied. 'I really do sound like a teenager, don't I? So embarrassing.'

'You don't have to go. You can stay.'

'I don't think so, Freddie.'

'Why not?'

She was struggling to do up the zipper on the back of her dress and looked as if she was going to cry.

'I don't know . . . I feel stupid.'

'Don't feel stupid.'

Freddie got up and hastily wrapped a blanket around himself, feeling embarrassed by his nudity when Kate was nearly fully dressed in front of him. Once sorted, he went up behind her, and helped her with the zipper. It was more intimate than he wanted it to be, being so close to her back, to the nape of her neck, only visible because Kate was holding her long hair out of the way.

'I'm scared we're going to get confused about things,' she admitted. 'That was nice, what happened just then. But . . . I just don't know what it means.'

'I don't either,' Freddie said. He thought he was being helpful, sympathetic, but it turned out that wasn't what she wanted to hear.

'I don't want to ruin our friendship,' she said sadly.

'Same here.'

'In which case, I'm just going to go. This wasn't meant to happen. I just think maybe we need a bit of space until we figure everything out?'

'OK.'

He sat on his bed, still and naked, for a long time after Kate left him. The light outside the window dimmed into dusk. Someone tried to ring (he guessed it was probably his mum, or maybe even Stella, anxious after how he'd left things with David earlier on), but he didn't even want to look at his phone. What was the point? It had been an absolute disaster and he couldn't handle any reminders of it. He felt bruised; not just his fist, but the whole of him. Almost as if he had been the one beaten up, not the one inflicting the damage.

Why couldn't I say anything? he thought. He loved the way they fitted together, so why hadn't he just told her that?

His stomach hurt with the intensity of his feelings. Watching her with his family, that rage he had felt when David had said what he had said, feeling her move with him for the second time – there was just so much to make sense of. Too much.

* * *

'Hey, is now a good time?'

Freddie had decided to call Baz while he waited for one of Damien's tiny espresso pods to turn into a cup of coffee. He'd never used the machine before (had never dared), but he'd seen his flatmate do it often enough. It was right there in the kitchen, in their shared kitchen, taking up all that room and looking so sleek and mighty, and Freddie had wanted a coffee.

He didn't know if it was the sex – which had really been quite something – or the inner coil of rage that was still there from his 'chat' with David earlier, but Freddie was feeling compulsive in a brand-new way. He wasn't thinking about germs, about needing to protect things by keeping himself clean, about counting things until numbers lost all meaning. Instead he was thinking about fixing things, about doing things, about making things happen. He wasn't angry at Damien or his coffee machine, but he was angry that he had never worked up the guts to use it. It might have been precious to Damien, he understood that, but it was just a cup of coffee. He could contribute to buy new pods. He could be trusted to use it regardless. He could be respected enough to share it.

'Hey pal,' Baz replied, 'everything OK with you?'

'I never slept with Camellia,' Freddie blurted.

'Right . . . Freddie, mate, is now really the best time for this? Are you sure you're all right?'

'That night at the Leavers' Ball? I thought we were going to hook up, but I caught her with another guy. She was all over him. Camellia was never interested in me. I never even talked to her about it. I just presumed, and then got lost in my stupid head.'

'Freddie, pal, you're sounding kinda worked up there.'

'I told you I had slept with her because I was embarrassed. I felt foolish, and I feel like I've been chasing that stupid lie ever since. I never slept with Camellia. I never even talked to her at that stupid party.'

'Freddie—'

'I needed to tell you. I'm sick of not saying anything, of pretending everything is all right, of bottling everything in. I feel like I've never actually done anything in my life. I feel like life just keeps passing me by because I'm standing on the sidelines. I don't want to be on the sidelines any more. I want to do something. I want things to happen.'

'Well, this is quite the revelation.'

'Sorry for saying it like that. For shouting or anything.'

'Don't say sorry now, mate, you're on a roll!'

'All these years, you thought I had slept with Camellia, but I never did. I've been a virgin this entire time, and I've been so embarrassed about it.'

'Freddie,' he heard Baz take in a deep breath on the other end of the phone line, 'I knew all along. Not the specifics, I wasn't sure, but I knew you were lying that night. I knew nothing had happened.'

'You never said.'

'I didn't want you to feel bad. I knew you were sensitive about it. I thought it was better that way.'

'Right, OK. Well now I feel even more embarrassed.'

'No, Freddie. Don't feel embarrassed. You have absolutely nothing to be embarrassed about!'

'I needed to tell you. To get it off my chest.'

'And I'm thrilled you did. I'm relieved you did. I've been worried about you.'

'You have?'

'I know we don't talk about our feelings much, and when we get together, Wayne seems to lower the tone somewhat, but we can talk about these kinds of things. We *should* talk about these kinds of things. You're my friend. And I'm yours. And I'm sorry that you felt you could never tell me the truth about everything.'

Freddie considered the tiny cup of coffee now in his hands. It all seemed a bit silly now.

'What's brought all this on, anyway? Do I need to be worried?' Baz asked.

'I met someone. A girl. She's called Kate. I really like her.'

He heard Baz sigh on the other end of the line, imagined him rubbing his jaw anxiously, like he did when he was trying to figure out the right thing to say.

'I think she likes me too,' Freddie continued. 'We've actually slept together – twice, in fact. But it's not straightforward. I can't seem . . . I can't seem to tell her how I feel. I can't seem to get the words out.'

'Why do you think that is?'

'I'm *terrified*,' Freddie admitted. 'I'm scared that she doesn't feel the same, that she sees this thing we have in a different way. I can't make sense of it. And I feel like if I don't say anything, if I don't risk anything, then maybe I can avoid getting hurt.'

'You're hurting now though, aren't you?'

Freddie considered that, and sighed loudly.

'What if I scare her away?' he asked his best friend. 'What if I lose this?'

'Freddie, you've been quiet your whole life, and that's fine. But sometimes in life you have to be loud. You have to make sure people hear you. Is it possible by telling her how you really feel that she'll run for the hills? Of course it is. But let's look at facts: you've slept together. She hardly hates you, does she?'

'We said we were going to stay just friends.'

'Do you want to be just friends?'

'I thought I'd be OK with that, but no. Not really.'

'You just have to tell her how you feel, but you know that.'

'That's not all that's happened today,' Freddie continued. 'Earlier, at my parents' anniversary thing, I punched David.'

'You what?'

'Right in the face.'

'Blimey.'

'I know.'

'Did he deserve it?'

'Absolutely, you should have seen it.'

'I wish I had!'

They chatted a little longer, until Freddie could hear Maisie calling for her dad in the background and Baz said that he was happy Freddie had called him, but he had to go.

Afterwards, Freddie finally took his first sip of Damien's precious coffee, now cold, and instantly spat it back out in revulsion.

22

She got the email while shepherding twenty schoolkids around the Renaissance rooms, and one particularly petulant twelve-year-old had wondered out loud why there were so many creepy skulls in the portraits.

'They're called memento mori,' Kate was explaining. 'They're put there to remind the sitter that life and good fortune doesn't go on for ever. That things will end one day.'

She was hesitant to go into too much gory detail. Three teachers from the group's school were milling around at the back, occasionally calling out the name of one kid or another who they felt wasn't paying attention. Kate wondered if she started talking about death, about symbols of death in art, whether they'd get annoyed and pull the kids away.

'That's gross, miss.'

'It seems weird to us today, but at the time, when it was painted, it was important. The kind of people who got their portrait painted would have been very wealthy, but they wanted to show people that they were humble too; that they knew none of their good fortune was going to last. That none of it really mattered.'

A couple of kids at the front were getting close to another painting now, pointing out other objects next to the sitters, wondering what they meant.

'Tell you what,' Kate said, feeling bold. 'We're going to stay in this room, but how about you all go off in pairs and find something in a painting that you think might be a symbol of something more important – like the skull – and then let's come back together in ten minutes and try and figure out what those symbols might mean.'

Kate had felt her phone vibrate in her pocket, but it was only when the kids had dispersed on their challenge that she was able to have a look.

It was an email from Elise.

She put the phone back in her pocket. Kate didn't have time to panic about whatever it might contain. She'd look at it later, when she had time and energy to let herself get stressed out.

'I've got to say, I've never seen them like this.' One of the teachers was standing with Kate now, as they both watched the children in their pairs, most standing in front of old paintings, pointing and discussing. 'You've really made this trip memorable for them, thank you.'

'I'm pleased to hear that,' Kate said, feeling shy.

'Oh, and don't worry about the gory stuff,' the teacher continued. 'I noticed you try and avoid it, but honestly, given what this lot normally talk about, the more disgusting the better!'

'There's a painting of Judith cutting off the head of Holofernes with a sword in the next room,' she suggested.

'Excellent! They'll love that!'

'So, I heard you were killing it,' Renee said when they had a chance to meet up later. Kate had stayed an extra half hour in the office, finishing up the report on the school visit earlier in the day so that she could meet Renee once her shift had finished. They had decided to catch up in the main gallery café, a place that was usually off limits due to the extortionate prices, but as they couldn't catch up nearly as often as they usually did any more, Kate thought that they both deserved fancy tea and cake, which would be on her, thanks to the novelty of her slightly increased wages.

'Who from?' Kate asked.

'I overheard Beth talking to one of the other managers. She was moaning, doesn't think she's going to get you back.'

'You're winding me up.'

'Nope. They stopped talking when they noticed me, but I think they're expecting you to get the job in the Learning and Development office permanently.' Renee took a huge bite out of her lemon drizzle cake and chewed happily.

'You think?'

'I know.'

Kate thought Renee was expecting her to be jubilant, but she remained quiet and cautious. It had been hard to feel enthusiastic lately. She focused all her energy into her work and then went home feeling depleted and sad. Her mind drifted to the email, still waiting unopened in her phone inbox. She didn't dare look at it.

'Kate, are you OK?' Renee asked. 'You haven't seemed yourself lately. Aren't you happy?'

In some respects, yes, Kate did feel happy. Her new role was going well, it kept her busy and she had responsibility. The team in her new office were great, and it was hard to see a reason why they wouldn't take her on full time. She could stay in the gallery, a place she had come to love, but actually have a career trajectory again. Once a job offer was confirmed, she could think about moving back out of her parents' house. But in other ways, she wasn't happy at all. Ever since she'd walked out of Freddie's flat, her body still awash with the fizzy afterglow of their second time together, she'd felt detached and empty.

But Kate didn't want to think about that. She didn't want to think about how she had essentially got up and walked away when her feelings had overwhelmed her. Didn't want to think about the fact that Freddie hadn't reached out to her since, how she hadn't reached out either. She felt guilty for how she had behaved and hated the feeling that lingered with her now. She didn't want to think about it.

'I'm fine,' Kate lied. 'But I haven't had a chance to catch up with you in ages. Tell me about Claude. What's happening with you two?'

'Claude is amazing, but . . .' Renee eyed Kate carefully over the rim of her teacup, and Kate got the sense that her friend knew she was purposely diverting the conversation and had decided to let it slide. 'He told me he loved me last night.'

'What? Why didn't you lead with that? This is huge!'

'Is it?' Renee sighed.

'Isn't it?' Kate returned, baffled.

'I told him that I thought it was a lovely sentiment, but that I couldn't return it,' said Renee.

'I thought you guys were perfect together.'

'I thought so too, but then he said it. And I couldn't say it back, not like he wanted me to.'

'You've only been going out with him for what, about two months? It's been really fast. Perhaps you'll feel the same way about him in time?'

'Oh Kate . . .' Renee sighed. 'He's always been more passionate about me than I have about him. And the passion is great – it's really fun – but it's not the same as love. Plus sometimes, he does these things. Stupid, little things. But they are, you know, annoying.'

'Like what?'

'He cleans up after me too much. If I leave an empty glass on a side table it's swooped away within moments. He makes the bed seconds after I've just left it. Oh, and he describes food in ridiculously weird ways. Chip shop chips? The really greasy kind? They "inspire" him, he loves their "wanton abandon of sophistication". He described a Pret sandwich the other day as the "Platonic ideal of all sandwiches that have come before and will come after".'

'Well, at least he's tidy—'

'There's one more thing . . .'

'Go on?'

'The other night, after we did it, he whimpered.'

'Whimpered?'

'Like, I think he wanted to cry, but he must have known that I'd beat him up with a pillow if he did, so he just held it in. Except it came out anyway, in this really pathetic little whimper. A lone tear trailing down his cheek.'

'Did you say anything about it?'

'I didn't, but he must have seen my face. It wasn't a good face.'

'I really did think he was perfect,' Kate reflected.

'I know you did. But sometimes the thing you think is perfect at the beginning turns out to be nothing. And then, the thing you presume is just going to be nothing turns out to be the big thing. Life sucks like that.'

Kate thought about Freddie. Thought about how big her feelings had become and how unexpected they were.

'You're thinking about that guy, aren't you? You're thinking about Freddie,' Renee said. 'That's why you're being all weird and mopey.'

'What? No, I'm not.'

'Did you break up too?'

'We were never together.'

'Are you sure about that?'

'I'm sure. We were only meant to be just friends.'

'And yet . . .'

'Renee, I'm not talking about it. It was nothing. Freddie is history.'

They sat in silence for a spell, Kate prodding her chocolate cake with her tiny fork, her appetite suddenly gone.

'Whatever it was, I've ruined it anyway,' Kate finally mumbled.

'Ruined how? You didn't whimper or anything, did you?'

'Oh gosh, nothing that embarrassing.'

'What was it then?'

'I just kind of . . . walked away.'

'You did what?'

'It's was over a week ago, and we were together – I actually went to this fancy family party with him, if you can believe it – and then I went back to his, and it was great. It was actually phenomenally great, but then I got up and I walked away.'

'I'm sorry, but I don't understand.'

'Neither do I.'

Kate pushed her plate of chocolate cake out in front of her and let her forehead fall to the table.

'I really like him,' she moaned into the Formica.

'Damn,' Renee replied.

'And I should have told him, but I got scared. And he's not the most communicative guy either, so now I think I've ruined it.'

'You could still tell him.'

'But if he felt the same way, don't you think he would have told me? I feel so alone here, and I'm so rubbish at all of this.'

'Oh Kate, no wonder you've been blue.'

'I'm sorry. I didn't want to think about any of this. I should be happy. I might end up with a new job. One that I like. My parents are supporting me, and so far that particular decision doesn't seem to be a total disaster, and I've had more action in the last month than I've had in the rest of my life. I feel like I should be grateful.'

'You're allowed to be sad. You're allowed to have complicated feelings.'

Kate sat back up in her seat, picked up her perfect china teacup, and sipped the last of her oolong, savouring the honey-like taste.

'I'm sorry you and Claude didn't work out. I liked him,' she said sadly.

'He was hot, but he was also pretentious, and thought I was a different person than I really am,' Renee sighed.

'You'll find the right one,' Kate encouraged.

'I don't know if I want to find just one,' Renee admitted. 'It seems so weirdly limited, to focus all your energy on finding just one person, and that person being for ever. Sure, I'd like someone, but only for right now, and only for as long as that lasts. Does that make sense?'

'You don't think there's a perfect person out there for you?'

'I think we're more adaptable than that. I think there are lots of people you can be perfect with.'

'I like that idea,' Kate said. And she did, for Renee. For herself, there was only one person she wanted.

'You could still message Freddie?' Renee suggested.

'I could.'

'But it's hard?'

'But it's hard. I don't know what to say. Don't know if I should be apologising or baring my soul, or what. Maybe it's easier to just let it go?'

'Just because something's easier, doesn't mean it's the right thing to do,' Renee warned.

Kate tried to smile and looked down at her chocolate cake crumbs. She knew Renee was right, but still wasn't sure what she was meant to do about it, what was appropriate and what was fair.

'I've got to go,' Renee said.

'I think I'm going to stay here for a bit,' Kate replied.

'Maybe, with your big new fancy job upstairs, we should make this a weekly thing. Next time on me?'

'I'd like that.'

Kate stood up to hug Renee before she left and then sat back down. It was time to look at the email. The first line was visible on the mail app, the ellipses at the end teasing her to click and find out more:

Hi Kate! It's been so long! Thought it would be nice . . .

Later, Kate decided. *I'll look at it later.*

She felt anxious on the Tube home. Kate had let herself fall away from her old girlfriends, but Elise's mail was the first time any of them had reached out to her like this in ages. If Lindsey had been there, she would have told Kate to ignore the email; Lindsey had never been keen on Kate's school friends (especially India), had pointed out in the past that they had different priorities, that it never felt as if Kate really fitted in with them. She'd never minded Lindsey's opinions, it wasn't as if her friendship circles ever mixed, but even so, Kate had always hoped that the friends she made in school would be friends she held on to for life. And then if life wasn't treating her well, and she felt insecure and lost, that they'd be there throughout until she found herself again.

They hadn't been, but Kate wondered if part of that was her fault too.

She'd been off radar for a while, but now her life was on the up again. Things were improving, and she was doing better. She wasn't a virgin anymore. Maybe Elise reaching out now was kismet, a sign that she was on the right track and everything was going to go back to how it was.

At home, Cinnamon greeted her at the door. She told her parents that she'd had cake after work and didn't fancy dinner, and then went straight to her room. Cinnamon bounded up the stairs with her, tail beating happily, and then jumped up to plonk himself across Kate's lap as she sat back on her bed, her childhood bedroom feeling crowded around her.

'Who's a good boy?' she asked him, giving him a deep, satisfying scratch behind the ears, something that made his back leg twitch with excitement.

Almost everything that had been left in the flat after Lindsey departed for Hong Kong was now packed into Kate's childhood bedroom. Teetering cardboard boxes and small storage containers stacked high formed a metropolis of chaos. She'd thought about unpacking some of it, seeing if there was any room in the loft for the less necessary items, like the box full of crockery and mugs, but Kate hoped that she wouldn't be here that long. She was hoping that she'd be able to move back out again soon.

As she let herself lie back on the bed, her eyes fell on a photo frame, the type that also doubled as an album, poised on her bedside table behind the sticker-covered lamp. She reached around the labradoodle to get it, and he whined at the disturbance. It only held twelve photos, all from a time when she actually had to go out to get the films developed. The first couple were of her parents, then there was one of Cinnamon as a puppy (such a good boy!), but the rest were of the old gang.

Kate had never considered herself pretty, but she was surprised by how good she looked in most of the photos. Her frame was a little larger than everybody else's, and she was taller, but otherwise they all looked like they were meant to be together, a pleasing consistency of attractiveness, glossy lipstick shining, eyebrows embarrassingly thin. There was one of just her and Elise, their faces pressed together as close as they could get. Elise hadn't started highlighting her hair by then, and it was about the same colour as Kate's. Their noses were about the same too, Kate's a little rounder, their cheeks equally flushed from the summer sun and make-up free. At the end of the album was a photo of the whole gang, *sans* India, who hadn't really been around back then. But there were Bella and Rosie, Lucy and Georgie, with Kate holding on to Elise right at the centre. They all wore tiny, strappy tank tops and had their hair arranged with perky little butterfly clips.

Wasn't I happier then? Happier than I am now?

Elise had been there right at the beginning of secondary school. They'd gone to the cinema on their own for the first time together, hung out at shopping centres on Saturday afternoons. When the other girls joined their group, Kate had tried her best to keep up with them. She wore the right clothes, listened to the right music, moaned about the right subjects in school, but it had never felt quite right. She had always felt as if she was performing for them, being the person they expected her to be. When she left for university, a part of her was relieved. When she'd found Lindsey and Pippa, she was elated.

She didn't miss her old gang, Kate realised. She missed what they meant, and what they had been to her, back when she was younger, the silly nostalgia of it, but she didn't need any of them now. They didn't feel like her friends, not any more.

She was also now starting to feel a little suspicious. After being left out of the wedding, and having been blocked across social media, it did seem a little strange that Elise was reaching out now.

Maybe she feels guilty, Kate thought. *Maybe I should give her a chance.*

But was I happier then?

Kate closed the photo album with a steady finality, and instead of placing it back on her bedside table, put it away in one of the boxes. Next she picked up her phone and deleted Elise's email.

23

The day was going well. He was feeling well.

His manager had asked him to attend the big all-company meeting in the afternoon, and to check that all the IT equipment was set up properly. It was never a task Freddie had particularly enjoyed, as it not only involved increased responsibility, but also meant he had to remain in the central meeting space, which was packed out with almost the entire company. If anything went wrong, all eyes would be on him, and if he couldn't make it work, it would be his fault. But today, Freddie didn't resent his manager's request. He felt capable and strong. He felt as though, even if the meeting went terribly, he could take it.

As it happened, the audiovisual equipment had been stowed badly since its last use, and getting the room rigged and ready took longer than it should have done. The CEO was there, visibly stressed as he went over his presentation, but Freddie realised, far more quickly than he did usually, that it wasn't his fault the CEO seemed upset and bothered. That CEOs had a million other things to worry about, and that Freddie's handling of the audiovisual equipment would likely be the least of his concerns.

Freddie looked around the meeting space once he was done. He had moved back to a corner as the CEO stepped forward to make his remarks, but remained focused and ready in case something failed and he was needed again. He realised how few people he knew. Many would have submitted help-desk tickets during his time at the company, so it was likely that Freddie had spoken to nearly all of them via email, but he couldn't remember the last time he'd socialised with anyone, or at least got to know them a bit. They seemed like OK people, for the most part. Maybe he would attend the next social gathering with them, or join them for drinks. He wasn't entirely sure why he found the prospect so frightening before.

'Thanks Freddie,' the CEO said after he had brought the meeting to a close. Freddie grinned; he had no idea that the CEO even knew his name.

It was Tuesday evening, just over a week since he'd had sex with Kate for the second time.

Kate had said that she needed space, and that was what he was giving her. He realised, after speaking with Baz, that it was probably a good idea to let his head clear, to allow himself a chance to get some focus. He had been feeling almost high that Sunday evening, pumped up with hormones and the thrill of the altercation with his brother, and had had enough therapy to realise that he needed time to calm down, to assess what was really going on rather than just how he was feeling in the moment. He'd texted Baz the next day, and Baz had agreed. He needed to chill out. Which, for Freddie, meant playing a lot of computer games and reading a lot of comics.

The one thing he felt guilty about was the distance he was also putting between himself and his family. Freddie realised that he needed time out from them, and that they probably needed time out from him, so aside from quick messages to his parents to assure them that he was fine and that they didn't need to worry, there had been no communication. No apologies. David hadn't been in touch at all. Stella had tried many times, but Freddie hadn't been ready. He wasn't sure if he was ever going to be ready again. It was possible that his relationship with his brother could never be repaired. It was also just as possible that David's pride would get the better of him and that he'd pretend the punch had never happened. It was still too soon to tell.

He wondered if the university building in Bloomsbury would feel different now. There was a moment just before he stepped into the room when he wondered what he would do if Kate was there. But he also knew that she wouldn't be. That he probably shouldn't be here either.

'Hey Freddie,' Andy said happily, once he had taken his seat. 'How is everything going?'

'Fine. I mean, quite good really. Considering.'

Hattie looked up at him suspiciously. She was wearing a dozen or so bangles on her wrists, which rattled as she moved. Freddie was aware that this was the most optimistic he'd ever sounded in this room, and that it might garner some attention.

When the door opened again, he was surprised at how suddenly charged he felt, but settled quickly again when it was just Cathryn and Mike.

'Hello Freddie, we didn't see you last meeting. Is everything good with you?' Cathryn asked warmly.

'I'm good,' Freddie replied, smiling.

'Ahh, that's lovely then!' Cathryn beamed as she sat down.

The first part of the meeting was taken up by Mike, who was angry that a friend of his had jokingly called him an incel, not realising how close to home the term struck.

'It just makes me so angry,' Mike said. 'Because dictionary-definition-wise, that's what I am. But I don't want to be. Because that's such an ugly word, and people who are proud of that are sick.'

'I did a deep dive into an incel forum once,' Hattie said solemnly. 'Not a fun place.'

'How do I make sure I don't become like them?' Mike asked.

'What's an incel, again?' Cathryn asked.

'It's short for "involuntary celibate",' Andy explained. 'Someone who wants to have sex, but isn't.'

'Aren't I an incel then?' she asked.

'The term's become associated with a specific type of man, who's basically misogynist, who thinks he deserves sex, and that women are withholding it from him for crazy reasons. It's a whole thing,' said Hattie, rolling her eyes.

'I don't want to be like that,' said Mike sadly. 'I don't want to be angry like them, I don't want to be bitter like them. But I also want to have sex. I want my life to be different. I hate what I have now.'

Freddie felt awkward. He realised that he was the only one in the room who wasn't a virgin, and wondered if they'd chuck him out if they found out.

'You can change it,' Freddie revealed, speaking softly.

'Sorry, I couldn't hear you there. What did you say?' Cathryn asked.

'I said that you can change it. That Mike can change it, if he wants to. It's possible.'

'Do tell us,' said Hattie, her arms folded across her chest.

'I think the trick is to not care so much about the sex,' Freddie said.

'Why do you think we're all here?' Mike returned.

'I mean it might be possible that the lack of sex isn't the problem. That it might be a symptom of another, bigger problem. I think my problem wasn't that I was a virgin. I thought it was my virginity holding me back, but it wasn't. It never was. It was other stuff. And maybe, by tackling the other stuff, you'll find that better stuff happens.'

'That's great advice Freddie,' Andy said warmly.

'What's my problem then?' Mike challenged.

'You're angry, for starters,' said Hattie boldly.

'I think that maybe it's worth Mike figuring all that out by himself,' Andy said. 'Maybe come back to the next meeting with whatever it is you need to work through? But we're not going to psychoanalyse you here.'

'I just want to be happy,' Mike said.

Cathryn leaned across and gave him the most nun-like face Freddie had seen from her yet: 'You can be happy. But none of us can tell you how to do it, or why you're not. You've got to figure it out yourself.'

Mike slouched down in his seat in resignation.

Just as Andy was about to lead them on, there was a light knock on the door, causing Freddie another shock of worry. This time it was Lizzie who peeked her face around shyly before coming all the way in.

'Hello everyone,' she said in a tiny voice.

'How are you doing this week, Lizzie?' Andy asked.

'Oh you know, ticking along.' She paused, looking nervous, and wet her lips before continuing: 'Steve wanted me to pass on that he doesn't want to come to these meetings any more.'

'Oh really?' Andy asked.

Hattie sat forward, intrigued.

'We had a little conversation, outside of the group. And I thought he was very sweet, as I've always said, but he really does have the wrong picture about him and me, you know, and I told him so. So he said that he's very sorry to everyone, but he's probably not going to be coming by again.'

'That's very sad,' said Andy.

'I know it's sad, but it's how I feel, and I'm happy that he respects that.'

Andy said that they would drop Steve an email to see how he was doing, and Freddie made a mental note to ask whether Andy could pass on his email address too. It would be a good thing, he decided, to check in on Steve and see if he could be a friend. Especially if he was trying to get over someone. It was something they had in common after all.

'Well, I went on another date,' Cathryn said, after it was clear that she had room to talk.

'How did it go?' Hattie asked.

'As well as could be expected. She was called Amy, a publisher. Something to do with science and textbooks, I think? All went a bit over my head. She was very serious.'

'Did you like her?' Andy asked.

'Well, I thought she was very cold, you know, but some people are a bit like that, aren't they. So we went to dinner after meeting for drinks first, and you know what, I just wasn't feeling it. I kept waiting for her to warm up, to smile. It all felt a bit business-like. But the weird thing was that she seemed to like me. Kept insisting that I stay longer, just have another drink.'

'Did you?' Hattie asked, interested.

'No, I just wanted to get home and catch up on this series I'm watching. That one about the serial killer. I do like a good serial killer story. Amy seemed a little disappointed, though. Isn't that funny? It's the first time a woman seems genuinely interested in me, and I'm not interested in her back.'

'How could you tell?' Freddie asked, the sudden question causing Cathryn to pause in surprise. 'How could you tell that she liked you?'

'Well, she touched me a lot. Like on the arm, grazing my fingers. Looking into my eyes and listening. I don't think she pulled out her phone once the whole evening. She just seemed to care.'

'Friends care though, don't they? How do you know that she didn't just want to be friends?' Freddie questioned.

Again he could feel Hattie paying attention to him, intrigued by his more frequent speaking up.

'I just knew. I guess it's like that. Maybe not for everyone, but for me, with Amy, I knew. But at the same time, I knew that I didn't feel the same way.'

'Do you think there's something more to that?' said Andy. 'I mean, if someone shows an interest, do you think that you might have instinctively backed off?'

'Oh, like getting frightened? You think that might be it?' Cathryn pondered, worried. 'I did think about staying. The place we were eating in was very nice – it served cocktails that came with little umbrellas and everything – but it just didn't feel right.'

'Cathryn is allowed to not fancy someone,' Hattie interjected confidently.

'I agree,' Cathryn concluded. 'I don't think I'm just waiting for someone to pick me. I think I'm waiting to pick someone myself, too.'

'I still don't know how you knew that she liked you. You knew how you felt, but how could you tell about the other person?' Freddie asked.

Hattie was staring at him. 'Is there something you want to tell us Freddie?'

'Kate and I went out,' Freddie said. He thought about not saying it, and he hesitated enough to make Hattie raise her eyebrows even more suspiciously, but then the words were there, and his mouth was talking.

There was silence, just for a moment, before Hattie tentatively asked: 'Like, *out* out?'

Freddie nodded in reply. He decided quickly that he didn't want to tell the group that they'd had sex. It felt too private; something that he wanted to protect from their scrutiny.

'Wait, are you talking about Kate from this group? You went on a date?' Cathryn checked again.

'Sort of,' Freddie said. He could do this in vague terms. They didn't have to know the details.

'I knew that she liked you,' Hattie proclaimed. 'I knew it. She was always looking at you funny, and I swear, I just knew it.'

'It hasn't ended well,' Freddie continued, not letting himself dwell on what Hattie thought she knew.

'What happened?' Andy asked.

'We don't have another Lizzie and Steve situation, do we?' said Mike, causing Lizzie to squirm before Andy shushed him.

'I don't know what happened,' Freddie admitted. 'I have absolutely no idea what happened. But it ended with her saying that she needed space, which I'm giving her, and me realising that I like her. A lot.'

'Damn!' said Mike excitedly.

'What would you say to her now if you could?' Andy asked.

'I'd tell her . . . that I think that she's the best person I know. That I feel like a better person when I'm around her.'

'Sounds like you're in love with her,' said Hattie. 'When has all this happened, by the way?'

'I guess almost since we met here. Maybe a bit after? I bumped into her where she works, and things just happened. Except, I don't know if they've happened for her.'

'You don't think she feels the same?' Hattie asked.

'Would she say that she needed space if she does?'

'You don't think you should ask her?' said Cathryn.

'I think . . . I think that I can't even imagine having that conversation. I think that it might kill me, to be honest.'

'OK, so, Freddie,' Hattie sat forward in her chair, stern with intent. 'Here's what I'm hearing. That you can't tell Kate how you really feel because you're scared that she doesn't feel the same way. But what if she *does* feel the same?'

'What if she doesn't? Sorry to bring this up,' Freddie looked apologetically towards Lizzie, 'but I don't want to hurt anyone, or make situations difficult. I don't want there to be any awkwardness.'

'I'm not going to lie and say I wasn't embarrassed when Steve told me how he felt,' Lizzie replied. 'But I still respect him for doing it. Just because I don't feel the same way, he's not a bad person for telling me.'

'What do you want to do, Freddie?' Andy asked.

'Sometimes I don't want to do anything. Sometimes I just want to forget her completely. It would be easier.'

'Nothing will happen if you do nothing,' Hattie said.

'I wonder,' Cathryn said. 'I wonder if you're just as scared of her saying she feels the same, as you are of her not.'

'What do you mean?' Freddie asked.

'I think you know. If she feels the same about you, then both your lives will change for ever. That's got to be tough for someone with OCD, who likes their routine.'

Freddie felt stung by that; a heightened electric sensation that was as thrilling as it was frightening.

Andy might have sensed that, as they started to draw the conversation away in another direction. 'Maybe we should focus on the fact that Freddie's had some quite profound feelings lately. They may be difficult, but you've acknowledged them, at least in part. And we should still celebrate that.'

Freddie looked up at Andy, who was smiling at him kindly.

'You might not have the confidence yet for whatever comes next, but you've made a start, right?'

Freddie nodded back at them appreciatively.

'I'm still convinced she felt the same way,' said Hattie, but Andy swiftly moved the conversation on.

Walking back through Bloomsbury, Freddie finally found the courage to call his parents.

'Freddie!' his mother cried, so loudly that it forced him to hold the phone away from his ear for a moment. 'Why haven't you replied to me? Or to Stella? We've been worrying about you! Have you spoken to David? What happened between you two? He won't say anything. Are you all right?'

'I'm fine, Mum,' Freddie sighed. 'How's David? Is he OK?'

'Won't you call him? Ask him yourself.'

'I think it's best that doesn't happen right now.'

'What happened, Freddie?'

'We had a disagreement, Mum,' he said as carefully as he could.

'But since when have you been violent? Was that really necessary?'

'Probably not,' Freddie conceded. 'I was just tired of it. Of everything, throughout my whole life. And let's just say that he wasn't particularly kind about Kate.'

'What did he say about her? I'll kill him!'

Freddie smiled but also felt sad all over again. He was pleased that his mum had liked Kate, but hated the thought of how disappointed she was going to be when she inevitably discovered the truth.

'I'm really sorry Mum, if I ruined the party.'

'Yes, well, I think it might be Stella that you have to talk to about that.'

'I might need time to build up to that one.'

'Hang on, your father wants to say something.'

He waited nervously as heard his mother pass the handset over to his father. Freddie couldn't remember the last time he'd spoken to his dad on the phone. He wondered how much trouble he must be in to warrant it.

'Son?' His voice was solemn, and serious.

'Hi Dad.' Freddie wondered if he could maintain his composure, whether his new-found resilience would break under his father's scrutiny.

'It's about time.'

'I'm sorry, what?'

'Look, I love my boys. I love both of you. And I'm never going to condone violence, you know that. In nearly thirty years, you boys have never once fought. Not physically at least. You've had your scrapes, and I recall David being heavy-handed when you were younger, yes, but you've never actually outright fought. Except, I always thought that it would probably be a good thing if you did. Does that make any sense?'

'Not really.'

'I think what I'm trying to say is that I know things have never been easy for you, that you've been . . .' He struggled for the words. 'I've always known that you're a sensitive one. But I just figured that one day you'd realise what you needed to do and stand up for yourself.'

'Dad . . .'

'David will get over this. Give him time, and he'll get over it. But how are you doing?'

'I'm fine, Dad.'

'Everybody's talking about your Kate girl. Are we going to see her again? I never even got the chance to say hello properly.'

'Oh, I'm not sure about that, actually.'

'Well, you've always done everything in your own time, Freddo, never been one to rush things. That's OK too, of course.'

'I know, thank you, Dad.'

'I'd better put your mother back on, she's making one of her faces at me . . .'

'Freddie!' his mother yelled, drawing a sharp line under the tears that had been starting to form. 'Just promise me that you're all right?'

'I promise,' he said. 'I've got to go Mum, I'm at the Tube.'

'Call me tomorrow, Freddie. Come and see us at the weekend.'

'I'll try. OK, bye.'

He wasn't at the Tube station. He'd been walking down Georgian streets and around squares that loomed and cast strange shadows in the dark.

It felt good, being brave. It felt really good. And it had unexpected results. Hearing his father talk to him like that seemed like a rare, lucid moment within a dream, a flash of clarity before everything went back to being blurred and inconsequential. His father didn't say much, didn't get involved much, but he cared. When it mattered, he cared.

Freddie decided to walk home and, as he did, he thought about what he would say back to Kate right now, if he could. He imagined every possible way that he could tell her that she was wonderful, and beautiful, and that he wanted them to be together, always. As he walked, he started smiling, thinking about how if he found someone new, if the opportunity ever came up again, then he'd be ready, even if he had to wait another lifetime for it.

24

'I'm really pleased that you wanted to meet up!'

His name was Patrick, and he seemed nice. At least, Kate wasn't getting any Ethan-like vibes from him. On his profile it said that he dabbled in an amateur orchestra (he played the bassoon) and his last holiday had involved Interrailing through Central Europe. His photos had revealed a cheerful, carefree smile and a readiness for fancy dress.

They were having drinks in a basement wine bar in Soho, a small place with low lighting and lots of cosy nooks to hide away in. Kate liked the place a lot, and was pleased when Patrick had suggested it.

'So tell me about your day?' she asked him.

He told her, and she listened as politely as she could, but barely took anything in. Patrick was as nice as Kate presumed he was going to be, but she had known the moment they met that it wasn't going to go any further.

It's not you, she told him in her head, as he explained orchestra cliques to her, and what you could tell about someone's personality type from what instrument they played. *I'm just not interested.*

'Can I admit something?' Patrick said. 'And I really hope that you don't find it strange.'

'Go on?'

'I clicked on you, and I was really hopeful that you'd click back on me. I was thrilled when we matched.'

'That's really nice to hear.'

'It's just nice, when you're going through these apps, to find someone you think might be on your level, someone who you can really foresee getting on with. I had that hope with you. Would you like more wine?'

Kate agreed to a top-up, felt she could do with it as her heart had started racing. She wished that it could be for good reasons, that her blood was pumping in response to his eagerness – he was so nice, after all – but the truth was that she was just dreading the moment when she would have to let him down.

One more glass, she told herself. She wanted to be polite, and didn't want to hurt his feelings. But every time he looked up at her, every time his body language suggested that he would like to get closer, that he wanted to know more about her, all she could think was: *You're not Freddie.*

She'd felt the same when swiping through on the dating app.

You're not Freddie.

You're not Freddie.

When Patrick had messaged her, Kate had responded not because of genuine mutual interest, but because it felt like something Renee or Lindsey would suggest she do. A distraction to make her feel better. A rebound to help her move on.

But now she was here, and she knew it wasn't going to work. Patrick was edging closer to her with every sip of wine he drank, and all she wanted to do was run away.

In the end they parted amicably. He suggested moving somewhere else to get food, she said that she should probably get home. He took the hint. But Kate hadn't been ready to go home, so she decided to walk alone through Soho, watching couples on dates like she watched the paintings in the gallery, a lonely outsider viewing from a distance.

She thought about texting Freddie, about seeing what he was up to, but it felt cruel, to herself and to him. She didn't want to confuse the situation more, for both of them.

A reminder came up on her phone with a notification for the next group meeting. Kate deleted it; she was no longer a virgin, so she didn't think she'd have a place there any more. But it did make her think of the rest of the anonymous gang and, seeing as Hattie's was the only number (apart from Freddie's) that she had saved, she sent her a message to see if she was around and fancied a drink.

A twenty-minute bus ride across town later, and she was sitting in a pub with Hattie, watching as Hattie's jaw slowly dropped further and further down in wide-open shock.

'Look at you, dating all over the place. Who would have thought it a couple of months ago!' Hattie said

'Patrick seemed so nice. Ridiculously nice. But I feel stupid for going,' Kate replied.

'Why?'

'Because I don't think there was ever going to be a chance that I would have allowed it to work. I was never going to like him back.'

'And why is that, do you think?' There was something in Hattie's face that made Kate feel nervous, an intent in her questions that she couldn't quite make sense of. She put it down to not really knowing Hattie very well outside the group context. Perhaps this was just what she was like in real life.

'There's been a lot of change in my life lately,' Kate replied carefully. 'My living situation, my job. You know those old school friends I talked about in group once? The ones who basically dumped me? Elise, who used to be my best friend back when we were in school, she tried to reach out, and I deleted the email. I wouldn't have done that a couple of months ago either.'

'Email though? Who tries to restart a friendship over email?'

'She wanted to meet up properly. To go over everything I think. Maybe make amends. Sometimes I think I should have gone, just to see. Do you think I'll regret not trying harder with her? With all of them?'

'No! They gave up on you first!'

'I knew you'd have opinions—'

'Kate, did you ever really like them? I'm not talking about when you were at school, but maybe I am. Did you ever choose them at any point?'

'I'm not sure . . . We were in the same classes. We saw each other every day. They were the people I hung around.'

'Did you ever take a moment to think about who *you* were, and what people you *wanted* to be around? You fell in with them, sure, I get that. That's what happens at school. But after that, after university. Who cares whether or not they liked you. That shouldn't matter. Did you ever actually like them?'

'I guess not.'

'They don't have to be bad people or anything, but you don't have to like everyone. You're allowed to dislike some people, sometimes for no reason at all. The great thing is that you get to choose now. You get to work out who you like, who you want to be around. And it's not just because of proximity. You could have called on anyone tonight, but you came to me. Why?'

'Because I trust your opinion. My head has been crazy lately, and I knew you'd think straight. And be firm with me. I appreciate that.'

Because Hattie always seemed to know exactly what the right thing was, and said it even if it wasn't appropriate to do so. That's why Kate liked her; there was no beating about the bush with Hattie, no second-guessing as to her true intentions. Hattie was all upfront honesty and big, obvious facial expressions. Unlike a certain other person she knew and was trying to forget.

'Good, that's what I like to hear!'

They clinked their drinks together and toasted their friendship.

'I guess I did choose Lindsey – we chose each other. But now she's got this great new life and is having all these adventures, and I miss her. Between that and this guy I've been kinda-but-not-really seeing, I thought that maybe . . . I don't know. I guess I've been feeling pretty desperate.'

'Wait, I thought you said you'd only met that Patrick guy tonight, and that he was a definite no. You'd seen him before?'

'Oh, no. Not Patrick. That was just tonight.'

Kate realised her blunder and hoped that she'd be able to get out of it quickly.

'So what guy then?' Hattie asked. Kate noticed something telling in her expression, a twitch of intense thought, like she was piecing something important together in her head.

'I misspoke. I meant the dates I've been on, with Patrick, and that other guy, Ethan. Nothing but disaster dates can make you feel pretty desperate I guess.'

'Look, I'm pleased you reached out to me,' Hattie continued after eyeing her carefully. 'Especially if you've been having a tough time. I was going to call you, actually.'

'You were?'

'Yeah . . . I remember you talking in group about your living situation, and moving back in with your mum and dad? And I thought, we're going to have a spare room in our place in a month or two, and maybe you could save me and my other housemate the hassle of vetting a stranger?'

'You're kidding?'

'Nope. The third room is going to be free relatively soon. Our housemate is moving in with her boyfriend – good luck to her, she's going to need it with that one. I'm not going to make out that it's the nicest house in the universe, and the area can be a little dodgy on Friday nights . . .'

'You're really selling it to me.'

'But the rent is reasonable, I love to cook for everyone, and we all chip in for a cleaner because, honestly, who has time for that? The other housemate is really chill. She's a designer and gets far too invested in *Love Island* for my taste . . . so what do you think?'

'I think that sounds pretty awesome, actually.'

'You really think you might be able to put up with me full time?'

Kate laughed and said that she was looking forward to the challenge.

'Great, so come over at the weekend and see the place. There's plenty of time to think about it, nobody's rushing or anything.'

'I'd like that.'

Hattie looked pleased, and Kate felt pleased. She went to the bar to buy them both some more drinks to celebrate, but when she returned to their table, Hattie looked more serious, and contemplative.

'So now that I've managed to get a smile on your face, there's one more thing I wanted to mention.'

Hattie averted her eyes, nervous about the topic, which Kate sensed was a rarity for her.

'It's about Freddie.'

'Is he OK? Has something happened?' Kate's heart pulsed unexpectedly, a sudden palpitation that forced her to swallow back a larger gulp of her drink than she had planned. It burned at the back of her throat.

'Well look at you, all concerned about him.' Hattie smiled wryly.

'I'm not concerned,' Kate lied.

Whatever, I don't believe you, Hattie seemed to say with a shrug, before she continued: 'He's fine, probably, I presume.'

'Right, so what then?'

Hattie's face shifted into something more calculated and thoughtful. 'Just settle an argument for me, OK?'

'What argument?'

'Me and Cathryn. We were talking after the last group, about you two. She says there's nothing, but I don't know, I think there's something.'

'Something?'

'Between the both of you.'

Kate fidgeted and gulped again. Suddenly her mouth was incredibly dry, despite the drink at hand.

'There, I *knew* it,' Hattie laughed.

'What?'

'You and Freddie. You like him, admit it.'

'Can we not talk about this, please?'

'You more than like him, don't you?'

'Hattie, I don't know why you're asking me about this. It's a complicated question with an even more complicated answer. Stupidly complicated.'

'I don't think it's that complicated. He's the one you've been kinda-but-not-really seeing. You like him, and he likes you. Simple as that.'

'I don't know where you got that, but you're wrong. Besides, there's no way you could possibly know how he feels about me. It's ridiculous.'

'Funny, that's pretty much what he said about you.'

Kate stared at her, heart now beating panic-attack fast.

'OK, so let's try it another way. Pure hypotheticals. If it did turn out that he liked you too, then how would you feel? What would you do?'

'Hattie . . .' Kate wondered why she was being tortured like this, why Hattie was bothering her with something that she was desperate to forget about.

'Kate, I promise. I just want you to settle this stupid argument between me and Cathryn. That's it. If Freddie liked you back, then how would you feel?'

Feeling tears forming and being powerless to stop them, Kate took a long, deep breath, and told Hattie everything.

25

Freddie checked the address on his phone once more before entering the pub. The emails had seemed innocuous at the time, claiming that Andy just wanted a chance to meet up away from the group, to check in on how he was doing without the pressure of everyone else being there, but now Freddie wasn't so sure. For one thing, nobody else had ever mentioned that they met up with Andy for one-on-one counselling time. For another, this pub was decidedly romantic. There were window boxes out front overflowing with spring flowers in clouds of reds and pinks, and tiny candles on most of the tables.

Having peered around every smoked-glass partition and not spotted them, he bought a pint and took a seat at a small, empty table. When he took his phone out of his pocket, there was an email from Andy to say that they'd be late and to hang tight.

'Freddie?'

Kate.

Kate was stunned to see him and embarrassed too. She was worried about the way she looked, her hair in a messy ponytail, a pair of old, scrappy jeans, and a coat designed to deal with the temperamental spring weather. This was not how she wanted to look when she bumped into him. She had wanted to be perfect and pretty.

She couldn't say anything to him at first, beyond his name, and then suddenly she felt foolish, and scared in case he thought she had been following him. She needed to make sure that he knew this meeting was a coincidence, that she wasn't a scary weirdo. But her mind tumbled, so instead of cool, calm and collected, she presented with babble instead.

'Hattie told me to meet her here,' she explained hurriedly. 'I might end up her housemate, if you can believe it, and we were going to meet here so that she could show me around her neighbourhood. Why are you here?'

'Andy,' Freddie said. 'They said they wanted to talk about stuff.'

'Right.' Kate sounded cynical. Freddie worried she thought he was lying.

But what sounded like cynicism to him was really the cogs in her mind turning. Kate was figuring things out.

'No, I promise,' Freddie continued. 'I went to the meeting. The one after that Sunday when we ... Maybe I shouldn't have gone, but I don't know. Anyway, I guess Andy got concerned, and they said they wanted to meet up to talk.'

'Oh, I believe you,' Kate reassured him. 'I think we've been set up.'

'Set up?'

'You spoke to the group? I saw Hattie the other night and she didn't say anything about it. What did you tell them exactly? How much did you tell them?'

'Well, what did you tell Hattie?'

'Nothing! I didn't tell her anything,' Kate felt flustered. She ran a hand through her hair, smoothing and flicking it back in a way she hoped would make it look less of a mess and more of a styling choice.

'Are you going to leave?' Freddie asked slowly.

'No,' Kate replied, just as slowly. 'I'm going to get a drink. And then I'm going to sit for a bit. If that's OK?'

Freddie nodded that it was.

At the bar, Kate instructed herself on some deep breathing. She placed both hands down on the cool counter and closed her eyes.

Freddie is here, she said to herself. *Freddie is here*.

He looked good as well, which was a huge problem. He looked lighter, something in his shoulders, and the way he'd looked at her when she came in – she hadn't imagined that, had she? The brightness, the focus on her, like there was nothing else that mattered in the world.

What was going on? Kate wondered as she paid for her drink.

'Why do you think they've done this?' she asked once she came back from the bar.

'Because they know I like you.' He said it after a pause, with his eyes cast down towards his drink, not daring to look at her. He knew he had words now, but doing the words plus the eye contact would have been far too much.

'They do?'

'At the meeting, I didn't tell them what we did, or what happened. I wanted to keep that for us. But I did tell them how I felt.'

'You did?' She paused, feeling tears and fighting them back. 'Why didn't you say it to me?'

'I'm saying it now.'

'Right.' Kate paused. When Freddie finally drew the courage to look at her, she was looking up at the ceiling, almost as if she was praying. 'Oh God, they know I like you too,' she finally admitted. 'Well, Hattie does, at least.'

He waited, almost like he was waiting for the punchline. It never came.

'When I met Hattie . . . Oh, it's so obvious now that she knew how you felt. It's because you told them all. That explains a lot. She pretty much had me cornered, so I told her. And now they've set us up, the bastards.'

'Why didn't you just tell me?' Freddie asked.

'I'm guessing for the same reason that you didn't tell me.'

'Fear? Humiliation? Uncertainty?'

'Sounds about right.'

Their eyes met, just for the briefest of moments, before Kate started to blush and look away.

'I feel like I really messed this all up,' he said softly. 'If I had only just said something . . .'

'You didn't mess anything up. I was the one who messed it up. I was a complete idiot. I *am* a complete idiot.'

'Maybe we can promise to just tell each other these sorts of things in the future? Instead of bottling them all up?'

'I will if you will.' Kate's laugh came out fraught and awkward. 'Is there going to be a future?'

'Do you *want* there to be a future?'

She was looking at him now, nodding with sad, hopeful eyes. He looked right back, and neither turned away.

'I need to know how you really feel about me,' Freddie said finally.

'Well, I need to know how you really feel about me,' Kate retorted.

'I asked first.'

'Fine.' There was a smile trying to break through, he noticed. She was forcing it down, but it was definitely there. 'I like you. Hell, I more than like you. I've been feeling it for ages. Maybe from the beginning, I don't know. But you're hard to read. And I got stuck in my head, convinced myself what I was feeling was nothing because I was scared that you didn't the same way. Happy now?'

Freddie smiled, reached for his pint, and took a long drink before starting.

'Kate, I don't always have the words. Even when I have them, they're hardly ever the right ones. But I'm working on it. After you left, I did a lot of thinking. I thought about all the things I wanted to say to you if I ever got this opportunity. I basically had this whole script in my head of all the things I wanted to say, but now you're here, it's like all the words have vanished.'

'These ones sound pretty good,' Kate offered.

She had that panic-attack feeling, like her heart was going to pound so hard and so fast that it would leap right out of her chest. But instead of being terrible, this time it was the opposite. It felt exciting, like she was on a rollercoaster about to plummet over the first drop.

Freddie wondered when the pub had become so quiet, and even though his voice was soft, barely more than a mumble, it seemed incredibly and inescapably loud. 'I think this might be what falling in love feels like?' he finally admitted.

'Those words sound great too.' Kate was smiling now.

'Want to go for a walk?' Freddie asked. Their drinks weren't finished, but he was starting to feel a little charged and jumpy, like he needed to move his legs for fear of spinning out of control.

'Sure.'

Once they were outside, Kate didn't know what to do with herself, where to put her hands, or where to look. So she did the thing she'd been thinking about for ages, the thing she wanted to do the moment she saw his face again. They stood in front of each other and she reached up towards him and offered a gentle kiss.

'Was that OK?' she asked, making Freddie wonder how startled he must have looked. 'I can brush my teeth if you like? I know we didn't do that last time, but that was different, and I don't know how the OCD thing works for you, so if it's easier and you want to wait, then—'

This time, when he kissed her, he wondered why he had ever been so mystified and scared by it. He could feel her smiling as he did it, could sense how she wanted to move and where he wanted to take her. Very quickly, as close as they were, it seemed like they could never get close enough.

'We need to make sure that we talk to each other,' Kate said sternly when they finally broke apart. 'No more trying to guess what each other is thinking.'

'Agreed.'

'And if you're ever uncomfortable, or need me to know about something, you have to tell me. All the anxiety stuff, and the OCD stuff, and anything else. You can tell me everything. Don't bottle it up.'

'Agreed. And that goes for you too. When you're nervous, or scared, or feel like rubbish. I don't always know how to tell, so you have to be the one to tell me.'

'That sounds fair. I'll try.'

'Anything else?'

'Nope, I think that just about covers it.'

They were back to kissing again, this time with a hungry eagerness. Freddie let his hands move around Kate's waist, and hers in turn moved up to clasp around his neck, cupping his face on the way there.

'We should go home,' Kate said softly. 'Except we're going to have to go to yours.'

'Are you sure you want to deal with Damien?'

'It's either me dealing with your flatmate, or you meeting my parents.'

'Good point.'

Their hands stayed firmly clasped together as they walked to the nearest Tube station. He was surprised by the easiness of it, of their hands joined together, of her shoulder pressing into him as they walked. Kate revelled in that sense of relief. That it was finally happening. For both of them, there was an instinct that this wasn't an ending, but that they had finally reached the beginning.

When they got to the front door of Freddie's building, Kate breathed deep, steadying herself: 'We've got a lot to be getting on with, haven't we?'

'What do you mean?'

'Well, I'd say that I've got about a decade of catching up to do, and a lot of things I've only ever heard about that I'd like to try. You must be the same, right?'

She watched the awareness creep to his face, along with a red flush. Then he seemed to swallow back his nervousness and smiled at her.

'Well, let's get started then,' he said happily, pulling her towards him as he turned the key in the door.

ACKNOWLEDGEMENTS

My thanks go out to all the people who believed in this book. To my agent Bryony Woods, and the team at Hodder, Melissa Cox and Lily Cooper especially.

Thanks also to everyone who supported me along the way. From my colleagues at my various day jobs, to the fellow writer chums who cheered me on (you know who you are). To my parents Elaine and Nigel who never fail to show unconditional support, and the rest of my family too, for whom this book might be a bit of a surprise!

Finally, thank you to the experiences who made me who I am today. There are a few life events that I have in common with both Freddie and Kate. I too had trouble shedding toxic friendships, and have battled with various mental health issues. If you're having a tough time and need help, I hope you manage to find a safe support network that can see you through.

MIND website: https://www.mind.org.uk/
OCD Action website: https://www.ocdaction.org.uk/